DAYS
AND
DAYS

DAYS AND DAYS

A STORY ABOUT SUNDERLAND'S

LEATHERFACE

AND THE TIES THAT BIND

CHRIS MACDONALD

Published by ECW Press
665 Gerrard Street East
Toronto, Ontario, Canada M4M 1Y2
416-694-3348 / info@ecwpress.com

Editor for the Press: Michael Holmes
Copy-editor: Jen Knoch
M I S F I T   Cover design: Caroline Suzuki
Cover illustrations: Chris MacDonald

To the best of his abilities, the author has related experiences, places, people, and organizations from his memories of them. In order to protect the privacy of others, he has, in some instances, changed the names of certain people and details of events and places.

LIBRARY AND ARCHIVES CANADA CATALOGUING
IN PUBLICATION

Title: Days and days : a story about Sunderland's Leatherface and the ties that bind / Chris MacDonald.

Names: MacDonald, Chris (Tattoo artist), author.

Identifiers: Canadiana (print) 20240405064 | Canadiana (ebook) 20240414055

ISBN 9781770416703 (softcover)
ISBN 9781778523403 (ePub)
ISBN 9781778523410 (PDF)

Subjects: LCSH: Leatherface (Musical group)—History and criticism. | LCSH: Rock groups—England—History and criticism. | LCSH: Punk rock musicians—England—Biography. | LCSH: MacDonald, Chris (Tattoo artist)—Travel.

Classification: LCC ML421.L422 M13 2024 | DDC 782.42166092/2—dc23

This book is funded in part by the Government of Canada. *Ce livre est financé en partie par le gouvernement du Canada.* We acknowledge the support of the Canada Council for the Arts. *Nous remercions le Conseil des arts du Canada de son soutien.* We would like to acknowledge the funding support of the Ontario Arts Council (OAC) and the Government of Ontario for their support. We also acknowledge the support of the Government of Ontario through the Ontario Book Publishing Tax Credit, and through Ontario Creates.

Canada Council   Conseil des arts
for the Arts   du Canada

ONTARIO ARTS COUNCIL
CONSEIL DES ARTS DE L'ONTARIO
an Ontario government agency
un organisme du gouvernement de l'Ontario

Ontario

ONTARIO CREATES

PRINTED AND BOUND IN CANADA   PRINTING: MARQUIS   5 4 3 2

Get the ebook free!*
*proof of purchase required

Purchase the print edition and receive the ebook free.
For details, go to ecwpress.com/ebook.

MIX
Paper | Supporting responsible forestry
FSC
www.fsc.org   FSC® C103567

CHRIS MACDONALD

LEATHERFACE REHEARSING IN THE BUNKER.
SUNDERLAND, 1999.

In 1988, Frankie Stubbs, Richard Hammond, and Andrew Laing formed Leatherface in Sunderland, England.

"The greatest British punk band of the modern era . . . no punk rock group ever mastered melancholia like they did, a scant few have carried the raw pain their songs did without buckling."
— James McMahon, *The Guardian*

"Dickie began a solo . . . It wasn't just punk. It was beautiful."
— Peter Catapano, *New York Times*

"The thought of an alternate reality where Frankie Stubbs was lauded as a Great British Pop Lyricist — on the scale of Morrissey or Damon Albarn, say — is tempting, but if cult appeal doesn't always allow the cults to pay their bills, it may have helped Leatherface to maintain their dignity."
— Noel Gardner, *The Quietus*

"The greatest cult bands of recent decades — The Pogues, The Replacements, The Pixies — have been musical universes unto themselves. By that standard, Leatherface fits right in."
— Andrew Marcus, *Phoenix New Times*

Sarah Anderson of *NME* listed Leatherface's *Mush* as one of the "20 Lost Albums Ripe for Rediscovery," and the forty-ninth best album of 1991.

"We've come to expect Stubbs's emotional Louis Armstrong/Tom Waits bellow, letting loose his raw, wounded, thoughtful sentiments, and he's an unstoppable force again."
— Jack Rabid, *The Big Takeover*

"With a working-class lyrical perspective comparable to a big-hitter such as Bruce Springsteen, Leatherface were the epitome of the cult band."
— Ben Myers, *Louder*

"Leatherface makes your heart beat as fiercely as your boots."
— Silke Tudor, author of *Gimme Something Better*,
writer at *Hi Fructose Magazine*

"After all, leader Frankie Stubbs's sandpapered larynx resembled Lemmy's legendary gravel throat, and the band's attack resembled the punk/metal heroes gone pop."
— Tim Stegall, *Alternative Press*

David McLauglin, *Kerrang!* listed Leatherface's *Mush* as one of the best punk albums since *Never Mind the Bullocks*. "Frankie Stubbs's infamous rasp, rising like a bellowed croak over the top of hurried, frantic drums and subtly dynamic guitars, as he delivered lines of affecting melancholia."

"Just because it's classified as punk rock doesn't mean that it isn't a universal thing. People should know, or at least have the opportunity to hear them because it's beautiful. It's uplifting, inspiring, and enlightening."
— Chuck Ragan, guitarist and vocalist, Hot Water Music

"Frankie Stubbs may be the best songwriter I've ever heard and most of the world doesn't know it yet."
— Brian Fallon, vocalist, guitarist, and lyricist for
The Gaslight Anthem

"I switched through songs on the van's stereo, anxiously looking for the right one to compliment the moment, eventually landing on the Leatherface song 'Plastic Surgery.' A perfect moment."
— Laura Jane Grace, lead singer, songwriter,
and guitarist, Against Me!

Dave Grohl has Andrew Laing's autograph.

"It's what Frankie decides to write about, and then how he writes about it. It was instantly recognizable, and instantly compelling. It was all so dark, but also so light. And then you've got Lainey back there with two sledgehammers for arms. It just gets me so fucking pumped up."
— Chris Wollard, vocalist and guitarist, Hot Water Music

"I stood in on drums for two gigs in 2009. The Kingston show was without a doubt one of the best nights of my life, absolute heaven. A beautiful memory I'll cherish forever. One thing is for sure, Leatherface were up there with the Clash for me."
— Duncan Redmonds, Snuff, Toy Dolls, Guns n' Wankers

When Chris "Big Rock" Schaefer, legendary tour manager and driver to acts like Adolescents and GBH was asked who his favourite band to work with was, he replied, "Leatherface." When asked who the worst band he'd worked with was, he also replied, "Leatherface."

"Leatherface tunes are raw and emotionally charged, like a sonic sledge-hammer forged from the fires of punk rebellion."
— Talli Osborne

"Frankie Stubbs, a true lifer and king of the British underground, continues to soldier on across the world with the enchanting spell of his and the band's classic, epic, life-altering songs."
— Eamon McGrath, musician and author

"Leatherface's fingerprints are on most every band that has come after them."
— Craig Hlavaty, *Houston Press*

"I can't remember a lovelier time than watching Leatherface play every single fucking night. With Leatherface you'd never want to miss a minute of any night. It was just a wonderful thing."
— Simon Wells, Snuff, Southport

"*Mush* just had this sort of undefinable x-factor. It was this perfect sounding record for the kind of music it was. It was like an AC/DC record, it was sort of perfect, it just leapt out. Sonically it was just ten out of ten for what it was."

— Laurence Bell, founder of Domino Records, in an interview with *Negative Insight*

"The lyrics are what made them special. However, their best song was 'Hops and Barley,' so they couldn't have been that special . . ."

— Sean Forbes, Rough Trade West, Wat Tyler, Hard Skin

"I remember the exact feeling, it was literally like warming up a little bit, I don't want to sound like Julia Roberts or something . . . But I warmed up a little bit, thinking this is the greatest record I've ever heard."

— Davey Quinn, Tiltwheel

"They were a band that never stopped impressing me, and they always made me feel things, even made me cry, made me feel emotions that other bands just couldn't."

— Austin Lucas

"If you listen to the guitar part of the chorus of 'Capsized,' that is, basically, a different rhythm, that is me not knowing how to play 'Dead Industrial Atmosphere.' . . . It's the verse of that, and that's what I did. . . . It was a very deliberate, bullshit process that I invoked, because I'm sitting there, and I want to write a song and I got nothing. Who do I love right now? Fuckin' Leatherface. What song do I love right now? That song."

— Sergie Loobkoff, Samiam

To the editor of the magazine from long ago who encouraged me to keep writing.

PREFACE

This book tells two stories, woven together. One is a tale of friendship set during a backpacking adventure through England, Scotland, and Ireland. The other celebrates the influential yet underestimated U.K. band Leatherface and the impact their music had on me over the years and throughout that trip. Previous band members, colleagues, and friends have generously shared personal insights, which are recorded in these pages. This is not intended to be a definitive biography, but rather a personal account of my experiences with a group of people that inspired me immensely. If nothing else, it's a thank you. There have been many members in the band since the beginning, but I've chosen to focus on those who were in Leatherface at the time of our journey.

FOREWORD

DAMIAN ABRAHAM

When you look at the history of punk, so much of it was shaped by the tastes of the people who sold the records. What was brought in and recommended by these stores and small distros could have an immeasurable impact on the music produced by a scene. Given that we are all products of our influences, it is interesting to imagine the difference in Bad Brains' sound had Sid McCray not picked up a copy of the Viletones' *Screaming Fist*. Staying in D.C., what would Revolution Summer have sounded like if Yesterday & Today hadn't stocked Empire's *Expensive Sound*?

For many in Toronto, their worship of Leatherface can be traced to Full Blast Records. The tiny, lower-level, west-end store was the city's late-'90s epicentre for punk scholarship. While Rotate This might have been "cooler" and Who's Emma more DIY, Full Blast was the city's nerdiest punk record shop. Whether it was Japanese "Burning Spirits" hardcore, American proto-punk, or Scandinavian garage revival, Full Blast was where my educational pursuit started. In this way, the people behind the counter became like professors — in other words, I "punished" the shit out of them daily. Some of them humoured me more than others. As it was, frustratingly, in actual school, time has made me realize that I learned the most from some of my most curmudgeonly teachers.

Some days it was clear the last thing in the world Simon Harvey at Full Blast wanted to do was serve as the punk-Google for my endless inquiries. To this day, the future owner of Ugly Pop Records remains one of the deepest punk music heads I have met; and there were certainly days I wasn't deemed worthy of his knowledge. But when I was, I would sit at the learning tree and absorb as much as possible. This would be how I first learned of Leatherface: "Oh, you like Hot Water Music and Avail? This band blows that stuff away."

What I heard come out of that little store stereo completely blew my mind. Given the band's name and the "raging" hardcore records I had bought from Simon up until that point, I was expecting something along the lines of Left For Dead or Voorhees. And while this definitely raged, it was melodic and beautiful instead of brutal and pummelling. At first blush, it sounded like Lemmy fronting the Buzzcocks or Joe Cocker singing with Hüsker Dü. Before the first song had even finished, I sputtered: "Can I buy this?"

"This is my copy," Simon said, deflating my hopes. "You can't find Leatherface records, anywhere."

And he was right: prior to the release of the Hot Water Music split, finding a copy of anything by Leatherface in the wild was an impossibility. It seems almost absurd at this point in our collective descent into streamed reality, but for a few years, they were a band that always seemed frustratingly out of reach. Their existence was almost myth-like: they were single tracks on mixtapes, or something played for me all too briefly by people privileged with record ownership. In my desperation to find these artifacts, I even bought *Leatherface Gets Religion* by Kill Ugly Pop, in the deluded hope that it was somehow related. In the pre-Discogs world, you lived on hope.

All this meant that when I finally found a beat-up used CD copy of *Mush* amongst the copies of Ace Of Base and R.E.M.'s *Monster*, at a random CD store a few years later, it felt like the heavens had opened just for me. By this point, I had the Hot Water Music split and a bunch of their songs spread out over a dozen or so tapes; but I had yet to sit down and really listen to a full Leatherface record.

So much of what gets hyped to us fails to meet expectations; with *Mush* I had the opposite reaction. Every track felt perfectly tailored to a preordained slot in my brain. It was as though I was listening to a cherished mixtape from another life. Even the few songs that previously failed to really hit for me, presented in their proper context, now made sense. Every piece of praise that I had ever heard lauded on this record felt completely just. Then the question became: why isn't this huge?

Yes, even then I recognized the commercial limitations. In a world dominated by songwriting teams and algorithms, maybe a Leatherface night on *The Voice* is a bit ridiculous. But I'm not complaining that Psycho Sin never played on *Late Night with David Letterman*: Leatherface makes music that feels like it should have a larger place in this world. It feels almost like there's a Mandela effect at work: the band played the NME Stage at Glastonbury in '93; it didn't headline the Pyramid Stage with 100,000 fans singing along to "Springtime."

And I'm certainly not the only one who feels this way. Leatherface was one of the first domestic signings to Laurence Bell and Jacqui Rice's Domino Records — which means the people that would later help bring Franz Ferdinand and Arctic Monkeys to the world felt this music needed to be heard by the masses. (Laurence is thanked on the first Blitz 7", so his credentials are beyond reproach.) Sadly, this would be the closest they would get to mass acceptance.

Leatherface is a band that was destined for something greater than their cult status within a cult. As much as their greatness is accepted by those who know, they remain defiantly just below the surface in a sense. Despite *The Guardian* naming them "the greatest British punk band of the modern era," I still find myself proselytizing to people about them, even in England. Maybe they are too real for a world obsessed with edifice.

Their timing was less than ideal. A mainstream breakthrough for Leatherface certainly looked less and less likely as the seeming earnestness of the indie era slipped into the Britpop era's return to rockstar posturing. In a music industry where the most photogenic get to write the history, what hope did a group of real dudes from Sunderland have against sharp-dressed Londoners or Manks with perfect cheekbones? Perfect songs were no match for secret Sony deals and good connections. It always bothers me when Britpop is positioned as the U.K.'s "grunge moment," because that had clearly taken place contemporaneously, with the melody-core explosion of bands like Leatherface, Snuff, Thatcher On Acid, Wat Tyler et al. Britpop was a much easier sell in the "everything's OK now" depoliticization of the Blair era.

Like many of the greatest bands, Leatherface was relegated to the margins. The band was a cherished gift for those fortunate enough to uncover it — people who were driven from then on, almost like a religious convert, to bring others into the fold. But as Jon Ronson wrote of Frank Sidebottom, while the margins might be where all the coolest and most interesting people dwell, they are also the most vulnerable to falling off the page. *The Last* (a Domino Records release) fulfilled its titular role and brought the first era of the band to a close.

A four-year hiatus came to an end when the death of bassist Andy Crighton spurred the band back to action. Leatherface's heartfelt tribute "Andy" opened their side of the Hot Water Music split and heralded the beginning of the band's second chapter. Over the next decade, they would add three more incredible albums to their canon ... admittedly with some questionable cover art choices. For a long time, one of my deepest regrets was that my final high school exams made me miss seeing Leatherface on their first U.S. tour, post-reunion, with Dillinger

Four and Hot Water Music. I had to start my stint roadie-ing for the Swarm just days later.

It would be another nine years before I would get the chance to see Frankie Stubbs sing those songs. This time, in the form of a one-off solo performance on a bill with my band (Fucked Up) and the Dillinger Four. He had come to Toronto to perform at a wedding and, since the Dillinger Four guys were in town just chilling ahead of a show with NOFX, it was decided that the three of us should do a surprise gig at Toronto's Sneaky Dee's. In the run-up to the show, I hoped I'd have the opportunity to meet Frankie and tell him not only what his music meant to me as a fan but also how much of an influence he had become in my own approach to doing vocals.

The day of the show, however, things went a little weird. First, Fucked Up did a very short, live, televised performance from one of MTV Canada's washrooms. While initially intended to be a three-song set, a mini-riot broke out as soon as we started playing, as the people in attendance rushed a barricade trying to get into the small bathroom. The control room cut to black before the end of the first song and told us to leave because the police had already been called.

Hastily making our exit, we arrived at Sneaky Dee's to the chaos of an oversold, hometown show. This meant trying to find ways to finagle as many friends and family into the sold-out room as possible. I was exhausted by the time we hit the stage, and I don't remember our set at all. Dillinger Four, the world's greatest band on any other night, were faced with a weird crowd. In a bizarre incident at the midpoint of Paddy Costello's mid-set head shaving: an argument about skinhead cultural appropriation broke out on stage between Paddy and a drunk friend of ours.

The day's only redemption came with finally getting to experience Frankie's voice live. Performing with just an acoustic guitar, he brought a moment of calm to a day of chaos. Much the same way that white noise can lull a person into slumber, the gruffness of Frankie's voice has always had a soothing effect on me.

The harsh vocal is the most misunderstood vocal in rock. It flies in the face of all other vocal styles. For my tastes, most of the elements that make for "good" traditional vocals are the very elements that ruin a harsh vocal. Things like control, finesse, and even timing impede the true reason for vocals: pure emotion. Not in some post–Hot Topic bullshit "emo" way, but as the honest presentation of emotion. And because of the emotional intensity, the nuances of it — its melodic qualities — can be lost on some people.

Jennifer Herrema once said that the hidden melodies in the music of Discharge and GBH had been a key influence on Royal Trux's sound. Frankie's voice has that power on me. He didn't need to switch to a melodic voice to convey melody. He forced the melody out. There was no need to adorn it with choral backing vocals, Pro Tools, or synth lines. The melodies in his songs were forged into them.

A year or so later, I had a chance to live out a dream and not only see Leatherface but play a show with them. Because of our tour routing we had missed the band's Toronto show, but we made sure to jump on the date in St. Catharines, Ontario, if for no other reason than to get to see them.

Little did we know it would be their last North American tour.

If I had known then that it would be the only time I'd see the band, I would have fought through the post-set, tour exhaustion, stood up front, and screamed my heart out. I would have fawned over them — about what they meant to us. But we can never really appreciate something until it is gone, can we? Instead, my interactions with Leatherface, beyond the obligatory "hello" during soundcheck, consisted of standing beside Dickie Hammond in the men's room and talking about H.D.Q. as we washed our hands. I watched the show from the back and sang along to myself, content with the thought that I would surely see Leatherface again down the road.

In a way, it is fitting that Leatherface finally played Southern Ontario during their last crossing of the Atlantic. As a result of some post-colonial hangover, English bands tend to find greater reception in Toronto. North America can sometimes be a tough slog for even the most beloved British bands, but Toronto has always seemed more susceptible to the sways of anglophile hype. This is not to say that Leatherface ever benefited from any *hype*, just that the preconditions for this geographical area's love of Leatherface are not without historical precedent.

And as the Process Church, Toronto would be home to one of the largest chapters of the Leatherface cult outside of the U.K. . . . along with, maybe, Gainesville, Florida. Just like in Gainesville, the band's influence has been worn on the sleeves of many area groups. The then Toronto-based Deranged Records would give the band's *Discography Part Two* compilation a reissue. But perhaps the love from here is best summed up by the labour of love that was Toronto's Rubber Factory Records' two-disc Leatherface tribute: bringing local and international bands together to celebrate the band.

It couldn't be more fitting, therefore, that Chris MacDonald's book originates from Toronto. It's in keeping with a deep tradition of loving, investigating, and championing this band, which permeates a large part of our punk scene. Being a part of that tradition, I am forever grateful to Chris for being up to the task of writing *Days and Days*. Leatherface is a band whose history and legacy need a book to contextualize it. While this book brings together voices in celebration of a band, it also serves as a group therapy session, as we collectively figure out what we saw that the outside world didn't. I hope it also brings more people into the world of Leatherface. Cults only gain power by growing . . .

Shout out to Chris, Johnny (Rubber Factory Records), Gord (Deranged Records), Simon (Ugly Pop), and anyone who helped champion this band.

R.I.P. Dickie, Andy, Andrew, and Ian.

"WE'VE ALL LIVED IN TIMES OF WAR.
I CAN'T UNDERSTAND ANYMORE.
WE'VE ALL LIVED TO START A WAR
AND I CAN'T WATCH THESE THINGS ANYMORE."

— "TRENCHFOOT," STUBBS

I clawed my way through the swarm of raised fists, neon mohawks, and leather jackets, hunting for a better vantage point. It was like swimming upstream in a hot river, twisting between rocks. Floral drug sweat, beer-soaked dance floor, teen anger seeping from the walls. Shoving my way toward the victorious moment, I clambered onto the shoulders of the human summit. There were hands on my back, gripping my belt, heaving me forward when my feet landed on the stage. I stumbled from the crest over the monitor but didn't fall. My eyes raised to the ghouls in a sea of twisted limbs, their faces like Edvard Munch's *The Scream*. My body was drenched. The band sounded like the type of thunderstorm that opens your eyes at night, electrifies your scalp, and makes your heart drop. A rudimentary beating made the spiked drum kit tremble. Jerry Only and Doyle moved like glitching film on either side of me, shirtless, wielding their instruments like weapons, their slicked hair falling to a long point between their hollow eyes. I paced among the visceral theatrics across the stage. *The fucking Misfits.*

The year was 1996, and Michale Graves had replaced legendary frontman Glenn Danzig as lead singer. The twelve-year hiatus brought a vicious crowd to the Opera House in Toronto, even without Danzig's presence. It wasn't long before the show spun out of control.

The lights strobed. Deafening distortion blasted from the amplifiers. I was blindsided by someone who felt I'd overstayed my welcome. They pushed me from behind and sent me tripping. This jarring hit spurred immediate anger. My foot came within inches of Doyle's guitar when I spun and kicked. I'd have been burned alive if looks could kill. Graves swung at me fast. I dodged the first attempt before he came at me again with a vengeance. My chest crumpled as he slammed me down. My plan to crowd surf for the first time vanished like the air in my lungs.

With a cheek pressed to the stage floor, there was a skewed view of the reaching hands before me. I knew my shoe was gone for good. In this moment I didn't understand the violence. I was so small and skinny. My intention was only to get a good look at the band, then jump.

When Graves shifted his weight to get a better hold of me, I writhed closer to the edge. Now people were pulling at my shirt, gripping my arms. But the frontman pinned me again, wailing on me with his fist inside a studded leather gauntlet. Lightning cracked behind my eyes. My friend Jason lunged through the hysteria and took hold of Graves from the floor below. I caught glimpses of him delivering solid punches to the singer. A horizontal row of Crimson Ghosts smiled their crooked grins from the back wall as the rest of "All Hell Breaks Loose" battered to its end without vocals. Graves let up when he knew he'd met his match. Jason dragged me to the safety of the pit, one sock dangling from my foot. Boots crushed my toes as we stepped through the puddles of booze toward the exit. People hollered in my ear. I couldn't understand what they were saying.

We sat in the darkened schoolyard north of Queen Street with thin ribbons of blood drying on my face. My smoking hand shaking, the other searching for cuts through my hair.

"Did you — did we — just fight the Misfits?" I mumbled with my head down between drags.

"Yeah, I think so." Jason's eyes were wide in the moonlight when I looked up. My head felt broken and was buzzing like television static. Adrenalin was coursing. He continued, "You just got the shit kicked out of you by one of your favourite bands." Although I smiled, I realized then that being eaten by something you love was a lonely feeling. The bellow from Jason was hearty. Having life mock me like that was ideal for him.

"I'm gonna need new shoes. My wallet's gone too," I said, looking at my soaking sock. Our friend Kevin drove me home.

I knew when I'd discovered punk that there would be danger. I fluttered to its light to be singed and sent tumbling. But it was too late, my naïveté had been confronted by the brutal aspect of it that sometimes followed. We were caught in the web. Connecting with others who felt similar contempt brought relief. But it still didn't change anything. I knew that part of me was dying. The thing is, I'd heard something in a basement on Islington Avenue a few years before. What began as a whisper was slowly getting louder.

The first indication of friendship happens like a flare in the night. It only takes a second for the person next to you to say one thing that makes you laugh your ass off or show you something beautiful before you're bound forever, even if only by memory. For Jason and me, it happened coincidentally in a parking lot somewhere near the Opera House, years before the Misfits concert.

"Hold up a minute," he said, eyes sparkling before looking toward the ground. Those nights were Tolkien, hushed talk of Black Riders, Sabbath, and crumpled tinfoil full of green leaves. On that long-lost evening, an electric apricot light roared above the east end parking lot where we stood amidst the scent of burger smoke wafting out from Dangerous Dan's — home of the stained minivan seat. Home of the Colossal Colon Clogger Combo. I spotted a ripped Cineforum flyer on the telephone pole clad in stapled armour. It reminded me I was home. Salvador Dalí's face disappeared as the corner of the paper folded over him in the wind. We wore youth across our flushed cheeks like pink warpaint. Insouciance radiated from under the weighted lids that cloaked our burned-out eyes. If opposition was a crucifix, we were devout and clung to it tightly.

I felt content because I could sense what was coming next. It justified my instincts. My friend's eagerness was a force I wasn't going to escape from. And that was okay because I didn't want to dodge it. I was beginning to know Jason like I knew those streets.

"I'm going to play you a song." And there it was, spoken as if I should be surprised. I smiled inside because there was never a time when I didn't want to hear a new song. Perhaps he was beginning to know me like those streets as well. We had little direction, nowhere to be, and no pressing commitments besides annihilation. But within all the uncertainty we both knew the other was searching for something.

He sat down on the crumbling abutment with his gold-red hair falling over his face. Young Kurt. He wore a Bad Brains shirt that was fraying at the shoulder — a poster child for the '90s hunched over a beat-up, stickered acoustic guitar. It was the same one he dragged all over town.

"Better be good," I teased. The kid played music like he was shy but he wasn't at all. I found my cigarettes and slid one between my lips, tilted my head, and watched the flame sear the end. It was important to light up with as much confidence as possible. I pretended the smoke hadn't stung my eye.

A voice came at me like rustling leaves, full of crepitation at its scraping edges. A contrasting image played in my brain of him pissing on an expensive carpet in the middle of a living room at some rich kid's party. *Somehow, this is the same person. Jesus.* Lyrics tumbled in breathless succession, like a Dylan song but with a punk edge to it. He sang at the end of every verse: "Today would be just as good as any other day to die." The sentiment sank deep into me while the guitar played out its lonely melody. I could only smoke and be reminded of how things aren't what they seem. The way people will surprise you.

I've been thinking about how in that moment our recklessness and pessimism may have suggested a truth in those words. But I could tell we both felt as electric as that sky above when the strings stopped ringing. You never know how far you'll be carried when someone's candour lights up the horizon for the first time.

"THERE'S DARK SATANIC MILLS,
THERE'S GREEN AND PLEASANT HILLS.
WE COULD BE RIDING THROUGH LANCASHIRE,
WITH ALL ITS WITCHCRAFT AND STALE INDUSTRIAL AIR.
YOU CAN HEAR A MELANCHOLY DESERT SONG
AND SMELL GEORGE ORWELL AS A FUNERAL GOES ON.
THERE'S PLENTY WITH A LICENSE TO PROSTITUTE
AND ROOM TO DEVELOP THE ULTIMATE BUILDING.
THE AIR IN HERE IS DEAD INDUSTRIAL AND SO AUSTERE.
THE AIR AROUND HERE SMELLS OF RELIGION AND VAUXIES BEER."

— "DEAD INDUSTRIAL ATMOSPHERE," STUBBS

LONDON, ENGLAND — YEARS LATER, LATE AUGUST, 1999

Before the two of us drifted into an abysmal slumber collapsed against the tiled wall in King's Cross subway station deep in the heart of the London Underground, Jason had nudged me and nodded his head back toward the exit. He was gesturing for me to look at the scene farther down the platform. The humming white light at the peak of the convex ceiling washed the half-cylinder in a milky-green film, giving everything a sickly undertone. I leaned forward off my backpack to peer beyond Jason's slouched body. Missing the last train to Leeds forced us to call the station home for the night when it had stolen the remaining midnight passengers. Its departure left the platform still and empty, except for us and a mass of blanketed human. A man's head protruded from the top of the covering and rested against the wall. With his chin tilted upward, eyes closed, and mouth agape, he looked strikingly like Jesus. A pair of pale legs capped in black high-heeled

26

high-heeled shoes spilled from under the shroud and across the platform. This gave the impression that the man had a pair of women's legs attached to his body, only backward. One of the stilettos looked like a hoof from my perspective as it scraped the floor, echoing in the empty tunnel. I tried to make sense of the scene with my sleepy eyes. The curved corner of Jason's parted lips told me that he was going to start chuckling. He was waiting for me to see what he was seeing. As his laugh became audible in his strung-out state, I understood only then as the veil bobbed faster and faster, and as Jesus's mouth opened further, what was really happening.

"Christ," I gasped. My travel companion's laugh turned to an exhausted cackle. His rosy, round face often donned this look. Music was one of the few things he took seriously back then. The volume of his delight seemed to gauge the absurdity of a situation. A ginger goatee sprouted from his chin like a healthy flame below his thin smile. We were both twenty-three, but I could've been his lanky younger brother. A thoughtful side of him was reserved for times when he'd say, "Hold up a sec" in a parking lot and make you listen to a song he'd written. For most of our trip, his expression read: "What the fuck are we doing?" or "Chris, take a look at this shit." It was a demeanour I was becoming more familiar with as our journey unravelled. He was not tall or obedient, had a cask of whisky for a chest, and fought like a tiger. The '90s poster child had morphed into kind of a beast. We cut our fists and eyes side by side more than a few times as we'd grown older, but unlike mine, his mother, Linda, had given birth to a true fighter.

Our dynamic was complicated. We were both bad news, only in different ways. I didn't live for confrontation the way he did. But I'm grateful he saved my ass a handful of times. Even his Irish last name, Dwyer, sounded like trouble. I guess some stereotypes exist because we keep living up to them. Now that the leg of our backpacking journey had led us to England, I could sense moments of uncertainty, tension, and dynamite ahead of us. This potential danger was the knot in my gut I couldn't untie. Keeping Jason out of any situations that might be problematic along the way was the challenge I now faced.

Because we missed the last train, our only alternative was to sleep in King's Cross station and catch another the following morning. Daybreak would have us en route to Leeds to see Hot Water Music from Gainesville, Florida, play at the iconic pub at 71 Vicar Lane, the Duchess of York. This was one of the most famous live music venues in all of northern England. We would meet up with our Canadian friends Danielle and Jenny at the show. Jason and I would then spend a night after the gig in Sunderland with Andrew Laing, drummer from the legendary punk band Leatherface. How this came to be was still hard to fathom. I'll tell you how it all went down, about my friend and me, and a band that made a lasting impact on a group of kids from Toronto, as well as so many others.

"BUSINESSMAN, BUSY MIND, CONTRITE, LIKE SHITE,
NOTHING LIKE INJUSTICE, NOTHING LIKE A SONG TO SING.
CHOOSE TO GIVE ICONS OF OUR AGE
AND CHOOSE TO LIVE WITH ONE FOOT IN THE GRAVE.
I WANT THE MOON.
I DON'T EXPECT TOO MUCH FROM HONEYMOONS."

— "I WANT THE MOON," STUBBS

ISLINGTON AVENUE, REXDALE — 1992

Jason and I came from separate crowds that merged. Out of the gate we were wild, reckless, and loved getting high. Those things bound us in the beginning. Our relationship strengthened as we learned of our desire for adventure and discovery. We shared a love for all music, but mostly punk, and we both felt compelled to write songs. The drive to understand and express ourselves became a home that kept us warm for many years to come.

Jason would make the trip from Woodbridge to our school. Some days we would descend the dirt embankment to the Humber River flowing parallel to my high school. The river's accessible locale served as an ideal escape route when needed. You'd be getting your ass kicked on the football field at the edge of the hill as the PE teacher blew the whistle and yelled, "I'm gonna put your *ass* in a sling!" This was the cue to slide down the dirt ridge in a cloud of dust. So long, suckers.

Looming over the water at the bottom of the hill was the bridge that served as our refuge during our high school years. The structure was an open-air clubhouse and our umbrella when it rained. You could get inside the top if you were brave enough to take the step out to the steel girder where the bridge met the road. The fifty-foot drop was enough to paralyze you. With only the thin edges of the vertical beams to cling to, you'd hold your breath, take the stride, and rely on nothing but your instincts. There was just enough room to squeeze into the crevice between the earth and the beams when standing on the girder. The only sounds in the cool, dark cave were the muffled cars and trucks rumbling across the concrete overhead. It was like a secret passage you could follow along the concrete ledge. The Humber River trickled brown with boulder clay below us, where the Huron-Wendat, Six Nations of the Grand River, and the Mississaugas of the Credit once built their communities. Where wildflowers sprouted like yellow and pink fireworks between the jagged rocks at the side of the bicycle path along its banks. Where the biggest garter snakes you've ever seen slid like ribbons through the undergrowth. Where as kids we'd lure the last of the Toronto catfish from its murkiness using marshmallows as bait.

By the time the teacher peered over the edge of the hill muttering "little bastard," you'd be gone, baby, gone. We'd smoke cigarettes, get high, escape from reality, and do what we needed to do away from authority. Anything to escape the monotony. Life was about breaking the chain then. It still is, I just do it differently these days. People would stroll beneath the bridge oblivious to the leering punks above. This made us feel smarter than them. We made ghost sounds that would echo through the steel rafters. The people would hurry off. I was beginning to understand that a small part of anarchy was discovering hideouts where no one could find you. The thought wasn't fully formed yet, but it sometimes felt as if I was standing in an open field when I looked around the industrial cave.

We would hang around on the rock that lined the trickling creek below our secret hermitage. Our gang of fifteen punks and skaters was always together — mohawks, plaid, boots, skateboards, freedom, fuck the world, fuck the police. We were barons of the afternoon light with GBH's "Generals" playing through a pair of lo-fi Walkman headphones.

Some days were dark though in that time, at that age, with those clothes and safety pins and careless state of mind. Some days the shadows of youth would keep us under its spell and prisoners from the sun. We were caught in the web. Our actions would shift direction like the wind.

Something awful happened once by the river, on a search for power beneath a hot sun. We were heaving stones into the steel above. With a weighted clang, a rock bounced off and fell to the brush. I could feel the girder reverberating inside me. Another throw left the air ringing like a gong. When a bird flew up seeking shelter, we didn't stop. To this day I've tried to understand why we kept at it, before it drifted down like a rag. I screamed inside but silence punched me in the gut. We stood breathless in the heat.

I went to class that afternoon to escape the crowd. I couldn't shake the awful feeling. Visions of trampled bodies and dead birds plagued me as I stifled the urge to puke. As I put my head down on my desk, I could smell the summer sweat near my elbows and the green paste cleaning solution the janitors used. We never talked about the event again. It was like we were numb, and did it to understand our boundaries. Maybe we do these things because the hard remorse makes us feel human again. It's brutal, but sometimes a sacrifice must be made for the greater good. And desperation comes with a price. It's so difficult to admit these atrocities and it burns deep down. Oh, how the great sweeping of our moods would change from dusk into night. It was a scary place to live, and we had only ourselves. We learned to take the bad with the good. Most days were okay at that age, with those clothes and safety pins and that careless state of mind, searching for power. But I hear that heavy clang sometimes.

A transformation came the night I rid myself of the tragic '90s skater haircut. My friend Rob lived with his girlfriend Michelle in a house near Albion Road. The strip malls in this neighbourhood were quilted with signs and shop names of every shape and colour. Street corners came alive in the mornings as vendors strung their flags up in the wind. Rob had a mini half-pipe in his garage spanning the surface area of the floor. The crowd would party at his place after skating all afternoon. I remember that fateful dusk evening, the orange sun falling over Rexdale. There was a pressed carpet beneath a scattered pile of chipped skateboards. We were slouched, smoking and drinking in a semicircle. A crammed ashtray on the coffee table looked like a still life of a mosh pit. The music got louder, the atmosphere primitive. Everything dizzied into a haze of wasted laughter with the Exploited shouting about sex and violence from the speakers. We jumped off the sinking sofa to follow in step with Rob's mod dance gaining slow, circular momentum in the centre of the living room. Shirts came off. Chairs toppled over. I was the runt falling to the rug, feeling the burn across my elbows. Beer bottles went careening like bomb shells when someone kicked over a case at the edge of the kitchen. All of this happening in front of the curtainless window.

In the midnight hours I sat in the low light of the kitchen with my friend Aron kneeling in front of me: "You ready, MacDonald?" His ability to make life feel less cumbersome was something I've always held dear. The clippers vibrated my skull as they came up the back of my head and across the front. A ginger lock drifted down like a feather to the linoleum beside my duct-taped Airwalk shoe. *My parents are going to lose their shit.* Something glowed inside at the thought. When it was all said and done, someone else was staring back at me in the bathroom mirror with a shaved head and a Misfits-style devilock. There comes a time when we all must leave the safety of the husk. For some, this emergence is slow and timid, for others it's like a switchblade.

I was spending more time with Jason than anyone else because of our connection to music. We'd get high at this kid Darrell's house when we weren't down at the river killing time. Darrell went to high school about as often as I did. Most days you could find him selling dime bags from a room in a basement apartment he shared with his Jamaican roommates. Masculine characteristics had embedded themselves in his stubbled teenage face. It was hard to tell if he was eighteen or twenty-six. A true-blue burnout, Darrell laughed an octave higher than everyone else.

There was always a group of strays walking with us to his place. Darrell sat in the captain's seat in the middle of the room as we crowded into his dingy space, finding spots on the bed or the floor. The way his chair sagged and clung to him had me imagining Darrell was its lifeblood. That it would release him only in the morning to attend school and wait hungrily for his return. The arms of the chair were flat and wide enough to house a faux crystal ashtray, a Zippo, and his Du Mauriers. A small television with a mess of cords spilling to the floor was perched on a night stand. There was an NES and a *Duck Hunt* gun, but I never saw him play it. Several pieces of Scotch Tape on the wall seemed to be the only decorations. Darrell's housemates would find their way in after the joints were fired up, grinning as they tiptoed into the room.

We listened to Grasshopper, Eric's Trip, Dream Warriors, Pennywise — anything and everything. It always sounded exactly like what we needed.

Jason introduced me to Leatherface in that basement. My friend pulled a cassette tape from his pocket like a detective placing evidence down on the table in front of the accused. Slow and calculated. I eyed the cover art — a photograph of mushrooms viewed from below. The gills underlit against an orange backdrop. The image seemed to radiate in the dim room.

"You need to hear this," he said in a serious tone.

Jason pressed stop on the black boom box. All went deathly quiet except Darrell shifting in his squeaking chair. He would do this in an attempt to rid the room of silence. Lighters often sparked during these occasions, and I could hear the tobacco burn from a deep drag. Jason was eager for the moment to progress. He slid the cassette into the stereo and pressed the play button down with a click.

A song called "I Want the Moon" began with a driving guitar riff and steady drums, the high-hat cymbal hissing like a beer can with a hole popped in the side. The music had a mid-tempo rock 'n' roll sensibility, but the guitars growled like it was 1977. The abrasive vocals started barking after the intro, the singer's throat full of broken glass and cotton. A ride cymbal chimed hard on the back beat and clanged like the bell at a railway crossing. A fist pounding on a table. A machine revving in the dust. The claustrophobic song shoved me in the chest as the words tripped over themselves. The intonation in the singer's voice changed to that of a desperate animal caught in a trap as the chorus hit: "And IIIIIIIIIIIIIIIIIIII want the moon!" The line ripped high and anthemic. "I don't expect too much from honeymoons." *What is he singing about? Did he just say honeymoons?* A music video played in my head of the band against a spray-painted backdrop with the singer bent over and belting into the microphone. I watched the scene of fluid outlines moving in technicolour static with my eyes closed and my hands clenched together.

"Where did you get this?" I asked, my voice under water. I was very stoned and the music was so good that it almost made me afraid to speak.

"This guy at school gave it to me, Pat. He's really into English punk. Great, right?"

I was enthralled. The singer sounded like Lemmy's younger, punk rock brother with a vocabulary that could give any of the poets I'd been exposed to at that point a run for their money. He sounded like a prizefighter swinging in a title bout. The whole thing was relentless. When a song called "Not a Day Goes By" started, I'd never heard punk rock guitars sound so beautiful. This moment brought me back to music class when my teacher played us Pachelbel's Canon for the first time. She turned out the lights and asked us to close our eyes, and to truly listen. I kept my eyes buried in my arms to hide my tears, acting like the lights were too bright when she turned them back on. The extended intro of "Not a Day Goes By" was pulling hard at something inside me. I knew it was intentional, that something was coming. What I didn't expect was how momentous the whispered first line would be: "A time when everything was evergreen." These words slammed into me. The song's urgency spurred an instant need to express myself. It was beaming with hope. I knew I wouldn't be able to move forward in life without it.

No one spoke for some time. Their voices didn't register with me if they did. The chorus of "Not Superstitious" rocked me. I've never heard anyone's voice sound like paper being torn into a megaphone. So much emotion, so much being said. It was fuming and heavy, but also composed and intelligent.

There was a story unfolding on an ethereal level about the cover art of *Mush* as the songs filled the room. Jason told me the band was from Sunderland, England, a place I knew nothing of. What I did know was that the English punk I was familiar with sounded nothing like what I was hearing. Unlike the others, this anger was complex and impassioned. I saw grey skies, smokestacks, and rain in my mind.

It was impossible to absorb the entirety of the record in one listen. I felt overwhelmed as it continued. Like experiencing an enormous ship passing next to you in the night with its power — height, mass, expansiveness stretching too far to see. All I could do was feel its presence.

Something deeper happened in Darrell's room that day. Its message was still a spore, but it had everything to do with finding sensitivity where I'd least expect it. Finding what felt like an answer in a world I'd yet to understand. These feelings were like lightning inside me.

Jason let me borrow the tape. The walk home brought something akin to enlightenment when I thought about the avant-garde messages I'd listened to earlier. I stopped to pull the cassette and cover from the clear case. The liner notes were difficult to read in the summer light. I learned the names of the members: Steve "The Eagle" Charlton, Andrew Laing, Richie Hammond, and the singer's name was Frankie N. W. Stubbs. My thoughts raced as I walked on. My brother would come for a visit soon and I couldn't wait to play it for him.

A MOMENT OF TERRIFYING HONESTY

I told a lie shortly after the life-changing day in Darrell's basement that's lingered in me since the words left my lips. It's the kind of fabrication that haunts a person and comes for you in the middle of the night.

It happened during a conversation with one of my brothers. I hadn't seen him in some time and was elated to be standing in the dark with him.

"Whaddyou been doing?" Joe asked before lighting a cigarette.

"Been playing music with friends, writing some tunes."

"Oh yeah, cool," he said.

"Yeah, man," I replied. "We have this one song, it's so wicked. You're going to love it."

"Yeah?" he asked, expelling a swirling cloud above our heads. I sung the melody and words that weren't mine.

"A time when everything was evergreen. Evergreen and seemingly ideal."

"That sounds cool." But I knew he was humouring me. The words weren't dancing in his head the way they did in mine.

My heart pounded.

Jesus Christ, what was that? I was hot with shame the second it happened. To realize in those burning minutes that my brother's approval was worth more than dignity felt awful. I wished I could take it back and play him the song. He would hear how incredible this new band I'd discovered was. Coming to terms with being a sham is a lonesome feeling.

He dropped the butt after a minute and crushed it beneath his shoe.

Can you feel it stinging like a paper cut? Stinging like a sibling's indifference about your make-believe achievements? I like to believe that sometimes we lie in our younger years to propel ourselves toward the truth we're searching for.

The entire contents of the platform in King's Cross station lay coated with a fine soot from decades of trains pounding through the cavernous warrens below. Staring into the yawning mouth of the tunnel, I remembered a time when my old friend Aron and I climbed past the gate and ventured into the tunnel at Islington subway station back in Toronto.

His dusty-blond mohawk bobbed above his lanky frame in front of me as we slinked into the shadows. We found a stairwell fifty feet inside that led to a second storey above the tracks. Our boots echoed on the metal steps as we climbed, quick and cautious. Two motionless fans the size of ship propellers were at the top with a pale light shining from behind them. We climbed between the blades into the confining chamber on the other side. The two of us sat for a moment inside the strange space before deciding to leave. Visions of the propellers stirring to life ran through my head as Aron climbed out. There would be blood.

I watched the scene in my mind's eye. *The remnants of my friend spraying across the walls. Everything turning red.*

This memory faded as I turned my attention to the Underground's recognizable insignia — a red circle with the word "underground" written within a blue rectangle that cut through the centre. I remember thinking about mods, England, the Queen, and the Clash. I thought about underground bands and how the best things in life make you dig a little to find them.

My mind soon wandered back to the disorienting train ride that brought us to King's Cross station as I drifted. It was still shimmering inside me. A last glance was taken at our surroundings that lay in stark contrast to the day before. The journey still could be felt, the vision clear and beautiful.

I opened my eyes with my head resting next to the window on a makeshift pillow fashioned from my sweater, the steel wheels groaning below. Jason sat diagonally facing me on a blue checkered seat, his figure like a ghost in the glass. He'd just finished reading a devasting chapter of Ann-Marie MacDonald's *Fall on Your Knees*. It was the first time I saw him cry. Soft lights glowed from above. The scenery outside was superimposed over our reflections as if it was telling a deeper story. Like we were living two realities. This womb-like swaying of the train car enveloped us after the commotion and furor of the weeks before. My mind wandered to all I'd seen, to all that was moving me. I thought about relocation and how good it felt. How Jason and I had found the adventure we'd come for. Hours passed quietly. The outside scenery focused then unfocused in a gliding metronome of paint streaks. Expressionless farmers looked up from their tools at the passing train while we gazed back at them. Children waved. Like a darting needle, the train stitched together the green swatches of countryside. We coasted across deep rivers where white birds drifted weightlessly above. Beads of rain came from the darkening sky to slide along the window, disappearing just as they reached my eye. Their existence only momentary. Long blades turned on the windmills in distant fields. We skimmed and rocked through villages and towns with vehicles painted in oxidized reds and blanched yellows. Everything looked like miniatures from the model railway magazines my dad used to buy me. The lowest point of the falling clouds shanked and split by the conifers flanking the mountains. A calm came over me that paralleled the way "Not a Day Goes By" made me feel in the weeks after I'd first heard it. The whispered opening line had been resonating inside me ever since. It was trying to tell me something. I caught a wider scope of the peace I was searching for in those long hours of solitude on that train.

I would slide in and out of sleep, waking to the rumbling dark with the silhouettes of silos and churches streaming by in the night. In a few hours, we'd catch the ferry across the channel to London. *How many hours have passed? Has it been a day, two? What will England be like?* We would soon be meeting our heroes. The steel kept rolling and so did the thundering of my dreams.

Looking like a pile of crumpled laundry stacked against the wall in King's Cross station, we attempted to sleep with little avail. I pulled my hoodie back and a blinding white fireball washed out the peaceful recollection of our train ride. I saw something skitter near us. My vision cleared to reveal a taut, fearless rat. The rodent's whiskers twitched as it searched the floor with its glossy eyes, undaunted by the half-dead humans. Jason was sitting stone-faced against the wall, staring at the vermin. I cloaked myself in darkness again in a daze of exhaustion. Rats, monotone drones, random bangs, distant automated announcements, the threat of authority coming to tell us to leave. We drifted like smoke through the night until we heard grumbling from another passage far away inside the labyrinth. Lights came pouring from the black hole. The ground shook below us. My fingers traced the Canadian flag I had sewed to the flap of my traveller's backpack. I felt self-conscious as I slid my sleeve down to my knuckles. Clammy hands have always been a default setting in my moments of expectancy. This time a mixture of fatigue and anticipation brought it on. It was time to move toward a strange new future.

```
"I LIVED HERE LAST SUMMER.
IT WAS BETTER THAN DYING COLD.
WHILE WE WATCHED THE SCORCHING SUN,
WE ALL WENT BLIND AND DIED.
IT WAS ALL SO NICE.
A PEASANT IN PARADISE.
AND WILL WE REMEMBER THIS?
IT WAS ALL SO NICE,
A PEASANT IN PARADISE.

- "PEASANT IN PARADISE," STUBBS
```

ANDREW "LAINEY" LAING — LEATHERFACE, COCKNEY REJECTS, ANGELIC UPSTARTS, RED ALERT, H.D.Q., BULLTACO, RUGRAT

Four years before joining Nirvana, Dave Grohl played drums in the American punk band Scream (Dischord Records) from Washington, D.C. Scream performed at what Lainey remembers to be the Punx Picnic in Birmingham, England in either 1985 or 1986 alongside Lainey and Hammond's band, H.D.Q. Lainey reminisces that watching Scream play that day was one of the most critical moments of punk rock he's witnessed. The PA cut out during Scream's set for reasons unknown. But the D.C. five-piece didn't let the adverse circumstance hinder them. Instead, they used it to their advantage. Singer Peter Stahl got the crowd so amped up that they screamed the lyrics loud enough to be heard over the music. They were offered the opportunity to live their band name. Lainey got goosebumps and says he'll never forget it.

Dave Grohl approached Lainey later that day with two H.D.Q. LPs and asked the Sunderland drummer to autograph them. Grohl thought for certain H.D.Q. was American based on their sound and was stunned to learn they were British. Grohl's acknowledgment of Lainey's talent helps reaffirm that Andrew Laing was a damn fine drummer.

I asked Lainey twice what it was like growing up in Sunderland as a boy. Both times he launched into talking about skinheads and Madness. Perhaps Lainey skipped childhood altogether and was thrown straight to the wolves. Maybe he wasn't born at all. Maybe he materialized in a flash of lighting in an alley on a stormy night with a shaved head, a pair of Docs, and a bottle of red wine in his fist. Regardless, England was in need of another drummer. Someone upstairs created Lainey to save Sunderland's punk community from drowning in a sea of bass players, who seemed to multiply like gremlins when it rained, and it rained often.

His older brother was a rock 'n' roller and his younger brother was a "Teddy Boy" — a subculture of British youth interested in both rock 'n' roll and R&B music. Teds wore clothing inspired by the Edwardian period and were reminiscent of zoot suits. Their dress rebelled against traditional British culture at the time.

Because Lainey was influenced by his younger brother's musical sensibilities and gravitated to bands like Madness and Selector, a natural fascination with brass instruments developed. He always wanted to play the saxophone but never got the chance. As delightful as it is to imagine Lainey cruising the strip in shades and a zoot suit with a sax, when he heard the Sex Pistols from his friend Rob Bewick (H.D.Q.) there was no looking back.

The first music to move Lainey before the impact of punk and ska was a rare single recorded by Elvis Presley and Jerry Lee Lewis — "Save the Last Dance for Me." Hearing these two artists together for the first time stopped him in his tracks. Lainey remembers thinking, *I hope I can do something like that one day.* His recollection of the misty moment comes across with a sincerity I don't think I've heard from anyone. He continues, inspired by the memory, "Out of everything I've recorded, there's one song I love to play, and I still listen to it today, and it's

'Peasant in Paradise.'" His voice gains momentum and excitement: "The lyrics, and just that phrase, 'peasant in paradise,' that was us. That's who Leatherface was — just four lads from Sunderland, and we travelled the world. And the one thing that we all had in common is when we got into that practice room, or walked onstage, we *became* a band. We *became* Leatherface. When we got home, we kept our family life separate from the band. But when we were onstage, we were a phenomenal band to be honest. It took a lot for somebody to walk onstage after Leatherface, I tell ya." As he says this, it's impossible not to believe him. "To this day, I've never worked in a band that's been able to perfect what we did. I've never been in a band where writing a song would come together in so many different ways. I haven't been able to do it since. Everything now, especially with Cockney Rejects, it's just like .... verse chorus, verse chorus, little bit, verse chorus. Leatherface, there would be a beginning, then melodically build up until you'd get smashed in the face by force, and it would drop down again, then go into a finale. The way I used to think of us all the time was that we were an orchestra. Like how in an orchestra, you'd have the conductor doing all the waving movements nice and soft and then build it up and come up to the finale. I've never been in a band since that captured that; I don't think I'll ever be in a band again that would be able to capture that. It's been a real privilege to work with the people I have."

Lainey's first band had his younger brother on vocals, Rob Bewick on bass, and Lainey on guitar. "We would just sing about stupid stuff," Lainey says, smiling through his beard. He realized at a young age that playing an instrument and holding it in his hand just felt right. He would gravitate toward anything similar. "If there was a hammer and a nail and a piece of wood, I was fine." During his high school years when he could be seen dislocating shoulders on the rugby field, he joined his first band to play a live show. It happened after he responded to a flyer posted at the local youth centre. The kids were in search of a bass player (surprise, surprise). Lainey decided to give it a go. Their first gig as the Animated Coathangers happened at a notorious Sunderland venue called the Old Twenty Nine, a building that was once the Boilermakers Arms. After opening in the '70s, the proper rock club saw everyone under the roof from the Toy Dolls to Angelic Upstarts. The pounding of local heavyweights Red Alert rehearsing could be heard below in the basement as the Animated Coathangers ripped through their six-song set. Lainey remembers glass and sawdust covering the entire surface of the floor and felt as if the thin planks under his boots could give way at any given moment, sending the young punks tumbling down, crashing on top of Red Alert in a pile of splintered timber, broken pints, and shaved heads.

Lainey was influenced by the sounds of the street — Cockney Rejects, Red Alert, and Angelic Upstarts — and somehow managed to go on to play drums in all three of these bands. He even played bass for The Business once. How many people do you know who grew up to play in not one, but three formative bands of their youth? Not many, one might suspect. He talks about playing in these bands like it was an everyday thing, as if he's talking about how he takes his tea in the afternoon. Maybe punk is just to be expected in England and is as commonplace as construction work is to employment. But his humble nature could make you miss the weight of these accomplishments.

Lainey met Dave Golledge at some point and jumped at the chance to play bass with Hex. They were influenced by Crass and Conflict and Lainey describes them as the first band he played in to write, perform, and record what he considered to be "proper songs." And that they did. Their demos are strong, full of melody and impressive musicianship. Hex rehearsed at the Bunker like most punk bands in Sunderland. This was where Lainey first laid eyes on Dickie Hammond, a good friend of Golledge's. His admiration for the guitar player soon led him onward to play bass alongside Hammond in H.D.Q.

Their drummer went AWOL though on the day that H.D.Q. were set to record their debut LP. This is the exact moment that Lainey looked at the drums like they were a piece of wood, and decided he could drive nails through them. Lainey sat behind the kit and taught himself how to play and became H.D.Q.'s new drummer. The band pushed the recording session a week. But there was an issue: the band couldn't keep up with Lainey. This may sound like a novice's folly, but Stubbs didn't see it that way. It comes as no surprise that Stubbs was the first person to notice this. At that time he was playing guitar with Hammond and invited Lainey to the garage behind his house where the three of them had their first jam.

It wasn't long after that Leatherface was born, followed by the debut LP, *Cherry Knowle*, recorded and released on July 9, 1989. This was an exciting period in Lainey's life as he got to witness the band come to life.

"Frankie has a span on the guitar with his fingers — I've never seen anybody else play with a wider span than what Frankie's got. I would look at his hand while he was picking and think, *How the hell is he playing that?* He would break it down, and I'd think, *Jesus Christ, that's incredible.* Dickie and Frankie had completely different styles of playing, but you'd put them together, and it was just perfect. Dickie was really good at chugging, and then Frankie would put something acoustical over it, you'd have thunder behind it, and then there would be an almost classical bit cutting through. And it worked every time."

Hammond still played with H.D.Q. while Lainey still played with Sofa Head, who went out on the road with Snuff after the release of *Cherry Knowle*. It was on this tour that Snuff vocalist Duncan Redmonds heard this debut LP for the first time. The revered frontman couldn't get enough of their sound. So much so that one time Redmonds told the organizers of a Newcastle show that Snuff wouldn't be playing unless they added Leatherface to the bill. They listened to Redmonds's demand in fear of Snuff sticking with their threat. Word was spreading fast of this new band from Sunderland. Their fanbase grew faster than they ever would have expected because of it, and life became one long tour. They saw Europe more times on tour than they played single gigs back home. "We were blowing bands off the stage," says Lainey. "We'd finish, and people would say, 'Who the fuck was that?'"

There's no debating the breakthrough success of their third LP, *Mush*. Lainey admits that the record has "a power so raw I don't think we could ever capture it again." But there's another record the drummer holds near and dear to his heart — 2000's *Horsebox*. It had been a few years of radio silence for the band. The expression "absence makes the heart grow fonder" rang true for Lainey. "Fancy a go?" Stubbs asked the drummer after years apart, to which Lainey replied, "Yeah, I'll have a tinker with ya."

The band reformed with David Lee Burdon on bass and Leighton Evans on guitar in place of Hammond. Lainey looks back at this time fondly, remembering how fresh and renewed he felt stepping into rehearsals with this group of friends. They all seemed to connect at the right time. "It was a perfect storm. Frankie was writing great songs, and the bass lines that Davey would come up with sounded simple at first, but as you started studying them, you realized they were quite complicated. When we got in that studio and started recording, aye, it was just perfect." Lainey sings the track "Grip," which by all standards earned a spot on the top shelf of best Leatherface songs ever recorded. You can tell the drummer is proud of *Horsebox* and speaks of their progression during this time in their lives as a milestone.

"The way I look at it, it's like having a Sunday dinner. There's no way you can get a dinner right unless you get the potatoes right and the carrots right. If your carrots are raw, then it's off. But if you get everything right, it's a spot-on dinner. That's how we worked, we'd go in there and get the perfect Sunday dinner." These guys aren't English at all. Not one bit.

Lainey says one aspect of their sound that separated them from other bands boiled down to time signatures. They found it entertaining when the entire band would all be on a different count but somehow harmonious. What they thought could be a simple eight count turned out to be eight and three-quarters on many occasions. They did things that the other bands in their circle weren't capable of or would even consider. They would spend hours on one drum beat. Sometimes Stubbs would sit behind the kit and show Lainey a basic version of what he wanted. Lainey would then perfect it. Stubbs would also give Lainey a list of beats he was looking for. They would record each one. Stubbs would go home and write songs over top of them.

"The best way I can put it is it's like a tree. If the roots are strong then the tree will grow. If the roots are weak, then the tree's going to die. And that's the way I've always based everything. If the bass guitar is solid, and the drums are solid, that's the backbone of the band. And while those guitars are playing, as long as that backbone is running through, and the roots are there, everybody else is like the branches growing off. And it continues, until even the lyrics, they become the leaves."

Lainey's endured a long road through punk. He's met characters wilder than we could ever imagine. There is still one gig that plays as vividly in his head as the night it happened. The excitement in his voice grows as he begins to recount the story. I can almost feel the butterflies in his stomach. His voice sparks as he starts, "There always has been, and will always be one gig . . ."

Leatherface was at the top of their game. An unstoppable touring force, cramming clubs everywhere they went. They'd almost become the bands' band, the people's champion — the Italian Stallion of Europe. A heavy buzz was already mounting before the show on the particular night Lainey mentions. The promoter of the event came in the green room to inform them, "Alright, lads, there's a band from America coming down to the club tonight because they're big, BIG fans. They're called Poison Idea."

It wasn't long after the promoter told them the news that the back door banged open. In strode five of the largest, toughest looking dudes Leatherface had ever laid eyes on. They walked in the room slowly, each of them carrying a crate of beer. "Christ almighty, who the fuck is this?" Lainey mumbled to himself, but he knew who it was. The singer, Jerry A, was pushing three hundred pounds. At least a few of them weren't far behind that. Bandanas, beards, cut-off shirts, shades (at night). Lainey says he's never seen a group of humans walk into a room the way Poison Idea walked into that venue that night. Those who witnessed the band's unexpected invasion had no choice but to cower to their presence. These were Oregon's finest fuck-ups, adored, condemned, celebrated, and respected across the world as the epitome of what hardcore punk rock was supposed to be. Leatherface sat down with Poison Idea and got to know them on a personal level after the Brits' set. Lainey had never met a group of more genuine humans in his life. "They were just brilliant people."

Lainey became convinced Jerry A was trying to kill them all with booze as the bands became close. This feeling started in the middle of a Leatherface set one night as Jerry A strolled onstage between songs and handed Lainey a pint of mystery liquor and made the drummer down it in one pull. He has zero recollection of the second half of the set, only of stage-diving later to Poison Idea.

Another night, Leatherface was graced with a rare day off on a tour through Europe. Poison Idea were playing that evening in the same city, as coincidence would have it. They invited Leatherface to do a short set even though they weren't listed on the bill. Leatherface had never seen that much booze in one band's dressing room. The stockpile of beer was two cases thick and covered an entire wall, floor to ceiling. There were boxes of liquor as well and tables full of food. A lord's banquet. In the corner were a few cases for Leatherface with a bottle of red wine propped on top. This was the night that Lainey witnessed the true carnage that Jerry A could bring. The whole club stood in horror as Jerry A chugged two entire bottles of Jim Beam in one go between songs. Not one. Two.

The two bands piled into the van and headed to a local restaurant after the gig. The vehicle pulled into the parking lot, stopped, and the door slid open. As Jerry A attempted to step out, the giant man went crashing to the pavement like a bag of unmixed cement. They managed to get him back on his feet and helped him into the restaurant, where they got him safe and seated. The server began placing glasses of red wine down on the table, but as fast as he could put them down, Jerry A snatched them up and guzzled them back. He grabbed Lainey's drink and downed it before he could get his hand on the glass. It took five grown men to carry Jerry A up to his room by the time they got back to the hotel.

The next morning Lainey was sitting outside his room on the balcony, feeling contemplative and taking in the view of the Alps before him. A raspy voice called from above, "Hey, Lainey," snapping him from his tranquil state. Lainey looked up to find Jerry A's tremendous, hairy belly hanging over the balcony railing. In his fist he clutched an open bottle of Jim Beam and he shouted down to the drummer, "Have your morning taster!"

Poison Idea were the real deal living on the fringes. They stepped over the line, channelling the essence of life, death, drugs, alcohol, and punk, and embracing its volatile existence. They made no excuses for who they were or for their honesty. This was stimulating to the members of Leatherface. They could relate to Poison Idea's bravery to live the way they wanted to live. Many of Jerry A's tattoos strategically covered the scars littering his body from falling and slashing himself on the broken glass that accumulated onstage during their sets.

"They loved the drink, but meeting them was absolutely brilliant. They were such a phenomenal band. Thee Slayer Hippy [Steven Hanford], what a fuckin' drummer, absolute fuckin' beast. I cannot believe I got to see them play with him on drums because he was fuckin' incredible. Didn't matter how much he had to drink, he didn't skip a beat. He was incredible to watch. The two best drummers I've ever seen are Vinnie Paul from Pantera and Thee Slayer Hippy from Poison Idea. I'm not joking."

Knowing that Dave Grohl has his autograph tucked away somewhere in his record collection is something Lainey was proud of, but he talked about his time with Poison Idea as though it were a lifetime achievement award.

"I HAVE A THEORY, THE THINGS YOU DO AREN'T GOOD FOR YOU.
A HYMN AND A RHYME AND A PLETHORA OF ASHTRAY ABUSE.
A BUCKET FULL OF SUNSHINE AND A MISSILE TO USE.
I'D LOVE TO SEE YOU SMILE
OR AM I JUST WASTING MY TIME AGAIN"

— "I DON'T WANT TO BE THE ONE TO SAY IT," STUBBS

LEEDS

It was a short walk from Leeds railway station to the Duchess of
York. We were stoked the venue was so easy to locate. The building
became the type of place where many celebrated musicians got their
start. You name the band, they've performed there — Bolt Thrower,
Green Day, Oasis, Poison Idea, U.K. Subs, Peter and the Test Tube
Babies, NOFX, GBH, the Jesus Lizard, the Cranberries, Nirvana,
Radiohead. Cobain was even rumoured to have spent the night on the
upstairs sofa, which looked like it had survived the war. This iconic
grassroots venue was the type of place that a proud English music
scene still cares about today, long after its closure in 2000. Its contribution to music culture in the city may be second to none. Before
the Duchess of York was born in the early '80s, the venue was known
as the Robin Hood Inn, a staple hangout for boozers, sex workers, and pimps. After all that blistering rock 'n' roll, the club's since
been gutted and fashioned into a Hugo Boss. If you listen closely,

I wonder if you can still hear the faint screams from the generations of discomposed youth?

We stepped up to the address on Vicar Lane with the name in gold letters above the door. The view between the pink and yellow band flyers in the window looked inviting. It was early, and the lingering smell of stale lager filled the air as we walked through the door. Two p.m. seemed as good a time as any to indulge in a pint. We took a seat on a bench against the wall behind a small round wooden table near the door. The daylight from the window poured across the worn floorboards. Dark, carved panels of rosette wreaths ran below the burgundy-red walls above. Gold chandeliers were set inside a bourbon-stained, wood-panelled overhang. There was something Art Deco about the curved archways that led to other sections of the pub. When we spotted a poster for the Hot Water Music show, it reassured me that the night would bring music and familiar faces. The warm feeling of having a hideout embraced us for the remainder of the day.

The beer went down easy in the afternoon light. We would be driving to Lainey's after the show. Morning would see us off to Huddersfield for a few days to visit Jason's family, then back to Sunderland to spend some more time with Lainey. Optimism was rising.

We explored Leeds before having too many drinks, lugging our packs through the streets, absorbing the energy of the city. Leeds presented a combination of old-world charm and modern buildings. Big brand stores and arcades filled the high street. We found an area full of action that entertained us for some time. Seeing the pretty women everywhere gave us stamina. I dipped into a market to buy a sandwich. We sat on a curb smoking and eating, watching people move past in all directions.

Jason perched like a bulldog as he sang a Stompin' Tom Connors song out to someone walking by. It was the one about the big spuds. I looked down. The person ignored Jason, expressionless as they passed. "No Stompin' Tom for you, huh?" he asked them. The passerby didn't answer. Then he looked at me and my sandwich. I knew what was coming and knew I couldn't dodge it.

"God, you're like a hummingbird."

"Huh?" I responded, looking up from my sandwich.

"Yeah, like a little hummingbird, flying around eating little bits at a time." I smiled at the creative analogy.

"I'm hungry," I said.

"It's because you take a shit every other hour," he said, laughing. "That's why you need to keep eating."

"Fuck you, bud."

"You're like a ferret."

Huh? I began to feel flushed. He knew, so he laughed again.

"Thought you just said I ate like a hummingbird."

"But you shit like a ferret." His impish grin grew wide. I couldn't help but smile too.

"What does that even mean?" I asked in a tone as dry as the salmon sandwich in my hands.

"Means you take too many shits, MacDonald."

The point in our journey when our everyday actions annoyed the other had become inevitable. When you realize your travelling companion's as charming as the petrified socks buried in your pack. My appetite irritated him. No matter how much I ate or drank, I remained a skinny runt. This was a mystery to the Irishman. I couldn't help this phenomenon or change my metabolism. In my younger days, I spent some time being hungry. Now that I had a few bucks to spare, I welcomed the taste of a mediocre sandwich on a grey afternoon.

We shrugged the tension off and watched people go by. The first time we'd done this together was on a winter day at the Eaton Centre in Toronto. Since it was 1992 or '93, Jason would have still had a head of hair. It may have been one of the first times we hung out. He was born a brat. I was a trouble maker in the making. He sensed this and wanted me by his side. We smoked a joint outside before stumbling through the doors into the mall to get warm. The heat hit us hard and I became very high. Everything echoed. People walked in all directions. The light radiated as you imagine it would from heaven. We sat on the steps near the doors where all the skaters and punks hung around. Salt under our frozen shoes. Christmas music chiming. The game began with little effort.

"Look at this guy," Jason muttered. He had a combover and looked shady. The man wore a tan trench coat that made a swishing sound when he passed.

"Looks like a Larry," I said, and Jason laughed at this.

"Larry drives a Buick," Jason added.

I thought for a moment. "Oh yeah . . . He just lost his job at Chrysler, they found him secretly driving the Buick." I muffled my snorty stoner giggle into my sleeve. I couldn't stop. Jason chuckled as quietly as he could behind his hair. He was skilled at keeping his laughter silent.

We watched on.

"This is Shelly, she's awful," he said about a severe-looking lady. She paraded past us with a cardigan draped across her shoulders. Her heels clacked like distant fireworks. She loathed scumbags like us. I buried my face some more. We played the English version of the game while sitting on a set of steps somewhere in downtown Leeds, smoking and laughing.

We found a record store and killed some time browsing. It felt comforting to be in an environment that we knew well. We both bought the same live New Model Army double disc album called . . . & Nobody Else. I handed the CD to the clerk, wondering if they'd approve of my choice.

RECORD PEDDLER, YONGE STREET, TORONTO — 1995

I emerged from the subway stairs in the shadows of the financial towers, my combat boots kicking through the melting snow on Bloor Street. A red and yellow Co-op cab swerved and honked as its tires turned through the slush. White clumps slid from the green awnings of Stollerys, the menswear shop on the southwest corner. The sun was warm on my face. March always felt like spring to me, and I've always pretended it was.

I'd ride the Bloor-Danforth subway across to Yonge station from Dufferin, then walk south. My first stop was always Rock Variety, a famous head shop where you could buy a Cramps shirt and fancy rolling papers for cheap. The red font on the blue rectangle sign always looked like a candy bar wrapper to me. Their window display was full of Jimi Hendrix and Chili Peppers shirts with a large Canada flag with a red marijuana leaf in the centre. Inside was crowded with psychedelic posters, patches, tie-dye everything, and glass pipes. The owner was a short man with a long grey handlebar moustache and chains around his neck.

The Record Peddler boasted an extensive selection of punk, thrash, and metal and was near Rock Variety. My route never changed, and inevitably led me to the window display of Doc Martens near Wellesley, where I'd dream of the boots I couldn't afford. I'd cut through city hall to Queen Street afterward. That's where the other independent record stores like Vortex, Kops, and Rotate This could be found.

The thought of having something new to wear that day lit me up while I browsed the clothing racks in Rock Variety. I can still smell the mothballs. A black Danzig shirt with a graphic of a goat-headed Jesus hanging from a cross lured me. I craved this, but it wasn't what I needed. It had been a few years since I'd first heard *Mush* in Darrell's smoky basement. I left the head shop with a reunion in mind.

It always felt like I was walking into Metallica's album cover for *Ride the Lightning* when entering Record Peddler. The facade was painted blue with white lightning bolts around the windows. The glass door full of show flyers (Snowdogs, Hev's Duties, Infernäl Mäjesty, Random Killing) always opened into a wave of thrash metal. The entire inside was covered with posters. Record Peddler's owner, Ben Hoffman, opened the doors to the iconic business in 1977, a fitting year for a store specializing in punk. An intimidating cast of characters worked behind the counter over the years including Brian Taylor of the Toronto punk band Youth Youth Youth and Adam Sewell of Monster Voodoo Machine.

I had zero facial hair with a shaved head and looked much younger than I was. Whoever was working that afternoon didn't acknowledge my presence as I entered. This record shop lived up to its reputation for posturing. I hummed the Misfits song about attitude under my breath as I slinked to the back. You couldn't blame them. I looked like any Yonge Street punk in a plaid jacket and army pants — a dime a dozen.

One of the first 7" records I bought from Record Peddler was released by a band called Exit Condition. They were a melodic hardcore punk band from Stoke-on-Trent, U.K. I loved this record with all my heart, and more so when I found out it was released on Pushead's label Pusmort. For those unfamiliar, Pushead is Brian Schroeder, an American artist best known for the artwork he created for Metallica, Misfits, and Dr. Dre. I needed to find the Exit Condition record after hearing them on a local radio show called *Fast and Bulbous on the Spot* broadcasted from York University. The show was co-hosted by Stephe Perry, a respected contributor to Canadian punk and hardcore music and an important voice in Canadian community radio. I would lie in bed and listen with only the blue light of the receiver dial glowing, squinting my eyes, writing down every song that resonated with me. One of them being Stephe's band — One Blood — who by all standards could be the best hardcore act to ever emerge from Toronto. I owe a lot to Stephe Perry. One day I will thank him for his kindness and generosity. Equipped with a long list, I would try to find the bands at the local record stores.

My vinyl collection consisted of about thirty records at that time. It was a small but impressive assortment. Jason's knowledge of music ran deeper than mine, but I had a few cards up my sleeve. Exit Condition was one of them. It felt like he tricked me out of the record after asking me if I wanted to trade it for another 45 from a band I'd never heard of. He assured me I would love them, and I took his word on good faith. When I reached home, I put the new music on my turntable and hated it. A wariness of Jason crept in that day. I suppose I could sense a hustler inside of him because I knew it was somewhere in me as well. If I can be kinder now to our younger selves, we were fuelled by desperation back then. In those early days of our friendship, we had no concept of what truly was at stake.

There was no Leatherface in stock under "L" in the vinyl section on that afternoon in March. I found one album titled *Minx* with the CDs. Something inside me surged at its sight. I yanked it from its place as if someone else were reaching for it. But the glow inside me dimmed as I looked at the price: twenty-six dollars. A CD in 1995. Why was it twenty-six dollars? I approached the person behind the counter with it in my hand. He already seemed irritated.

"Is this the right price?"

The clerk looked up with a blank expression. "Yup," he said, looking away. A moment of silence followed.

"Why so expensive?"

Small exhale. Don't annoy me you little puke.

"Import."

"Oh . . ."

I walked away looking at the cover like a kid in 2024 looks down at a cellphone. It was milky inside its faded plastic casing. I wanted it even more now that it seemed unattainable. The cryptic photograph on the front was of a little girl running and laughing with a camel in the background. It reminded me of *Mush*. I flipped the album over to look at the back. The second track, titled "Books," caught my attention. I needed to hear what Frankie Stubbs had to say about books.

I found myself walking to the front like a robot and handing over the music regardless of what little cash was left in my pocket. *Fuck it.* You only live once. Besides, something about Leatherface was again calling me. Like a traveller standing in customs talking to the border guard, I waited with my foot tapping. The clerk raised his eyebrow. This look suggested that if I was going to spend that much on watered-down English punk, then I was a turd, but this was probably my own insecurities talking. He flipped and eyed the CD on both sides as if examining my passport. The clerk glanced at me and began writing up a receipt. He handed me the brown paper bag and seemed happy to have me out of his face. Despite the vibe at times, Record Peddler was a formative staple that had everything a kid like me needed. I headed back out into the crisp air of Yonge Street stoked to have some tunes. New music meant promise. I couldn't wait to get back home.

The space I rented was in the back of a shabby rooming house where twenty other people lived. Next door was a punk named Tony from an older, more stoned generation. He was perma-fried and listened to the weirdest shit. I never once recognized a single song coming from beyond his door. The only thing of value in my room was a decent stereo I bought from the pawn shop at Gladstone and Queen that is still there today.

I lit a smoke and opened the window to let the cool breeze in. The navy-and-rose-patterned sofa I'd dragged in from the curb had two springs shooting up through the foam. They hadn't split the fabric yet and it still looked nice, reassuring me that things aren't what they seem. You needed to be strategic about where you sat. I found the sweet spot on the cushion, then slid *Minx* in the player and pressed play.

Imagine a heavy storm's blown over and left rain drops dripping in fast succession from an eavestrough above a porch. It's late April. Now give the rain a sound, in this case distortion. Only a tiny amount for every drop, as well as a different note for each. Adjust the treble a little — that's it, give it a hint of light. Now picture yourself on the porch, where the "electric guitar–like rain" is dripping from above while you sit in a chair next to a window. In your lap is a heavy feather pillow. Pooled in the centre lies a handful of coins. With a drumstick you begin thumping the pillow in perfect time with the drops.

That's what the first seven seconds of this record sounds like.

Stubbs comes running up the stairs out of nowhere with his shoes clapping on the wood as you sink into the beat. He's growling low and holding a bouquet of flowers, eyeing the window beside you with caution. The singer seems worried that he might wake the child sleeping in the room next to the porch. He commands your attention with his fierce whisper so you can't look away.

The song is "Wallflower" and it dips and dives like the swallow hovering in the grey afternoon. Stubbs waves the fisted flowers from the porch like a conductor, choreographing the rain, the thudding pillow, and the bird up in the sky — like it all follows some surreal, dream-like orchestra.

Minx sounds like old friends who know how to play music with one another. Hammond, Laing, and Crighton follow every nuance together as one. Both *Mush* and *Minx* are full of lyrics that fit perfectly in their place. But the songs on *Minx* are like poems unobstructed by the confines of music, as if the instrumentation could have been built around the words. The poetic undertone was shining. This was melancholia. Jack Rabid (critic, *The Big Takeover*) states that although Stubbs spent many years internalizing the punk rock surrounding him, it was Joy Division that "truly turned his head in 1979." The brooding, esoteric undertone makes so much sense now. This deliberate change in mood was an attempt to keep things fresh. Stubbs also took the advance given to him from the record company and upgraded his recording equipment and tracked the whole thing in his studio. This offered the singer many more hours to place words exactly how they needed to be.[1]

I was entranced by what Stubbs was singing about once again: "And I love the way it turns." No band I knew (nor punk music in general for that matter) spoke about the world in such a way. The thoughtful stance was fearless. This was the essence of true punk for me. I smoked and listened, smoked and listened some more while pondering the words. Stubbs materialized in my mind as someone in the corner of the pub reading Salinger, and rarely speaking to anyone. A loner. Those who knew his band knew nothing of him as a person. An ambiguous figure. A ghost in the street. I was convinced from that day on that this was the person singing those songs.

My eyes scanned the inside cover. It had pictures of young children and a baby. Little did I know at the time, one of the little girls was named Beth, the daughter of Graeme Philliskirk, a long-time friend of the band. Graeme would become their bass player later in life. Soon the end of the album was upon me. The last song was called "Pale Moonlight." It began with a guitar tone reminiscent of "Stark Raving Normal" by the Blood from London. It seemed like a reminder that Leatherface hadn't forgotten what it meant to be tough. The song left me in a state. There was a definite change in character happening within

---

1   The information in this paragraph came directly from Jack Rabid's personal notes written in 2015 about the reissue of *Minx*.

me. When I lit another cigarette, a notion was unravelling — that if I kept listening to this band, they'd make me a better person. It made me feel like there was a vault down in me with something of great value inside. The key, however, was nowhere to be found.

I didn't have much besides a broken sofa, a stereo, a few smokes, and a new Leatherface CD. But I felt as if I'd been rescued. With the cool wind of early March sliding through the crack in the window at dusk, I knew then the warmest spring I'd spent was the winter I first heard *Minx*.

SIMON WELLS — SNUFF, SOUTHPORT

It was a miracle the guitarist could open his eyes at all. The monotonous rumble below was doing nothing to aid his breaking skull or settle his churning guts. It's unlikely any man has stood toe to toe with the hangover Wells faced that morning. The founder of north London's punk rock group Snuff peeled his face from the crumb-dusted floor of J Church's tour van rollicking through Spain's Monegros Desert. Images of the past week flashed through his mind like scenes of a strange film. From the darkened cargo area, he could make out the voices of Lance Hahn and Gardner Maxam from J Church. This alleviated his panic, because for a moment he thought he'd been kidnapped by the vaquero who'd poisoned him the night before.

Wells played drums in a band called Your Mum then, who was supporting J Church through the U.K. leg of their tour before they headed to Europe for six weeks. J Church was a fairly well-known American punk band from San Francisco that emerged from their former band,

Cringer. The band asked Wells if he'd consider being their roadie for the remainder of the tour. He was unemployed and had no other obligations to speak of. Wells agreed with enthusiasm. As J Church, Wells, and their driver, Christy Colcord (Lookout Records staff), made their way to southern Italy, a string of bad luck descended upon them — the next four tour dates were cancelled. The income made from the shows was their only means to fuel and food. It was a dire situation. J Church was still finding their footing as a band in 1991, and attendance was somewhat sparse in those days. They had enough to fill the gas tank after pooling all of their cash together. It would get them to the next gig in Spain. The remainder of the money left enough for a baguette each. The lot of them didn't eat for three days once the bread was gone. They rolled through Saint-Tropez and Monaco and other places of great wealth with empty bellies and pockets, sleeping on beaches, hoping things would turn around when they reached Spain.

As they reached Zaragoza, the capital of northeastern Spain's Aragon region, they were greeted by a thirsty crowd that recognized Wells from Snuff. It wasn't only at the Zaragoza show that Wells felt like a celebrity, Snuff had sold out concerts all across Europe at that time. Wells was noticed at most J Church gigs. The guitarist was enjoying the press and indulging with fans. He laments that if only the organizers of the Zaragoza show could have greeted them with as much gratitude, their rider may have consisted of something other than a large bowl of salad and a few strawberries. Not what was needed after consuming next to nothing for three days. "A salad, after not eating for three fucking days. It was the worst rider I'd ever seen," his dusty voice still living the pain of the moment. "I was going to be drinking hard with these boys!"

The band still had no money because they wouldn't be getting paid until after the gig. The lettuce and liquor sloshed around inside their empty stomachs. A lack of food brought a lack of judgment. Wells found himself at a nightclub at three in the morning. That's when the vaquero came from the darkness and the crowd, surrounded by his goons, wearing a ten-gallon Stetson. The big hat was all that could be seen through the flashing neon. That and a half-pint of whisky in each of the man's fists.

"You English?" the vaquero asked. Wells sensed the brewing challenge. He replied with as much confidence and pride as he could muster, eyeing the booze with caution.

"Yeah, I'm English," Wells said. That's when the man raised the drink to his lips and gulped at the liquor. Streams of amber ran down his chin. He smiled like a madman as he swallowed the last mouthful. His goons danced around them. The born-and-bred Englishman knew the damage a half-pint of whisky could cause. Wells refused the offer. But the vaquero wouldn't accept defeat.

"C'mon, you're English, NOO?!" he egged him on. Wells took the glass and tried his best to show him what a northwest Londoner was made of in a moment of wounded pride. He came close to finishing the brutal offering before his eyes and brain went black. The guitarist didn't come around until he was being lifted from the pavement outside the club.

Wells woke wrapped around a toilet somewhere in Zaragoza with the members of J Church trying to lift him from the floor of the bathroom and get him downstairs. His body was rendered limp with alcohol poisoning. He could do nothing but lie on the floor of the van like a corpse as the vehicle sped out of town toward the desert. All functionality had been disabled by the drink. He became concerned that the van was not a van at all, but rather a rolling coffin driving him to his grave.

Nothing inspired Wells more than the afternoon the young man walked into Rough Trade Records in northwest London in 1987 and took a chance on the new Hüsker Dü 7" titled *Eight Miles High*. Wells looks back fondly on the days before the internet. It was a time when somehow a person could still know about every new record being released. His ear was always to the ground then. He was overcome with inspiration when he put on the Hüsker Dü record. His only thought was, *This is it. I want to make records now.*

Andy Crighton lived on the next street over from Wells in northwest London as kids. It wasn't a picturesque place in 1976. Crighton, the future Snuff/Leatherface bass player, grew up in the house that both he and his mother were born in. It was an old home full of history. Crighton and Wells began playing guitar together when the boys were thirteen. Crighton was obsessed with Killing Joke and the Stranglers, and together the two of them played along to those records as best they could. The spirit wore off on them. Most of the kids back then grew up smoking and drinking. "Andy never had any intention to stop drinking or smoking. He'd buy a bulk box of tobacco, a hundred packs, only because it was a little cheaper. We all thought maybe at some point we'd eventually quit. But not Andy. He knew he was never going to quit anything, ever in his life. He was all about the bass, completely committed. Committed to smoking, committed to drinking, and committed to playing music. He could accept his lot in the world. Whereas I wanted the grass in the next field, Andy was content with what he had and who he was and what he was doing at the time. I don't know if that was a great thing or bad thing, it was just his thing. By the end, Andy's alcoholism was so bad, Snuff would be in the middle of a song and the bell would ding for last call. He'd put his bass down halfway through a verse and go to the bar and order three pints." Wells continued, "The place would be sold out, but he didn't care. None of us knew how to deal with his problem, and eventually it killed him. Leatherface could never find the right bass player in the early days, but when Andy got there, there was no doubt about that anymore because Andy's bass was solid. Andy served the song, which is all you can ask for in a musician, is to serve the song, to remove your ego out of the equation. He always did what was right for the song. He never showed off, he was a slave to it, and one of the greatest. It was just so right, and you knew this because many times you couldn't even hear it. Andy would make us all sound great. What more could you ask? He was an unsung hero."

Wells formed Snuff after hearing *Eight Miles High* and learning all he did with Crighton. Crighton played bass and Duncan Redmonds played drums and sang. The band took off faster than expected. When you hear their chanting vocals coupled with their reliable formulas, it's easy to understand why it didn't take long before filling clubs was a regular occurrence for the London trio. Their first incarnation of the band sounds similar to their last and has held a solid stance among U.K. punk culture. When their first full-length, *Snuff Said* (a play on cockney accents), was released in 1989, the record sounded unlike anything else at the time.

Snuff soon ventured north to Tyneside way as they became more prominent on the scene. The atmosphere was different, though, in Newcastle and Sunderland. As unsavoury as their home was, when they got to the North East, Wells admits that staying in the van with the door locked seemed like a wiser idea. Their first gig in Sunderland was at a club filled with tables right up to the front of the stage. The place reminded him of a jazz bar. Wells noticed something curious as the venue filled with showgoers; an empty table with a reserved sign below the microphone remained empty no matter how many people entered the room. A man with a crew of tough-looking blokes soon weaved among the people as if they owned the joint and sat down in the vacant seats. With a drink his hand, the guy stared up at Wells.

After the gig, this mysterious stranger approached Wells and introduced himself as Norm. Back then, Frankie Norman Warsaw Stubbs went as Norman Frankie Warsaw Stubbs. Norm told Wells that he had a band called Leatherface and convinced him they should be the supporting act for Snuff. There was something about Norm's demeanour that Wells couldn't say no to. He agreed without even hearing them. Snuff returned to the North East to play a benefit in Darlington supporting rape crisis centres, with Leatherface as the opening act. Dickie "The Dog" Camm was one of the many bass players that Leatherface chewed through in those days. Redmonds recalls the Sunderland band stepping onstage in balaclavas and Dickie "The Dog" saying into the mic, "We're Leatherface and we're rapists," before Stubbs gave the bassist a telling look that suggested the Dogman's position in Leatherface would be short lived. They stole everyone's hearts with what would have been a bare-bones set of songs from their first LP, *Cherry Knowle*. Wells said to himself while they played, *Shit, they sound like us, only tougher*. Redmonds says the band "launched into a wonderful, grinding, rasping, melodic wall of noise. They blew me away. So gutsy, so powerful. I loved the way the two guitars worked together and have loved them ever since."

Leatherface sent their demo of *Cherry Knowle* to Snuff's record label Workers Playtime. It showed up in the post while Wells was visiting the office. The songs blew them all away from the opening track. Wells was left wondering how it was that they could have sounded so similar to Snuff without ever hearing them before. But the mystery began to unravel.

This small circle of punks created a unique sound. One of the notable characteristics is the use of the U.K.'s longest-running guitar manufacturer, Gordon Smith Guitars, in their music. As legend would have it, their earliest guitar bodies were fashioned from the mahogany bar tops ripped from inside the pubs around Manchester. Gordon Whitham and John Smith collected these bar tops sodden in beer and whisky and breathed new life into the wood. These guitars weren't popular and were the cheapest in the shops back then: one of their models could be bought for 120 pounds, including a case. They were rudimentary builds with little finesse, but the manufacturers prided themselves on their no-frills design. You wouldn't have found a sunburst on a Gordon Smith then. The general public knew they were being made in a garage somewhere and that could have been part of the attraction. These guitars had something going for them despite their unpopular look — a rare resonance that contributed to the unique, sombre undertone heard in North East English punk. Could it be that deep within the grains of wood was the laughter and the tears of yesterday, a region's history ringing through?

Hammond and Wells discovered they both owned and played the same guitar, a Gordon Smith GS1. What was more of a coincidence was that on each guitar was a sticker for Dan (a local band from Darlington). They knew then the ties would be strong. Hammond was very close with Gordon as well as Smith in those days. Wells started getting his guitars through Hammond because of this.

What these English punks also had going for them was that they'd mastered the iconic D-beat, a hardcore punk drum beat invented in England during the late '70s and '80s. The D-beat borrowed the stock American punk beat, essentially a sped-up polka beat, and added an extra kick drum hit into the mix. One of the earliest examples can be heard in the Buzzcocks' "You Tear Me Up," released in '78. Wells describes it as putting "the funk in the punk." It was one of the first things I noticed about Snuff when I heard the song "Another Girl" from their 1989 debut release, *Snuff Said*. You could hear how natural the D-beat came out of Redmonds. Almost as if he'd been raised listening to it.

Out of all the bands that Leatherface had a harmonious pairing with, it's true that the first cut is the deepest. You might speculate that no relationship has been as important as their time spent with Snuff. They played so many shows together that to count them would be futile. Wells states with confidence that the best punk shows in the U.K. at that time would have been Snuff, Leatherface, and either the Abs or Broccoli. Tim Scott of *Vice* said that despite Broccoli's terrible name, "The influential Scottish band's album is stacked with layers of melody and urgent and emotive raspy punk."

Wells continues, "In those days, if you walked down the street with Snuff and Leatherface, you wouldn't have to worry about anything. With Lainey being a black belt, everyone felt safe." Wells says he witnessed Lainey make waste of two loudmouths for saying he looked like Right Said Fred.

When considering Leatherface's distinction from other punk music, Wells speculates their signature sound can be traced to Stubbs's love for the Police. He believes that if you took the Police's songbook and played it with a distorted Gordon Smith guitar, you would find the spark that ignited the Leatherface sound.

"When it was Dickie, Lainey, and Norm in the lineup. By the time he got to *Mush*, 'Not Superstitious,' 'Not a Day Goes By,' Norm was fucking hitting it right on the post. He knew what he was doing by that point. The hardness of their life really came through in songs like 'Dead Industrial Atmosphere.' It *was* a dead industrial atmosphere there. The glory days were gone. There was fucking nothing left for people, and I think you could hear that in their music. You can feel that melancholy and past glories in his words, you can hear it in the guitars. All of those towns grew up around coal, around pits and coal mines, and when Margaret Thatcher closed the coal mines everyone was pissed off and had no future. Industry in the U.K. died. These people worked with their hands and had hard jobs. You could feel it in the places you went, Mansfield and such, they were old pit villages. There was fuck all else to do. The only way to get their heart pumping was to go out on Saturday night, to make themselves feel like there was something worth living for. There was violence those nights too. It was a different time and a different age. Norm really reflects the culture of where he comes from, and it's a beautiful thing. I will always be thankful for what he gave to us. I can't remember a lovelier time than watching Leatherface play every single fucking night. On tour with other bands, it was different, but with Leatherface you'd never want to miss a minute of any set on any night. It was just a wonderful thing. It's so honest. Norman Frankie Warsaw Stubbs, what a fuckin' songwriter. Yeah, Leatherface will give me the feels every time, they really will. They were my favourite band, no two ways about it. If I ever see Frankie again in this lifetime, I'll be happy, if he's only come around to smack me in the head."

From the floor of the van, Wells could feel the vehicle veer from the road. They turned into the parking lot of a service station in the middle of the Monegros Desert, where the van finally came to a stop. Colcord turned the engine off. There was only one other vehicle in sight — another van parked about a hundred yards away. Colcord sat examining the other automobile after Hahn and Maxam had jumped out. The only words to grant Wells enough strength to lift himself from the floor since leaving Zaragoza were when Colcord said, "I think someone just got out of that van over there with a Leatherface shirt on."

Wells dragged himself through the heat of the asphalt parking lot like a man emerging from the desert's death grip. He pulled the door of the service station open and let the cool air hit him on the face. His lips parched. Eyes searching for the Leatherface shirt.

A mirage is a naturally occurring optical phenomenon where light rays bend via refraction to produce a displaced image of distant objects. Wells stepped deeper into the station with his brain still in the throes of alcohol poisoning and his delirium peaking. His sense of reality was challenged when he saw Stubbs, Hammond, and Crighton relaxing in chairs. The three of them were laughing and drinking cold lagers.

A chorus of Englishmen echoed through the canyon walls.

Crighton could see his childhood friend was in dire straits and lent Wells some money. This was the last time Wells saw Crighton before he passed away. Wells never got the chance to pay him back. There's only one person that Wells thinks of when he hears Leatherface's "Not a Day Goes By," this kid named Andy who lived one street over from him in northwest London, who loved smoking cigarettes and who taught him his first guitar chord.

My dry salmon sandwich left me feeling like I'd swallowed a mouthful of sand. I needed beer. We spotted a large boat landlocked in the grass while walking back to the venue.

"Whoa, it's a boat . . . in the grass," Jason said.

"MOTO."

"Huh?"

"Master of the obvious."

There was a pause before Jason responded.

"Asshole."

"I think it's a pub."

"Really?"

"Yeah look, there's a sign for drinks."

"No way . . ."

"Let's go."

"Beer."

The boat bar in Leeds is now called Dry Dock. I have no idea if it was called that in 1999. We walked inside to find the innards sheathed in floor-to-ceiling wood. The only comparable thing I know of is Inter Steer on Roncesvalles Avenue in Toronto.

We found a cozy nook in the stern of the boat, a seating area three steps higher than everything else. After hearing next to no music for days, our eyes widened at the sight of a jukebox in the corner. The music player shone like a lighthouse. Two young women sitting close by snuck glances in our direction. It felt like they were laughing at us because of how rough we looked. With pint in hand, Jason dropped some coins in the slot. The Offspring's *Americana* seemed to be the only thing close to punk. I loved them in my younger days. *Ignition* and *Smash* were both great albums. I knew a tune from *Americana* that would give us what we needed. And no, it wasn't "Pretty Fly (for a White Guy)." I pressed the code for "The Kids Aren't Alright." I love this song because the guitar lead in the beginning reminds me of Judas Priest's "Breaking the Law." The music was loud and glorious. We were glowing like the lights on the chrome music machine. We'd been saved. We spent the afternoon drinking in a boat on the grass, only hours from seeing Hot Water Music live.

"Hi, I'm Fionna," said one of the young women with a smile that revealed her tiny teeth. Her short black hair smelled like a salon. I spotted an impressive Japanese tattoo on her arm. We introduced ourselves and they seemed entertained by our Canadian mannerisms.

"Eeeeeee . . . what happened there?" she asked, pointing to the tender pink slice marks all over my hand.

"Yeah, I cut myself a few times," I said, amused. It had happened on the train a few days before.

She looked back at me with a puzzled expression. "How?"

"Oh shit," I said as the blood ran from my finger across the white cream cheese like a tiny red river through fresh snow. My brother Rob had given me a steel multi-tool made by Leatherman in preparation for my journey. He's an expert knife sharpener and the blade was doing what it was meant to do. The Leatherman is a Scout's dream that comes equipped with everything from a saw to a pair of pliers. Spreading cream cheese on a bagel while on a swaying train may not have been the smartest idea, but my brain wasn't functioning at full capacity. Jason squinted his eyes and smiled at me. He began to snicker when he saw the accident.

I got up and placed the bagel, knife, and cheese down in my seat and headed to the back of the train to get the napkins I'd stuffed in my bag before leaving Amsterdam. They were crammed in a pocket filled with plastic forks, ketchup and pepper packets, and whatever else I'd scavenged from the last fast-food joint we'd been in. I placed a folded strip of serviette over the wound and sealed the makeshift dressing with a piece of tape. Once I was seated and things were back in order, I continued to spread the cheese before cutting myself again.

"Are you kidding me right now?" I asked no one. The knife couldn't have been sharper.

A concerned-looking man with a soup strainer moustache and knit sweater seated across the aisle leaned forward and peered sideways toward me. I looked at him and flashed my best John Candy smile.

I stood and dropped my bloodied lunch back onto the cushion, then walked down the aisle again to my backpack, trying not to drip blood on the other commuters. Another serviette was folded and taped around the second gash. I tucked the tape and more napkins into the front pocket of my shirt just in case. One couldn't be prepared enough.

My hand was in a terrible state. I collected my lunch and sat back down, hoping to not make a scene. But I could feel eyes on me. The nicks were small but were seeping through the makeshift bandages. A piece of hairy tape dangled from my finger. I huffed in annoyance at the sight.

"What is wrong with you?" Jason asked, his question aimed at my precarious state of mind.

"Yup, all good, mind your own business," I whispered.

I set my things in order and began spreading.

I cut myself again. And more blood came.

GODAAAMMIT, Rob!

This slice left a long flap of skin waving like a white flag in the wind next to my knuckle. It was surrendering. This was true slasher cinema. Chainsaws and screams.

The passenger with the soup strainer cast a very uneasy expression my way. One bushy brow lifted this time. I looked at him and shrugged. He began to say something but I raised my hand. He closed his parted lips. The hand I'd gestured to him with had been holding the knife. Jason cackled.

"You're so fucked," he said in a whisper as loud as he could.

"I'm hungover, I think," I muttered.

"You *think*?" he asked, then added, "You're still drunk, MacDonald."

"It's my brother's fault."

"No, it's yours, you loser."

I looked at the knife, then at my filleted hand.

"They should've called this thing a Leatherface, not a Leatherman. It's a fucking horror show."

I bandaged up the third cut as best I could, managing to get the cheese on top of the bagel without a fourth incident. I could see the man across the aisle still gawking at me through the corner of my eye. He couldn't pry himself away from the gross display. I turned and raised my bagel in my disgusting bandaged hand to cheers him before biting into the bloodied breakfast. Jason scoffed, laughed, and rocked in his seat while the train rolled through the pretty Dutch landscape. When I was finished, I dropped the Leatherman back in my bag with the ketchup and the pepper. The funny thing is, Rob had given me the knife to protect myself.

Fionna laughed hard at the story and took a seat with us. Her friend gave us all a look of repulsion before moving to the front of the bar. We told Fionna all about our wild adventure thus far and she hung on to every word.

"Chris!" Jason shouted red-faced. "The French hip hop blasting from the mustard tent!" he yelled.

"Mustard tent?" Fionna asked, looking puzzled and amused at the sound of our ramshackle exploits. She urged us to tell her more. Between laughs Jason spit out how we woke up in a dirt patch in Amsterdam to some guy blaring French hip hop from the Dijon-coloured tent next to ours.

"What about the old man farting in the train station?" he yelled again so everyone else in the pub could hear him. A look of shock and delight appeared on her face. Jason launched into the story. "There we were slumped against the wall in Amsterdam Centraal, just fuckin'. . . ruined. Like, we had been drinking, without sleep . . ."

"How long had you been there?" Fionna interjected.

"Four days, I think," I added. "It's unclear, all a blur. We landed on Gay Pride weekend and had no idea."

"What? Holy shit." She sipped her beer.

"So, yeah, we're there, waiting to get on a train, when this old man comes shuffling down the hallway right in front of us." Jason tried to compose himself.

"He had on these plaid golf pants," I continued, and Fionna laughed at that, amused with how tickled we both were.

"He comes shuffling down," Jason continued, "he's got this long grey moustache that twirled right off the side of face, and as he passes in front of us, out comes this long, whistling fart that's like, beeeeoooooooooooOOOP." He imitated the sound of a slide whistle like he'd done it a thousand times. We all cracked up.

"That was Amsterdam saying, 'Shhhmell you later!'" I yelled, more laughter. Jason snorted through his beer at the memory because of how preposterous and absurd it was.

Fionna guffawed and took a hearty swig.

After learning of our plan to see Hot Water Music that night, Fionna decided she was coming along. We listened to the jukebox with our new friend until the time came to split.

The three of us slid back into the venue and reclaimed the exact seats from earlier in the day. As the light outside the window faded and the warmth of the venue's lights grew brighter, an hour of uncertainty set in. *Should I stop drinking? Take a nap? Eat? Take a walk?* Dusk is no man's land.

That's when Gainesville, Florida's Hot Water Music walked through the door with their gear — Chris Wollard, Jason Black, George Rebelo, and Chuck Ragan entering last.

Their arrival snapped me from my lull. Ragan scanned the room. He looked in our general direction then spotted us against the wall. Ragan put down his gear. The singer stared at us for a moment before realizing he recognized Jason from the Hot Water Music and Leatherface tour earlier that year. He smiled wide.

"What the fuck are you doing here?" he said in a hoarse voice.

The greeting made us all laugh. You could tell he felt happy to see a familiar face. "Ohhh, he's handsoooome," Fionna said under her breath.

People soon poured in like a river and before long the little pub was clamorous with shouting and clinking drinks. Tattoos and band shirts crowded the bar stools and it felt like we were home again.

Our friends from Canada then walked through the door like a shining light. Danielle strode in with her leather jacket. Jenny with her friendly smile. Danielle knew how to give a proper hug. "What's up friends!?" she shouted. One of the finest things is seeing friends from home when you're far away from it.

"THERE'S A LITTLE BIT OF SPRINGTIME IN THE BACK OF MIND,
THAT REMEMBERS WHEN THERE WAS A TIME WHEN WE DANCED
AND WE LAUGHED AND SPENT SOME TIME DRINKING WINE,
AND SOMEWHERE IN THERE, THERE'S A LITTLE CHILD WITHOUT A THOUGHT,
WITHOUT A DOUBT THAT EVERY CLOUD IS SILVER-LINED.
HE IS WARM."

– "SPRINGTIME," STUBBS

CHRIS WOLLARD – HOT WATER MUSIC, THE DRAFT, THE SHIP THIEVES

"May I help you?" Amanda MacKaye (Desiderata, Sammich Records) asked the nervy fifteen-year-old standing on her front porch. A realization flooded through the boy in that moment — that the person standing before him was the sister of Ian MacKaye, frontman of Minor Threat and Fugazi, also the founder of Dischord Records.

"Is this the Dischord House?"

"Well, this is our *family's* house," she replied with a look of suspicion. MacKaye looked past the kid and eyed the parents peering through the window of the minivan parked on the street. The vehicle had piloted the family from museum to museum around the greater Washington, D.C., area while on vacation, but a young punk can only entertain such trivial matters for so long. When he found himself in the same city as the Dischord house, dinosaurs and history weren't at the forefront of his interests. He'd already led his family on a wild goose chase to what

77

he believed to be the correct coordinates of the legendary house, only to come up short. He then made his family take him to a myriad of local record shops where he prodded every person in sight until someone gave him the correct directions.

"But, this *is* the Dischord House, right?"

"Yeeeah, do *you need something?*"

"I don't even know why I'm here," he admitted, flustered, before stammering, "I just felt like I had to come here. I . . . I see the Dischord ads come out in *Maximum Rocknroll* and, I don't understand. I need to know how to put out records." She either gave him her number because it was the quickest way to get him off her porch, or she was charmed by his wide-eyed fortitude. Either way, it worked. He got the contact. He called MacKaye many times and asked her many questions. The kid's name was Chris Wollard. And what's so compelling about him is he's not afraid to cold call you or show up on your doorstep. He phoned Michael "Popeye" Vogelsang from the Orange County hardcore band Farside when he was fourteen. Wollard would ask Popeye's mother when she picked up, "May I please speak with Popeye, it's Chris from Florida, again." Her laugh could be heard on the other end. But his persistence paid off. Popeye broke down the proper way to record music, which was by laying down rhythm and percussion first as bed tracks, then layering lead instruments overtop. This information blew his young mind. Integrity's first drummer, Anthony Pines, a.k.a. "Chubby Fresh," was also on Wollard's speed dial. He even called the booking number for Snapcase and started firing questions at whoever it was that answered. It comes as no surprise that he became the successful musician he is today. He's a hunter on a constant search to understand, to make records, and to make shit happen.

It's great drinking beer with Wollard over Zoom as he tells me it's hotter than hell that day in Gainesville. His hometown could be considered the polar opposite of Sunderland when comparing geography and climate. However, they do share a certain affinity: these are dark horse towns that produce a lot of heart.

Wollard lights so many cigarettes during our conversation that I can barely seem him through the haze. Things add up. Like how he's been able to maintain the rasp in his voice for over twenty years. His general demeanour has an early Tom Green charm about it. I'm talking about the pre-Barrymore days — when he would prank his parents, hide in animal corpses, and rap in Organized Rhyme. I enjoy the company of people that seem as though they're on the edge of laughter at any given moment. It's a good quality. This is how Wollard is that afternoon. I can tell the singer is amused by his own thoughts. His voice sounds like a cross between Chong and Ralph from the Muppets, both of which I think are cool.

"I paint houses and make rock 'n' roll for a living," he says.

"That's great," I reply.

He takes a moment to assess my comment before realizing I am being genuine. He smiles and affirms with confidence, "It *is* fucking great."

Hot Water Music formed in 1994. It was in these early stages that they started hearing the name Leatherface kicking around. But we're talking about Gainesville, Florida, in the early '90s — there wasn't a Leatherface record to be found anywhere, no matter how many rocks you turned over. The name would come and go like the southern sun. It's worth noting that the band's exposure to Leatherface can be attributed to two dudes named Pat.

Hot Water Music's first documented tour was a short stint up the east coast of the U.S. during spring break. Wollard recalls getting paid four dollars after a gig one night. Divided evenly between each band member, that left almost enough for a can of Pabst Blue Ribbon. The other band got paid eight dollars and were upset at Hot Water Music because of how loud they'd been. This was the same tour that Ragan and Wollard found a store front that was replacing its air conditioning unit. The band offered to help the merchant install it and earned enough bucks to get them to the next town.

It was on their second tour up the east coast that they found them- selves in Richmond playing with Pat Snavely's band, Whirlybird.

Booking shows was a much different process in the early '90s. You had a list of random people's phone numbers who played in random bands and who lived in random towns, and they had the contacts of random clubs. That's how it went. Wollard called more people than most though. Bands like Hot Water Music played in circles with strong community roots and where people generally looked out for one another. Crashing at someone's pad after the show to save the little money you made was commonplace. They ended up back at Snavely's house after a performance in Richmond, drinking and listening to music. Snavely asked them in the early hours of morning, "Hey, you guys into Leatherface at all?" When they told him they knew the name but hadn't heard the band yet, he replied, "I think you'd like 'em, you're really going to dig it!" Interest was beginning to take hold with every new mention of them. Snavely handed them a mixtape he'd made of the first three Leatherface albums while the band was leaving the house the next day.

They pushed the tape into the deck as the van rolled out of Richmond in the cool morning light with Leatherface playing from the dashboard speakers. But they didn't know the name of the songs yet because Snavely hadn't labelled the mix. Wollard describes the collective feeling in the van as something along the lines of "Whoa . . . What the fuck isss *this*?"

"It kept changing, it wasn't like an Oi! band or your typical punk or hardcore band, there was no metal in it. Some of it was just, like, blow-your-face-off angst. The guitar interplay was ridiculous. And you're sitting there, trying to figure out what they sound like. It doesn't sound different than everything I've heard, but you're trying to figure where their reference points are as writers. They were just coming from somewhere else. It was instantly recognizable, instantly compelling, but at the same time sounded very new. That's just because of the guys; their chemistry is their own. It was just kind of this magic fucking thing."

Not long after the first mixtape was gifted to them, the band's close friend Pat Hughes came around with another Leatherface compilation for them. It's easy to see now that the messengers of the punk gods are all named Pat. This mixtape came with no song titles like the first one. The mystery of Leatherface was coming in hard from all angles. Both crucial cassettes lived in the van and had no distinct owner. They were to be enjoyed only when driving with each other.

Ragan and Wollard would walk into record stores and head straight to the "L" section hoping to find something. Anything at all. Any shred of evidence that could prove the band wasn't just myth. They came up short time and time again. The mystery remained.

"Oh god, it was awful. Just *fucking* awful." This is how Wollard describes the band's first expedition to the west coast of the U.S. "Horrible tour, *juuuust* horrible. It was an exercise in self defeat and poverty," he continued. Their van then was a standard 1979 Chevy 10. An Ohio tank with no air conditioning or heat. It could have been the sketchiest vehicle chugging down the highway out across the American landscape. Can you see it? Can you see yourself driving down the interstate on the first day of family vacation? There's your smiling wife in the passenger seat wearing sunglasses and sunhat. The kids are reading in the back. Everyone's bellies are full of orange juice and pancakes as a rumble cuts the lull, and let me tell you something — the rearview mirror doesn't lie. It presents the Chevy 10 coughing smoke into the serene countryside. A big fucking bear on wheels. The steaming steel box rolls by with a wobbly wheel. You notice that the door is being held open to cool the beast down. Your wife is horrified, but also intrigued. Wollard turns to you from the driver's side as he passes. His grin widens below a pair of dark shades, a cigarette protruding from between his teeth.

It reached a point that when things would break on the Chevy, the parts would just be removed from the engine for good. It somehow still turned over and kept rolling though. They sold the van to their friends from the grindcore band Assück, who Wollard went on the road with sometimes. Hot Water Music then put $600 back into the Chevy. This got the vehicle running well enough to carry the two bands across the U.S. on many more miserable commutes. But that particular west coast tour was meant to be. It was part of Hot Water Music's bigger picture. In a rare stroke of luck, when they played San Francisco, they befriended founder of *Maximum Rocknroll* Tim Yohannan (also known on the scene as Tim Yo). The not-for-profit zine/publication was the largest of its kind to celebrate punk and hardcore subculture. What this relationship meant was that no accommodations had to be secured when they played San Fran. Yohannan would let them stay at the *Maximum Rocknroll* office. This could be one of the highest honours a punk rock band could be given.

To get your record reviewed by *Maximum Rocknroll*, you needed to send one copy to the reviewer and one copy to the head office so they could keep it with their archives. The zine's record collection was as extensive as it gets, stretching about seventy feet in length — longer than a semi-trailer truck. It's the best record collection Wollard's laid eyes on to this day. "Keep in mind," he says, "there was no fuckin' Neil Diamond in this collection, no Lynyrd Skynyrd, and no Boston either." They went straight toward the "L" section, expecting to come up short like the many letdowns before. What they discovered was like finding gold in a river. The office had every record released by Leatherface to date. Everything.

What a victorious moment. As kids, my brother and I would spread our Halloween candy haul all around us in a circle like a protective wall of sugar. I imagine Hot Water Music in a similar scenario with LPs and 45s pooled around them. After all that time, they were able to finally figure out what songs the two Pats had loaded onto their mixtapes, and what albums those songs belonged on. They saw the artwork and read the lyrics along with the music. The band stayed at the *Maximum Rocknroll* office for the next three west coast tours. They would bring stacks of blank cassettes with them and spend their nights recording music instead of partying in the city with everyone else.

They got to experience Tokyo's music "megastore" phenomenon when Hot Water Music toured Japan. They had never seen such a vast selection of music under one roof. The "L" section was as bountiful as the *Maximum Rocknroll* office because of how adored Leatherface was in Japan. They were able to purchase albums for themselves. Now they could give the lyrics the attention they deserved. They fell into a deeper level of love as they did. "It took a while to start understanding the scope of what was being said, then you start understanding them, and lyrically, they are unlike anything I've ever heard. Sometimes you can tell Frankie's pissed, and sometimes you can tell he's emotional." Their appreciation was mounting because of how much work it took to find these records. Every bit of fragmented information coming in fuelled them to know more. The boys from Gainesville were beginning to feel that Leatherface was *their* band.

"If you're talking about Leatherface lyrics, then you have to be talking about Frankie. In the same album I'm hearing the harshest criticisms of the world around us, and also some of the most beautiful words I've ever read in *any* song. There is only one Frankie: he's a thoughtful, caring person, and in some ways mature beyond his years, and other ways, still very playful like a young'un. There's a lot of stereotypes in punk songs, but his approach wasn't so reactionary, and he's never been scared to be vulnerable in a song, where I think a lot of people are. It wasn't your typical, 'I'm an angry young man.' I even asked him one time, 'Where do you come up with some of the things you're talking about? Because some of it, until you put it into that song, seemed like it should never be in any song.' Frankie replied, 'Well, those are just the things I think about.' He had a way of connecting his thoughts. He's also just a very observant person. It's not all about him and it's not all about his struggle in the world, there's many things happening, and many people in those stories. And man, the guy can just set a fucking scene, can't he? You start picturing things before he's even said a word. And he makes us start feeling things that aren't purely related to the lyrical content. He finds a way to not only have the words, but has the phrasing that allows you to connect to it so early on. Also, their willingness to not follow standard structures, because that allows it to be its own thing. They weren't scared to be themselves, and it's hard to do that. There's something about living in Sunderland that allowed their true selves to come out, as opposed, to say, if they tried to move to London. They're just one of those bands I've never, *ever* stopped being excited about."

It was mostly music to their ears when Hot Water Music learned that Leatherface was reforming. The news also caused anxiety for Wollard because Hot Water Music had recently recorded their version of Leatherface's "Springtime." The potential collision of events sent him into a tailspin. Wollard feared that Leatherface would think they were assholes. He didn't feel comfortable with any of it.

Wollard reverted to the thing he does best (other than play guitar and smoke cigarettes) and went on a mission of the highest order. It was an assignment that would forever change the course of Hot Water Music's history. He set out to get Frankie Stubbs's phone number.

It was like the whole of his teenage existence was a lead up to that very moment. He got out his pencil and paper, book of contacts, and got to work. "I was just calling *evverybooody* . . ." It's unclear how long it took to track down the number. Wollard guesses about a hundred phone calls. He tracked it down from a couple of punks in Atlanta after countless inquiries.

Wollard inhaled a deep breath and dialled the number, unaware of what a time zone was. The first call went to an answering machine with a message that garbled out something like "thisisfrankieleaveamessage" in a thick Geordie accent. But hearing the person on the answering machine say "Frankie" gave Wollard the hope he needed to continue. He was again directed to the answering machine when he called the next day at a different time. Wollard made sure his message was a little more elaborate this time. He called until upwards of eight or nine messages were blinking red on Stubbs's machine. Wollard picked a different time to call every day. Sometimes in the morning. Sometimes late at night, exhausting all possibilities in hopes of catching the singer. His determination became unwavering, and he thought, *At some point, I'm going to catch you at home.*

But still Stubbs alluded him. This went on for about two weeks. Wollard was tired of talking to the answering machine. The fear crept upon him that he might have shot himself in the foot and pissed off the singer to a damaging degree. He entertained the thought that he might have already blown his chance. Anxiety was building. A different tactic was in order. Something sneaky. Something *so bold* it would override Stubbs's assumed irritated state. Wollard got an idea. He picked up the phone one final time. As it went to the answering machine, he left a message telling Stubbs that if he had any interest in speaking with him about music, then to change his answering machine greeting to say so and to specify a good time to call. I don't know Wollard well, but I know he doesn't go quietly into the night.

He let it ride for a few days before dialling the number again. Sure enough, it went to the answering machine. But something was different. Though it still garbled "thisisFrankieleaveamessage" he could tell the greeting had been rerecorded. The voice had a different tonality. To his grandest surprise the greeting continued, "And if this is Chris from Florida, again, call me Tuesday at five p.m. my time." It was like landing on the moon. Wollard phoned at the time that Stubbs requested now knowing what a time zone was. Stubbs picked up.

"What do you want from me?" Stubbs said into the phone. Chris told him that he played in Hot Water Music from Florida and that they were huge fans of Leatherface. "Never heard of ya," Stubbs told Wollard, which wasn't a surprise. Wollard told the singer they'd recorded a cover of one their songs and planned to release it on a benefit album. He told Stubbs he didn't want to upset him, and only wanted his approval, or not. Either way was fine.

"What song did you do?" Stubbs asked, with a timbre insinuating that Wollard's reply would determine his fate once and for all.

"Springtime."

"Oh, okay, that's fine then."

Their conversation rolled along so easily that the lines of reality and fiction blurred. Having the singer on the phone was a mammoth victory after all those years. What would be the point of coming all that way if he didn't take a further shot in the dark? He pushed his luck. Wollard could see the totality of his plan in his mind's eye. It just might work. He conveyed to Stubbs that Hot Water Music was starting to acquire a following around the U.S. and that if Leatherface would come across the water, it would be a good thing for everybody. They'd be well received. Stubbs told Wollard that he would have to talk to Youth Brigade vocalist Shawn Stern, co-owner of BYO Records, which would be the label releasing the newest Leatherface songs. Wollard's anxiety rose another notch when thinking about having to talk with Stern, whose band Wollard had grown up listening to.

"If Shawn says okay, then we'll do it." One thing to keep in mind is Stubbs hadn't even heard a Hot Water Music song yet. "Call him tomorrow," he commanded.

"Will you give him a heads up that I'm calling?" Wollard asked.

"No."

The next day Wollard phoned Stern.

"HELLO," Stern boomed on the other end like a wrecking ball.

"Hi, is this Shawn Stern?"

"YEAH. WHAT IS IT?"

"Hi, my name is Chris. I'm from Florida and play in a band called Hot Water Music."

"YEAH, YEAH, I've heard of ya."

They talked and talked. Somehow it was decided between the two phone conversations with Stubbs and Stern that Leatherface would do a U.S. tour with Hot Water Music that coming summer. They would also release a split LP to promote the tour. All of this unbeknownst to the other members in Hot Water Music. The Leatherface songs were completed. Hot Water Music would have only one month to record their tracks. You can imagine the looks of disbelief on the faces of his bandmates when Wollard walked into the practice space and dropped that bomb. Sometimes you just have to not worry about looking like an asshole and pick up the phone and put it all on the line. The rest will follow if your intentions are true. Hot Water Music recorded their songs for the album on an ADAT recorder in a friend's living room. They followed up with two U.S. tours as well as a European tour with Leatherface. Wollard joined them every night on stage as a second guitarist for the duration of the European tour.

"Ya know, I'm still pissed," Stubbs spat at Wollard.

"About last night?" Wollard asked, feeling sheepish.

"Yup. But I'm glad to see you have pants on tonight. I don't ever want to see that again."

"I apologize, Frankie . . ." Wollard said, feeling like he was about to die.

This conversation happened between Stubbs and Wollard only moments before Leatherface's set at an open-air festival with ten thousand people standing in front of the stage. Neither of the musicians had expected that kind of turnout. Hot Water Music would go on after Leatherface. It is well-documented that Wollard's anxiety occasionally flares at the thought of playing live. It wasn't helping matters that both bands had been up very late. The morning of the festival saw the two bands the most hungover they'd been all tour.

"Honestly, we were a twisted wreck, we smelled bad, we were crabby, we were all scared. I was absolutely terrified," Wollard admits.

Stubbs was pissed off because Wollard wore shorts onstage during their set the night before. This was a hard no. Wollard was confused because shorts were fairly normal attire to him, seeing as his hometown was a humid swamp. But Stubbs didn't care, nor did he like it one bit. After the show he cornered Wollard.

"All these people are coming and spending money to watch you play music and you don't even have the respect to put on a pair of fuckin' PANTS?!"

"If that's the rule, I'm sorry, I had no idea. You never told me," Wollard apologized.

Wollard's uneasiness was ascending to mountainous proportions. Panic took hold when he heard the noise from the people in the grounds. "I'm sorry, dude, it won't happen again," was all he could think of to say.

Stubbs looked at him hard. "So, we've decided what your punishment is."

"Huh, what are you talking about?" Wollard coughed out, confused and rather offended.

"You have to wear these onstage for the next week," Stubbs said, reaching up and sliding a pair of sunglasses over Wollard's eyes. He pulled his head back trying to dodge Stubbs, but failed. When Wollard took them off he discovered a pair of sparkling gold Las Vegas Elvis shades. A shift came in mood. Wollard realized Stubbs wasn't pissed off at all. He was being funny. This simple act turned Wollard's unravelling state around. He could feel the tension leaving his body at once. Stubbs knew how to break down the seriousness. Wollard realized that Stubbs wasn't going to let such a silly thing ruin such a grand concert.

"We have a different idea of how we're going to open the show this afternoon," Stubbs said, smiling.

"Okay, what are we doing?"

"We're going to open with "You Are My Sunshine," a cappella, all four of us, and *then* we're going to start playing."

"That's how you want to start the set?" Wollard asked, amused.

"Yeah. It's going to be great," Stubbs said with confidence.

The energy in the shadowed Duchess of York leapt to life when Hot Water Music began their set. The Gainesville four dragged us into their world with the rhythm section locked in tighter than a prison cell door. Wollard and Ragan spat their brash vocals, jumping and rocking with "The Duchess" written in white on a black banner behind them. When they hit their stride and sunk deep into the groove like an eight ball into the corner pocket, man, could they ever move a crowd. Like when they played "Manual," every head in the place was nodding, controlled by the slow build of plinking and screeching guitars dominating the intro. The drums walloped and fell into place, securing the heavy tempo with both singers snarling over top. Ragan's mic teetered from the weight of his foot pressing the stage floor down. It bumped off his lips. Droplets sprayed into the hot stage lights above. This was Fugazi for a new generation, and everyone swayed.

The guitar in the intro of "Scraping" blared like a slow ambulance siren oscillating between two hypnotizing notes. Rebelo smashed the snare and cymbal together, along with a thundering strum from the bass — the two of them as quiet as a car tire through a window. They waited for a moment before Rebelo led the gang into a heavy, measured beat, a reminder of the band's jazz background. Both guitars rode the anticipation before opening up high above, full blast with the amps shaking. They see-sawed back and forth, then clung to one last resonating note, like an airplane disappearing into the horizon. The drums and bass rode out along the low road, carrying us into the arms of Ragan's vocals.

"Are you mighty? Are you what you think you are?"

With his voice full of forty-grit sandpaper, I fell inside myself. I was transported back to my studio apartment on Ontario Street where I lived with Jay Yates and Johnny Kells. For a moment I was not in England at all.

I had awoke one morning with both of my cats curled on my legs. There was a shaft of yellow light pouring in from the door across the hardwood when I rolled to my side. From its furthest point, a diagonal line cut back through the room. Dust drifted lazy and peaceful inside the glow. I could hear this amazing band I had never heard before playing on the stereo. The music echoed through the living room of our loft, just loud enough for me to hear. They sounded like morning heartache after a long summer night. I lay there, content with the world and listening. When I crawled from my bed and made my way closer to the music, there was my old friend Yates. He was always smiling like a friendly wolf, always happy, always snickering, always eating grilled cheese sandwiches. I asked him who the band was. He told me they were called Hot Water Music. The name made me think of coffee and how much I wanted one. I intended to listen to the record all over again once my mug was filled. That night in Leeds was the closest I'd get to that morning ever again.

I was talking with someone at the back of the room when Jason found me. He put his hand on my shoulder and pointed to a group of tough-looking dudes coming through the room. "Leatherface," he said in my ear with excitement in his baritone voice. People parted like waves against a boat. A communal buzz among the crowd surged. Heads turned to catch a glimpse of the gang-like band. I could make out Lainey, Stubbs, Evans, and Burdon. The energy climbed higher. This was my second sighting of them. The first was at the Showplace Theater show in Buffalo a few months before our trip.

It wasn't long after their arrival that Stubbs climbed onstage and plugged in a guitar. We watched in wonder and waited to hear what song he'd play with them. There was a moment of silence before Wollard moved closer to his amp, creating a noise that sounded like we'd flatlined in a hospital room. Wollard let the panicked sound grow louder, shaking his guitar before the band exploded overhead. We were shocked back to life with Leatherface's "Springtime." Stubbs soft-shoed during the intro with Ragan smiling wide. The two of them both growled out the words in a moment of suspended beauty.

Leatherface's presence brought a whole different animation. Everyone knew something important was happening, that they might be witnessing a once-in-a-lifetime event. Fionna shot hearts from her gleaming eyes at Ragan. Danielle sang her lungs out. Jenny's hair shook in a fever. Jason banged his head with one finger raised high. I bit my bottom lip and air drummed like the guy from "Pretty Fly (For a White Guy)." That night felt like a secret show in an undercover club. I feel thankful that I witnessed the Duchess of York's crucial contribution to the Leeds music scene first-hand. I only danced in the clandestine room for one night, but it was so special. Thank you, 71 Vicar Lane, for having me.

After stuffing our packs into Lainey's trunk, we hugged our friends and hit the road. The man could pilot a car down a dark English highway almost as well as he could play drums, and he pressed the gas down about as hard as his foot pedal on his kit. Bassist David Lee Burdon rode shotgun. Lainey was taller than Jason with the same heavy build and shaved head, and looked like he'd rolled a few kegs around in his time. My first time in an English automobile on the other side of the road was confounding. As we listened to Lainey and Burdon tell us stories in the dark of the car it became clear how gentle the two men were. Seeing them in the front seat felt so strange. I began to think that my life had become fictitious.

The drive back to Sunderland was about two hours. Both Jason and I passed out. We woke later to find ourselves in the mystical land that produced Leatherface, Toy Dolls, and Dave Stewart from Eurythmics. I looked into the darkness when we pulled into the driveway. It wasn't a mystical land at all. Through the window I could see an ordinary suburb full of trees and row houses just like anywhere.

I became transfixed at the sight of the oxblood carpet in the living room as we hauled our bags into the house. This was my introduction into the living spaces of the English. Little did I know, many more like it could be found within a stone's throw. Lainey turned on a lamp and put on some music before he poured us two Leatherface-sized glasses of red wine. I was scared shitless handling mine, so I made a conscious effort to perch on the edge of my seat. It felt only right to lean forward so that if I fumbled the glass, the wine would hit the red carpet.

It was like I had just opened my eyes and there we were with one of Britain's most regarded drummers. The man who'd played with legends like Angelic Upstarts, Cockney Rejects, Red Alert, and Leatherface. We were buzzing something fierce from the show. We talked about the days to come, drank wine, and listened to punk rock into the early hours of morning.

HUDDERSFIELD, YORKSHIRE

Uncle Ian's blue Skoda shot like a cannonball down the winding roads to the local football club in a desperate search for a pint. We screeched sideways into the club's parking lot nestled in the middle of the countryside. The football boys in jerseys milled about inside watching a match on the telly. Sunderland was down and you could hear the low, dismal chanting. Ian put two pints into our hands. He tilted his tweed cap, gulped at the ale, and looked up at the match.

"Hops and barley will be the death of me," I sang low next to Jason. I'd begun to feel normal again with the beer inside me.

"Actually, it's saving my life right now."

"I know, right," I agreed.

"We have to find out what Vaux beer is. Frankie's always singing about it."

"'The air round here smells of religion and Vauxies beer,'" I quoted. "I'm guessing it's brewed in Sunderland? Is it Vaux, or Vauxies?"

"I dunno," Jason said, wiping the foam from his mouth. "Even their beer is cult classic." He loved the idea of cryptic ale.

We ripped back through the green hills after the beverage while looking out the window at the stone walls zigzagging through the rolling fields. Jason's Aunt Jacqui came to the door and welcomed us both with hugs and smiles. They set us up with our own room and it felt so comforting to be inside a house with familiar things — a kitchen with dishes, a fridge full of food. Sofas with pillows, bathrooms with fluffy towels and warm water. Their house was a sight for sore eyes with the memory of our filthy night in King's Cross station still tender like a fresh wound.

When the rare opportunity to shower presented itself on our trip, we'd leap at the offer. Simple cleanliness felt like an immeasurable conquest for the home team. We felt revitalized after cleaning up and eating Aunt Jacqui's home-cooked meal. Uncle Ian decided to take us into town to the pub after dinner, another offer we couldn't refuse.

The Skoda ripped off again, swerving and skidding along the narrow roads. Hedges blew wild against the sides of the car as we blasted by on our quest for lager. We soon came to a village and parked outside the sandy block building that was the pub.

Most of the people seemed pleased to meet us and hear about our journey. From the locals I heard the thick Yorkshire dialect, Broad Yorkshire or Tyke, the roots of which can be traced back to Old English.

Ian passed us pints topped to the brim with golden ale. "Here ya go, boys." Beer spilled over the sides as the glasses clinked. We considered ourselves skilled draughtsmen but had the feeling we'd met our match. Jason's little cousin Michael joined us for the night out. I thought fourteen might be too young for the pub but I was wrong. Youngsters were allowed if accompanied by an adult. He sipped an Irn-Bru, Scotland's "other" drink.

The main attraction in the pub was a karaoke machine. We were right on time to catch "Total Eclipse of the Heart" sung by a woman in black leather pants, with red cheeks and crimped blond hair. "Way to go, Rose!" a voice shouted through the clapping as she finished. Rose strutted back to the bar like a proud pony and hoisted her white wine. They were about to shut down the karaoke for the night but Ian convinced the host to allow one more song. He then urged us to sing. We butchered "Cum on Feel the Noize," the Quiet Riot version, before finding a shadow to hide in for the rest of the night. Cold pints go down easy in the heat of shame.

We found ourselves talking with some younger locals. Whether our presence was well-received was up for debate. From what I could gather the young women enjoyed our company. The young men not so much. It was clear that people like us didn't come through Huddersfield often. I wore my favourite plaid shirt, otherwise known back home as a Lanark County dinner jacket. It was too big for me, as all my clothes were in 1999. I also wore a trucker hat with an embroidered heart on the front. Our visible tattoos weren't helping matters any.

We sat in a dim corner of the room. Next to us sat a young woman with some guys that looked our age. She sparked up a conversation. Her accent sounded so thick and drunk I struggled to understand what was being said at all. I was thankful when Jason assumed the role of translator between us. She appeared to be the ringleader of her gang. Her poofy hair bobbed as she smiled in the dim light. The encounter turned sour when her friend got aggressive with me.

"You look like a farmer, mate," he said with narrowed eyes. His friends hung their heads and smirked. He wasn't wrong.

"Well, my last name *is* MacDonald . . ." I replied. My awkward response seemed to be all I could muster and left Jason laughing at the lousy statement. They looked confused. "You know?" I continued, singing the opening notes from the song so many kids had tortured me with when I was a child. Making fun of myself always seemed like a good angle of defense. When in doubt, self-deprecation sometimes confuses the antagonist. I also could tell Jason was prepared to flip a table at any moment. The guys snorted into their beers with no comeback. See, no sweat. There was a clear divide between us.

"Arghtheytakinthepissoutofyouuuchris?" she asked me with a slur so impressive it could have come from a Saturday night at the Inter Steer.

"Sorry?" I asked, baffled at the muttered mess.

"Arghtheytakinthepisssssoutofyouthen, Chris?" she said again, smiling through the dark with teeth like a mako shark.

Jason chuckled in the background. For the life of me I couldn't understand the question. The myth about unbridled English slang was true. She looked confused as to why I couldn't get it through my thick skull, then smiled again. Jason spelled it out for me plain and simple.

"Are. They. Taking. The. Piss. Out. Of. You. MacDonald. You idiot. It means 'are they making fun of you?'" Jason said.

"Oh," I said, taken aback. Instincts told me it may have had something to do with that, but I hadn't been sure.

She reached up to lift the brim of my cap.

"I like yerrrhhhat," she said.

The boys became agitated with every bit of attention we got. Their stares became darker and the tension rose. We hit the road. I couldn't help but think encounters of a similar kind were coming our way.

"YOU WILL BE MY BROTHER.
YOU WILL BE THE ONE.
AND YOU WILL BE THE SETTING SUN."

— "SPEAK IN TONGUES," STUBBS

CHUCK RAGAN — HOT WATER MUSIC

An integral aspect of music is the live experience. I often imagine a swaying crowd of people living in the moment together. And to be a part of this communal song is moving. To be bound by fine, unseen threads. But sometimes the most powerful moments are intimate. The fewer bodies the better. When you're singing to your friends, or your friends are singing to you, or when you find yourself floating on a raft-like rooftop somewhere out in Richmond, Virginia, in the mid-'90s, drinking, smoking, staring out into the black, twinkling sky as your friend Pat Snavely plays you Leatherface's *Mush* for the first time. I wonder what Ragan was imagining in that hour. Or was he frozen in the moment as *Mush* passed by him in the night with its gigantic presence rumbling down in his guts?

When I ask him, Ragan replies, "I just absolutely fell in love with it immediately. Like, immediately. You know, the type of music I love and adore is kind of a strange mix of something rough, aggressive, and full of piss and vinegar, but still emotional and heartfelt. Right away I was taken aback, and they'd been a band for a long time before I'd ever heard them that night. I was wowed. I remember my first thought was how I'd really missed the boat (pardon the pun) on this one. Snavely sent us home with a tape, and we wore that thing out. To me, *Mush* is the one because that's the record that really and truly defines all of Leatherface, almost. But *The Last* is also very special."

It was around this time that George Rebelo and Ragan moved in with Pat Hughes, who Ragan boasts was a pillar of the Gainesville punk rock scene. Hughes owned a small DIY record store in Gainesville called Shaft Records, and these kids looked up to this old-school punk-rocker immensely. Whatever music he was listening to was the music they were missing in their lives. Hughes was the epitome of cool in this community and it sounds like his dedication to all things punk was second to none. Hughes took Rebelo and Ragan in. It was a strange sensation for Ragan because of how revered Hughes was. His room was stacked with thousands of LPs lining the walls, floor to ceiling, and was nothing short of a library. The topic of Leatherface's *Mush* was inevitable. That's when Hughes asked Ragan if he'd ever heard their first album, *Cherry Knowle*.

"I'll never forget sitting in his room, and he put on *Cherry Knowle*, and I was like, 'This is everything to me.' From the get-go, it hit me like a ton of bricks. The sound of Frankie's voice, the tribe of the band, the melodies of Dickie's guitars, how everything came together so perfectly. It's very rare that I hear something and say, 'There's nothing wrong with this.' There seems to be something we always pick out, because you usually know within thirty seconds, right? You can feel whether it's false or not. Whether it's your taste. And it's rare to me that something kicks off and you think, *This is fine*, and not only fine, but exceptional. Leatherface was one of those bands.

"To learn they were broken up was kind of devasting for me, and really odd because I'd never felt that way about any band before. Because I'd fallen in love with their music and fallen in love with an energy. I soon realized I'd never get to witness this in a live setting. Then, fast forward, and after Wollard gets off the phone with Stubbs, somehow we're taking Leatherface on their first tour of the United States. The moment where I found out that Leatherface was back together and coming to the U.S., I truly thought it was false. It felt like a joke. It didn't register that it would actually happen. It felt like someone was going to pull the rug out from under me. It was real, yet completely surreal. The more things started to come together though, and the more we planned it out, we started to understand that it *was* real. It was overwhelming and intimidating. How do you meet your idols, the people you look up to, the people you admire and respect? How do you do that coming from the walk of life that we all come from, which is punk rock and rock 'n' roll, where nothing matters? But for some reason I was starstruck. Completely overwhelmed and so excited knowing that it was even a possibility."

Ragan will never forget the first night of this tour when it all came to a head inside San Diego's Ché Café. His disbelief gripped him as he pulled the door open and walked into the venue. And yet, there they were, shimmering like a mirage: Lainey, Evans, Burdon, and Stubbs, who was asleep on the sofa with his hat over his eyes. He almost wanted to run his hand over them to make sure they weren't a figment of his imagination. There was a great rush that enveloped Ragan.

From the very first conversation with them he knew he was dealing with people poured from a different tap. These guys were tougher than most because of where they were from, but within this he also sensed a commonality. Gainesville, Florida, was rough around its edges then, and Hot Water Music had dealt with their fair share of disputes and blows in their time. Complementary views on music, the world, and the punk scene began to bind the two bands.

Ragan couldn't accept having Leatherface be the opening act though. This was a ridiculous idea in his mind. Jason Black understood where Ragan was coming from, but convinced him that a greater exposure to their music would be had if Leatherface were to open.

Nobody in the U.S. really knew them at this time. People would likely leave right after Hot Water Music's set if they were to go on before Leatherface. Ragan can't stress enough how walking onstage following a Leatherface set was one of the most difficult things he's had to do.

Ragan describes this tour as two bands becoming kindred spirits. He felt an openness with these new friends and looked up to Stubbs as an elder. When Ragan confessed to him that the last thing he wanted to do was go up onstage after watching them perform, Stubbs told him, "You're looking at it all wrong, son. I know what's going on here. These people don't know us, they know you. They're here to see you. We're here to play rock'n'roll. So, you need to decide if you're going to play rock'n'roll or not. Our job is to get up there and get people fired up and excited for the night. If they like our music, great. If they don't, fuck 'em. Your job is to get up there and play better than us, so what are you going to do?"

Hot Water Music studied Leatherface's every move from that moment on while the Brits ripped stages apart. There were times when Ragan, Wollard, Rebelo, and Black would be right there in the crowd singing at the top of their lungs and leaping from the stage. They learned to deal with how uncomfortable it felt to follow an act as intimidating as Leatherface by walking the green mile. But every night got a little easier simply by acknowledging the only option was to try their best and deliver.

"I then started recognizing and realizing all these people across the U.S. had never experienced the power and the poetry of Leatherface. That's when it clicked and I said to myself onstage, *We need to use this opportunity to let everybody know how important this band is*. And that's what we did. There are few bands on the planet that write songs where their whole package stands the test of time. I'm talking the music, the lyrics, the melodies. There's few that cover all the bases. To find an artist of any kind that can create something timeless, that can be understood on that level is special. To me, Frank's lyrics can be understood and appreciated by someone who read them one hundred years ago, or one hundred years from now. Truly. I believe that. I could listen to them anytime. There's only a handful of bands in my life that I can put on when I'm in any mood. This is rare. I can put them on when I'm at my highest of highs and lowest of lows, and it still makes sense and still does it for me, and I feel like it always will. To me the world's a better place with Leatherface in it. I've put it on for people who aren't interested in punk or rock 'n' roll in the slightest, and said, 'Listen to this, read this,' and seen them appreciate it. Just because it's classified as punk rock doesn't mean that it isn't a universal thing. People should know or at least have the opportunity to hear them, because it's beautiful. It's uplifting, inspiring, and enlightening. It's music that makes you think, question, and analyze. This is something the entire world needs to have and hold. And if it's not the band, the songs, or the lyrics themselves, then at least the energy and the message and the ethics that is Leatherface."

Ragan's voice softens as he recounts the night he performed solo in Manchester. Stubbs, his daughter, and wife, Lynsey, were in attendance. Ragan says he was as nervous as he was honoured, that it felt like his dad who'd never seen him play was somewhere out in the crowd. They had dinner together before the show, and after, Ragan had a special seat reserved for Stubbs and his family up in the balcony of the venue with a bottle of red wine waiting.

"That's who I was playing for that night. My song, 'The Boat,' which is more or less what Leatherface has meant to me. I dedicated it to him. It was just a really heavy night, emotionally. I had tunnel vision, and though I had this beautiful crowd in front of me, I was only playing for three people. All I could think about was the memories I've had with Leatherface, the gratitude I have for the entire band, Frankie, all of his lyrics, what they've done for me, my friends, and my community."

"LIVE, DIE ON YOUR FAITH.
LIVE LIFE ON YOUR DAYS.
IT'S BURNING IN MY EYES AGAIN.
THEY CAN'T TAKE THE SPARK FROM MY EYES.
WE CAN'T KILL THE LIGHT THAT SHINES.
WHICH BURNS, IT'S BURNING."

— "PALE MOONLIGHT," STUBBS

SHOWPLACE THEATER, BUFFALO — JUNE 6, 1999, A FEW MONTHS BEFORE OUR TRIP

I stopped to listen like a jackrabbit in a field. A familiar melody pounded from somewhere inside the theatre. *Soundcheck.* I stepped closer and put my ear against the wooden door. The muffled music became louder. *Should I go in? Will I get in trouble? Fuck it, I have to.* My hand grabbed hold of the brass handle and heaved, opening a floodgate. Sound gushed toward me. I could see all the way to the back where I spotted Leatherface onstage. I sprang into the building. They were bathed in pink and purple lights and playing their cover of the Police song "Message in a Bottle." A rippled gold curtain spanned the length of the stage behind them. My heart skipped. The song was exactly how it sounded on *Mush.*

A charged afternoon of road tripping had led me to the abstract moment as I watched, stunned, from the back of the room. I had finally put faces to the music. It was also my first time hearing them live. Both of those things were special because I was alone while experiencing them.

The last note of the song echoed in the empty venue. I yelled from the back of the room, then turned and pushed back out the door before being spotted. Friends gathered like a gang in the street outside the venue as the day turned to night. There was so much emotion and provocation.

After an amazing set from Discount, the moment we all had waited so long for arrived. The crowd let out a deafening cheer as the singer from Sunderland stepped to the front of the stage. Stubbs muttered into the mic. He was asking the sound person to turn up the vocals, "More, please. Mooore!" There was a moment of silence before I felt a piercing buzz in the bottom of my feet as the amplifier volume shot to ten. Andrew Laing hit the high-hat six times (two slow, four fast) before the band let loose the set opener, "How Lonely."

It sounded like a stampede of wild horses and screaming chainsaws. Lainey was shirtless and wore his ball cap backwards with camouflage shorts. He pounded the drums with unnerving speed and confidence amidst the searing guitars. Stubbs was dressed in a baggy lavender golf shirt that was too big for him. That's when I saw "the dance" for the first time.

The frontman's comical shimmy seemed out of place amongst the caustic noise, but looked as natural as a bird bobbing across a tree branch. It was an eclectic jig of pop sensibilities. He was as light on his feet as he was robotic. Imagine a life-sized mechanical toy after being wound up. He then loosened, sidestepped like a puppy learning to run, swayed his hips, shuffled his feet, and slid into a frontwards moonwalk all in the matter of a few seconds. The movements were hypnotic. This was a human in their element. I believe I heard Neil Young once say that all he wanted to do was sit in his truck and listen to his own band because it was the best sounding music he'd ever heard. Young said we start bands to make the music we always wanted to hear. Stubbs says they created Leatherface to sound exactly how they wanted as well. In all its roughness there was a perfection to them. He danced for so long he almost missed his cue before stepping back to the mic. The moment became serious when he leaned in with his Gordon Smith pointed at the ceiling and growled like a wolf. We all felt this and leapt to action. The singer looked how I had imagined him in my mind's eye when I first heard them back in Darrell's basement long ago. I felt shivers as I fell into the hive as we scrambled over one another, moving only by some innate instinct.

After "Peasant in Paradise" we reconvened for a drink along the bar. Our crowd stood in the pink light, clinking American-sized shots of Jägermeister while the band ripped through "Discipline." Someone tossed a long-stem rose onstage between songs. Stubbs fastened it to his shirt like a boutonniere.

Eyes smiled and flickered in the dark like little fires. We laughed at the cowboys at the end of the bar in Stetson hats and big belt buckles, whooping and hollering, spinning their partners around. A younger woman fell from the crowd and hit the floor sliding. Her hair splaying over discarded beer cans. She smiled as we helped her to her feet so she could elbow her way, tough as nails, back into the crowd.

When I heard the opening chords to "Pale Moonlight," I was drawn back into the sea, where we swayed like the tide to the moon's gravitational pull. The song has always felt like a body of water to me. There's so much weight inside it. Those beautiful chords were so loud and powerful that night. You could almost feel the rain falling from the ceiling. The whole place erupted into fists and light when the drums pounded into the chorus.

"'CAUSE WE'RE DANCING WITH THE DEVIL IN THE PALE MOONLIGHT! And I can try and get it right." I looked down and closed my eyes and let myself be moved.

They finished the show with their cover of Wat Tyler's "Hops and Barley," a huge chanting number reminiscent of Blitz and Angelic Upstarts. The raucous set closer would've had those beer guzzling cowboys trading their Stetsons for football scarfs and jigging in no time if it continued a minute longer. When the stage went silent, one of them yelled, "Encore! 'Freebird'!" Leatherface took off their instruments and disappeared.

The band had parted ways in 1993 but reformed years after the tragic death of friend and bass player Andy Crighton. This reformation came to our shores with Davey Burdon in place of Crighton and Leighton Evans on electric guitar where Hammond had stood for so long.

Hot Water Music's fascination with Leatherface helped the U.K. legends get recognized by a broader audience. I believe the love that Leatherface felt in this time became a driving force. During this tour they came to understand that they'd touched the hearts and minds of kids across North America. Tiltwheel's Davey Quinn was Leatherface's sound tech for most of this tour and said that both bands wouldn't stop talking about the Buffalo show.

The night sky hung above picnic tables behind a chain-link fence in the grassy lot a few doors down from the venue. To see my friends begin to form relationships with their heroes felt wonderful. Jason, Cactus, Jenny, Danielle, and others were following the tour across the U.S. During this time their friendship with the band became something they never thought possible. There was a glow on Cactus's face when talking with Stubbs about guitars. I observed from afar, drinking, taking it in. Jason's extroverted nature always stood out in a crowd, and he made a fast impression. He became acquaintances with members of Leatherface as well as Chuck Ragan. Lainey told Jason to give him a call if we ended up near Sunderland when he learned of our approaching European journey.

We drove home through the dark, smoking cigarettes and laughing in the glow of the radio light, buzzing from the power and hope that only youth, rock 'n' roll, and a warm summer night can bring.

"HE'S IN LOVE WITH THE ROTTEN OLD WORLD.
HE'S SO IN LOVE, HE'LL TAKE IT IN THE ARM OF HIS GIRL.
HE'S IN LOVE WITH A LITTLE WHITE GOD.
HE'S SO IN LOVE, HE'S FORGOTTEN ABOUT BEING A MOD."

— "LITTLE WHITE GOD," STUBBS

LEIGHTON EVANS — LEATHERFACE, JESSE

There seemed to be only a few discerning paths a young lad from Sunderland could venture down during Leighton Evans's high school years. Two of the more obvious choices were to join a band or play football. The majority of his peers chose one or the other, but Evans was adept enough to drift between both worlds with little effort. Though he was captain of the football team, something still nagged at him, tugging at his sleeve while he chased the ball around the field. Evans bought a cheap red electric guitar on a whim from one of the second-hand shops on Hylton Road with the savings from his birthday fund. When he tried to play the guitar at home, he was perplexed as to why it sounded so miserable. One of his more musically inclined friends tuned the instrument for him while visiting, proving Evans's purchase wasn't a complete loss. He applied the working-class determination passed down to him and learned how to play. It wasn't long before he found himself clad in a fur coat, shades, and standing onstage with a local act called the Carmodies.

The band was surprised to find they'd been written up in the local paper after one of their gigs. But it wasn't the type of press a group of budding musicians would've hoped for. Their name appeared in an advice column known as Aunty Beryl, where people could seek guidance about a personal issue. Someone wrote in claiming to have been at the Carmodies gig a few nights before. It seemed their "personal issue" was with the band's decision to include a cover of U2's "I Will Follow" in their set. They were appalled that a "mod band" would commit such an act. The majority of letters to Aunty Beryl were penned anonymously, but this rant was signed by Frankie Stubbs. Beryl had some helpful advice for Stubbs, but also some pearls about how the aspiring young mods should sort themselves out.

The situation left the kids confounded and dejected.

Born July 20, 1976, Leighton Evans grew up in Sunderland only a few miles from David Lee Burdon against the same dreary coal mining backdrop. These kids learned the ropes through trial by fire and inherited a tough-as-nails demeanour from those before them. Terms such as "mental health" and "anxiety" weren't spoken of in Evans's circle. He was born into a happy home, but trouble came easy in a place like Sunderland. Luckily, his passion and discipline for football kept him grounded.

As a kid he'd found himself flipping through his parents' extensive record collection which included artists like Thin Lizzy and the Police. The six-year-old slid on a pair of giant headphones that were plugged into the family record player, the kind with the long, curly cord. He placed a Beatles record on the turntable. When he dropped the needle down on that sunny day in Sunderland it triggered something deep in the young boy's head.

But it was the influence of Evans's older brother that turned the tide. He could hear a brave new sound coming from down the hall as his brother played the Smiths, Stone Roses, and Joy Division. These sombre sounds entered his psyche. He imagined the brooding poet Ian Curtis. The provocative music conjured shadowy images of suicide. Evans was drawn to the darkness, mystery, and romance in this new movement.

The Carmodies knew that if they were going to make it out of Sunderland, they would first have to record their music. The most convenient recording studio happened to be located inside the Bunker where Evans and company also rehearsed. This came with a complication though. It seemed that the same frustrated man who had written Aunty Beryl about the Carmodies also had ties with this studio. To what extent was unclear at the time.

Despite their distress about possibly coming face to face with the character that had publicly professed his aggravation with them, they decided to stick with their recording date. The Carmodies pulled up their socks and faced the predicament head-on with a stiff upper lip, as Sunderland chaps do. But when the band reached the Bunker, these worries escalated. Stubbs was there waiting for them. As it turned out, he was the engineer and owner of the studio. It was a difficult moment knowing they would be working directly with him for five days. Stubbs laughed like a madman because he knew the whole time it was the Carmodies who were coming in. The kids managed to see the humour in the prank, and everyone laughed about it later over beers. Evans and Stubbs got along after being forced to spend more time together as the demo progressed. The session went well, and the Carmodies even gained Stubbs's respect because of their willingness to stay the course.

This period was during the first hiatus of Leatherface. Stubbs was now playing in a new project called Jesse with a drummer named Spud (Peter Shield). It seems Stubbs has forever been hunting for a capable bass player to play with. Good bass players are as scarce in Sunderland as drummers are in Toronto. They would need someone soon for the band's upcoming tour in Japan and invited Evans to come audition for Jesse. Stubbs could see the kid had talent. Evans was floored by the offer even though he admits he'd never listened to Leatherface. He knew Stubbs's reputation though and began to think it might be foolish to turn down the opportunity.

Evans showed up at the first practice with Stubbs and Spud after learning the songs from a poorly recorded demo the prankster had given him. He was surprised to learn of the troubadour's idiosyncrasies — no vocals while practising. This was Stubbs's law then. By rehearsing this way, he could tell if the musicians knew the songs or not. Spuds's body engulfed the drum kit like it was a toy as he clicked his sticks together. A few bars into the verse and Stubbs gave Evans a look that said, *Shit, son, you really are a proper bass player.* What happened next was very unusual. The singer's body began to stir. Stubbs started shuffling about with his guitar, shoulders rotating, hips swaying, feet sliding around where he stood. The display could only be described as a sort of jig. Evans tried to look away but couldn't. It was mesmerizing watching the nimble man move around the jam space as happy as a clam.

This period after the Leatherface split was an isolating time for Stubbs. Lainey and Hammond had been invited by their peers to join other projects, which made the separation less painful for them. But nobody asks the lead singer of a band if they'd like to come play rhythm guitar in another project. Stubbs admits he would have enjoyed this very much. He started his own thing because the call never came. Evans and Stubbs grew very close in this time, playing together in Jesse.

The original members of Leatherface began to lick their wounds from the first breakup. After two years, Hammond started coming around again with his mischievous smile and dark spiky hair. The three of them would go drink at the pub where Lainey worked. Evans watched as these huge personalities merged. He could see how they might clash like titans or fit like snug components of a complicated engine. The four of them enjoyed each other's company, and for a short period of time they were like a pack of wild horses running together again. It wasn't long before the four of them found themselves standing in the jam space moments from playing "Little White God." Evans was seconds away from witnessing the true sound Leatherface could make when powered by the band's original forces. There was a precarious balance of raw emotion and nervous energy teetering amongst them. Like standing in a room with the dog that bit them, they stared into its eyes trying to disguise their fear.

Evans says it sounded like an earthquake and the hairs on the back of his neck stood up when the song started. He honestly thought the room might crumble under the stress of the thundering sound coming from the band. When the song ended, all uneasy emotions were replaced with joy.

Evans began to understand Leatherface on a deeper level after spending more time with his bandmates. He realized a portion of their revered existence hinged on larger-than-life characters full of incredible talent and passion. A musical harmony that sounded like impalpable light emerged as theses displaced planets drifted back into the solar system. He could see how elaborate and intelligent the heart of the music could be. Leatherface was an onion. New sounds and new ideas unfolded with every layer peeled. He felt some of this came from the guitars. Hammond's isolated guitar ideas sounded unintelligible at times. It wasn't until Frankie's guitar was dropped over top that the chaos became genius and morphed into a complex electric wreath. The band then hit the road en route to Germany in preparation for the upcoming U.S. tour with Hot Water Music.

The only vehicle the band could find to rent at the time was a cargo van with no windows in the back. They took what they could get and loaded up the gear. Leatherface was on the road once again with Stubbs and Lainey at the helm, and Hammond and Evans in the back. Hammond's and Evans's sanity wavered after nearly twenty-four hours of being stuck in the darkened cargo area without a view to let their eyes wander. Evans found himself staring down at Hammond's shoes as the guitarist's big toe started pushing upward at the top of the footwear to make it flex. He watched this for longer than he ever would have because there simply was nothing else to capture the imagination. The toe pushed up higher and higher in the shoe. He looked up to meet Hammond's mischievous smirk in the dark. His expression urged Evans to look back down at the toe. Evans lowered his eyes as Hammond gave the flexing shoe a shrill, elderly lady's voice which echoed loudly in the depths of the steel box. Evans burst into hysterics as Hammond's shoe launched into a narrative about all kinds of things, taking on a life of its own, as if it were a fifth member of the band. Everyone laughed until it hurt. Part of what powers Leatherface is humour, and it came all too easy to Hammond.

This reunion was short-lived. Hammond was off again after they'd completed the songs for the Hot Water Music split album. Stubbs went out on a limb and suggested that Evans take the place of Hammond on guitar to keep the momentum going for the impending album and the U.S. tour. The singer had another potential bass player in mind — this strange bartender kid named David Lee Burdon who played in a stoner rock band in town.

Uncle Ian dropped us off in town the next evening to experience Manchester's nightlife on our own. But excitement for a pair of hosers was difficult to find in proper Manchester. We were turned away by every disapproving pub and nightclub in the village. Years had passed since I felt that level of rejection. We decided to take a last desperate stab before heading home with our tails between our legs. There seemed to be only one place left for us to go. We would have to try the strip club. I could never walk up to one of these places without thinking of the first time Jason and I tried to get into one.

"I've got an idea, c'mere" Jason said, urging me to lean forward from the back seat of Yates's Oldsmobile. He ran his index finger through the car's ashtray before reaching toward my face. His was delighted by his own ingenuity.

"Yeah, give him a 'stache," Yates chimed in with his head half turned to the back, sideburns like giant furry boots on his face. I was seventeen and my face was like silk. I closed my eyes as Jason's pudgy finger pressed around above my upper lip before he turned red with laughter.

In my reflection in the rearview mirror, I looked like a bruised peach. They were enjoying my embarrassment. I played along though, because I too thought it was hilarious.

"You kiddin' me?! I look like a creepy Charlie Chaplin?" I asked. More laughter. I lunged forward between the two front seats and dug my finger into the ashtray. I smoothed, worked, and thinned my slate moustache so it extended to the edge of my lips. "That's better, shit looks tight," I said, checking the mirror again from the back seat of Yates's car.

"Cracker Zorro!" Yates yelled as we drove en route to the infamous strip club Whiskey A Go-Go.

The car pulled into the busy parking lot. Well-dressed businessmen strutted from their expensive cars in through the tall black doors. Jason chuckled when he spotted the large doorman standing like a wrestler in a tuxedo.

"K. Oldest-looking first, Cracker Zorro in the middle," Jason said.

"Play it cool, boys," I reminded them. "Plaaay it cooooool."

I walked through the parking lot staring down at my ripped army pants and baggy flannel shirt. Yates slid by the man with a nod. I stepped forward like I owned the joint without making eye contact. An arm came down in front of me like a gate at a railroad crossing just as I thought I was free. The doorman's meaty hand rested on my chest. I looked up at his face.

"Nice try," he said with a smile before ushering me off to the side. There was no point in arguing.

"One day I'm going to have a real soup-strainer!" I called to him as we drove out of the parking lot.

I was surprised the inebriated doorman at the strip club in Manchester could even stand. After a period of speculation, wobbly flashlights, twitchy moustaches, and fumbled foreign ID, he waved us through. As we entered, I questioned whether it was where I really wanted to spend my time. Jason and I stepped forward with timid expressions into the *Scarface*-esque ballroom of black marble, white lacey curtains, and synth pop. It felt as if we'd stepped back into an '80s glamour shot without realizing. The place twinkled like stardust. A bright light spilled across the pale thighs gripping the chrome dance pole. An older man with a wide scarf around his neck and a captain's hat sat in the front row. He wore a purple velvet jacket with an embellished golden patch on the breast. It was easy to tell by his fishhook eyes that the Captain was hammered. His lips were puckered like Donald Trump's and his head bobbled on his shoulders like it might roll off at any second. "Away from the Captain," I whispered. Couples eyed us from their tables. My skin crawled but my thirst propelled me farther into the lair.

"Whoa . . ." Jason muttered under his breath. We ordered two pints. I felt a wave of loneliness rise into my arms as I leaned across the mahogany bar. The bartender couldn't fool me with his slick dark hair and baggy white dress shirt. We both knew how bad it was. Jason and I watched the dancer twirl about with a feather boa for ten minutes before leaving the Captain, the leering swingers, and the '80s lighting behind. Sometimes you have to venture where you don't belong to understand where you do.

The next afternoon we said goodbye to Jason's family and boarded the bus back to Sunderland. We couldn't believe our eyes as David Lee Burdon walked up the steps and paid his fare. I was certain I was dreaming when he invited us to a Leatherface rehearsal happening the following day.

"A NATURAL DISASTER.
A BIT OF A BASTARD.
A MUTUAL FEELING
OF LEVELLING THE BLAME.
THE TRUTH HURTS
AND LIES DO THE SAME.
AS FICKLE AS AN AUTUMN DAY.
PRAISE THE LORD, HALLELUJAH JUST THE SAME.
BEFORE I TALK TO THE TREES,
I'LL HAVE A NICE POT OF TEA.
I WON'T BREATHE A WORD
BECAUSE IT HAS ITS MOMENTS AND THAT'S WHAT MATTERS."

—"HEAVEN SENT," STUBBS

DAVID LEE BURDON — LEATHERFACE, FORMER CELL MATES, DL BURDON & HIS QUESTIONABLE INTENTIONS

The twenty-one-year-old tried with all his might to keep his shit together while waiting onstage to play his first gig with Leatherface at the Garage in Highbury, north London. A condescending sound tech was projecting his irritated state about Burdon not knowing what a DI (direct input) was or how to plug his bass into one. The show was a benefit for the family of former bass player Andy Crighton, who had passed the year before, in 1998. A wound that was still fresh. It would have been frightening enough to play with Leatherface live for the first time, let alone be on the same bill with Snuff and Wat Tyler. But it was a much different concern altogether to be standing in the place of someone who'd performed their part so instinctively for the band. The emotional weight of this evening bore down on him. With everything on the line, the strange and wonderful road that had led him to that evening flashed before his eyes.

Burdon was born in Sunderland in 1977. The boy spent his childhood under the wing of his mother and sister against a post-industrial backdrop of picketing workers, unemployment, and the town's buckling coal industry. His childhood was sunny despite the grim setting, and on most days, he could be found riding his BMX for miles in search of the beach and freedom. It was Stevie Wonder's "Lately" that started a lifelong love for music, and it began with him first constructing guitars out of Stickle Bricks. The song brought tears then as it still does to this day. He spent a lot of time as he grew older flipping through the stacks of vinyl his dad had left behind. Soul, Motown, Springsteen, and Thin Lizzy soon had the kid dreaming of riding a motorbike to the beach instead of his BMX. His true calling came though when he laid eyes on Sid Vicious for the first time after the bass player kicked the mic stand over in a TV special celebrating the tenth anniversary of the Sex Pistols's gig at the Lesser Free Trade Hall. The band was the gateway into punk culture for many kids then.

After broadening his horizons and reading alternative music magazines, he stumbled on a feature about a mysterious band called Leatherface from his hometown. Burdon fell deeper into the world he longed to live in after discovering the radio show of John Peel, a highly regarded British disc jockey and radio presenter. The host would spin everything from British hip hop to psychedelic rock to punk. John Peel loved Leatherface, and so did Burdon after hearing them on Peel's show for the first time. He could now feel that Stubbs's songwriting and lyrical prowess stood in stark contrast to the working-class town where they lived. This contradictory presence drew him farther in.

Another local Sunderland College radio host named Patricia Lockhart offered a giveaway of Leatherface's *Minx* to the first few callers one night. Davey "Fast Fingers" Burdon had them on the line in no time and won himself the album he now considers a bible.

While attending a media class in college, an assignment was handed out to find and interview a published writer or artist within their community. This proved to be a challenge in Sunderland then. At the pub one night while contemplating this dilemma, he sparked a conversation with a woman named Angela. It turns out she'd have a drink with Stubbs from time to time. Angela suggested to Burdon that Stubbs might do the interview and urged him to call the musician. She said he was a kind person. The prospect had Burdon feeling inspired. Angela told him, "Make sure you tell him it was Angela with the big tits that gave you his number."

The kid dialled the number when he reached home after midnight. The singer didn't pick up and the call went straight to voicemail: "Thisisfrankieleaveamessage." Burdon left a message explaining his assignment and added at the end, "Oh yeah, Angela with the big tits gave me your number . . ."

He was surprised when Stubbs returned his call later after having been at the pub himself. The singer was angry. Stubbs scolded Burdon by telling him he didn't stand for sexism, and that he believed in equality for all. "But she told me to say that to you," he pleaded, his words falling on deaf ears. The frontman told Burdon to fuck off and hung up. It stung to be chewed out by someone he admired so much.

Burdon gathered up his courage to confront Stubbs after catching sight of him out at the pub on another occasion. He refreshed the singer's memory about the night he had told Burdon to fuck off. The kid knew the way into most Englishmen's hearts and offered a peace pint to smooth the situation out. Stubbs offered to do the interview for him after realizing Burdon was a good enough kid.

Stubbs began spending more and more time at the pub that Burdon bartended at. A friendship formed because of this. Stubbs would pay his tab and Burdon would refund him his money. Stubbs would give him recordings of Jesse and other musical projects of his in return. Burdon played bass in a stoner rock band at the time. He was aware of the passing of Leatherface's bass player Andy Crighton, but when Stubbs asked him to come try out for the position, Burdon didn't understand what he was hearing. He accepted the offer.

With a sixteen-year age gap between the two of them, and Stubbs's protective nature, the singer became a father figure to Burdon. The two bandmates had dropped ecstasy one night and went to see Lainey's other band, Red Alert, play. The show was at a venue above a strip club called Chambers. Burdon, his friend "Dumpsta," and Stubbs headed back to Stubbs's flat to relax after the show finished. They ran into two "chavs" (troublemakers) setting off fire extinguishers in the alley as they approached the building. Burdon walked up to them, hoping to join in the fun, but was knocked out cold after one of them attacked him out of the blue. The hoodlums fled the scene fast. Stubbs and Dumpsta helped the kid up the stairs and sat him down, placing a bag of frozen peas against his head. Stubbs then set off into the night to find the men. He let the two chavs know they had made a poor decision by attacking his friend when he found them.

Burdon stood looking out at the full house crammed inside the Garage. His bass was now plugged into the DI. His hands trembled. He was buzzed from the Red Stripes. It had boiled down to the most unnerving minute of his life.

The way "Springtime" detonated from the stage was unlike anything a kid from Sunderland could have ever imagined. The crowd screamed. Cameras flashed. He stood like a stone statue as Lainey forced him to blink with every crack of the snare drum. Burdon could only hold on for dear life and try his best to lock in the groove, which he did just fine for the next eight years that he played with Leatherface.

"WE'VE ALL SEEN THE BIG RED BUS,
WITH FACES GAZING EXPRESSIONLESS.
THE BREAKFAST JOINT THAT KILL THE BEAST,
HELPS SOW THE SEED FOR ALL MANNER OF DANGEROUS THINGS.
AND HERE IT GOES AGAIN AS MELANCHOLY AS THE LAST ONE,
AND WHEN YOU FEEL AS DOGMATIC AS THE NEXT,
THEN IT'S TIME TO READ INTO WHAT IT IS THAT YOU DO."

– "DEAD INDUSTRIAL ATMOSPHERE," STUBBS

SUNDERLAND

On the banks of the River Wear entering Sunderland you'll see evidence of past industrialization, where collieries, engineering works, and dozens of shipyards once thrived through the seventeenth and eighteenth centuries, back when a thick cloud of coal dust and the deafening noise of riveters filled the air. The town has been home to over four hundred registered shipyards, with the earliest one founded in 1346. By the early 1800's, Sunderland was building hundreds of ships each year and became one of the most crucial ports not just in England, but in all of Europe.

Death came easy at the docks because of how severe it was. The effect on family life was devasting because compensation for such tragedy was not regulated. Not until the twentieth century did medical officers get appointed to the yards. It was feast or famine. You could be sure unemployment and dire straits were close behind when the world felt like it had built enough cargo and turret ships. Workers wondered whether they'd be hired again as completed ships launched to sea. When the Second World War erupted and Britain's naval fleet fell prey to the enemy's submarine attacks, Sunderland played an important role in repairing these damaged vessels and building more to replace those lost in combat.

But Sunderland's incredible shipbuilding capabilities made its ports a prime target for Germany, and the townspeople lived in a state of perpetual fear. The incredibly dangerous working conditions coupled with the relentless threat of death from above made for a terrifying way of life. Despite all of this, it's been written that the workers maintained a sense of loyalty and camaraderie and managed to keep the atmosphere light with pranks and laughter during those dark days.

Sunderland's greatest fears were realized in 1940, and the city was attacked and bombed for three years. The worst of these raids occurred in 1943, and has been described by the *Sunderland Echo* as one of the war's most brutal. When bombs aimed at the ports missed their targets, they landed in the city centre, leaving the town in ruins. Hundreds died by the war's end.

As the war progressed and men felt obliged to leave the shipyards to fight for their country, the women of the city rolled up their sleeves and headed to the docks to keep the yards working at full potential. These dauntless women took up the skilled labour of welders, rivet catchers, and crane operators. They worked long hours to do their part and make ends meet and even took on extra work at night. Despite these essential efforts many believed this kind of work was meant for the men of Sunderland when they returned. The working women were referred to as "dilutes," a comparison to thinning with water. These shipbuilding women received little applause and little pay for their perseverance despite being given some of the toughest jobs in the war effort. Knowing even these basic points of Sunderland's history is perhaps a glimpse into the Leatherface members' feminism as well as their capacity to find humour when times were tough.

We were mid-conversation with Lainey when the door to the Ivy House opened and in walked Danielle, Jenny, Leighton Evans, Frankie Stubbs, and his girlfriend. A reunion of cheers and hugs was had. Stubbs went straight across the damask-carpeted floor for the panelled bar before I got a good look at him. He wore a faded green army jacket with a hood and had short hair. From what I could see of his face, he reminded me of De Niro in *Taxi Driver*.

The singer knew just about everyone in the place. I guess that's what happens after twenty years of going to the same pub. With his back turned to us, Stubbs greeted everyone along the bar. His presence electrified the atmosphere. I could tell by the roundness of his cheeks in profile that he was smiling. Our eyes followed him while he patted shoulders and shook hands. Everyone who seemed to lock eyes with the singer couldn't hold in their surprise. He raised both arms in the air like a ghost at the bartender. The man pouring drinks laughed uproariously, red-faced with one hand on a pint glass and the other on the tap. The scene looked like a Norman Rockwell painting full of exaggerated emotion.

The person I considered to be one of the most influential people of my generation then turned to our table with pints in hand. He walked toward us with a grin unlike any grin I've ever seen. His eyes were round and full of lightning like a wild stallion. Stubbs spat out a muffled greeting through a pair of fake, deviated, tobacco-stained "hick" teeth.

His smile grew wide. Spittle jiggled at the corner of his mouth as he guffawed through the cheap dollar store prosthetic. Stubbs's girlfriend covered her eyes with delight and embarrassment. The memory of the first time I'd heard *Minx* flashed through my mind: "I laugh at the world it's hysterical, and I love the way that it turns."

The words had come full circle and were resonating in me while I sat in a trance-like state. There was clarity. Years had passed since first reading the lyrics in the ramshackle rooming house where I lived. Five feet away stood the man who penned them. Any preconceived notions I'd been carrying with me shattered. I could do nothing but laugh and stare in wonder while trying to process it.

This charade went on for a long time, and it was difficult for him to pull out of it. The scene became hysterical like the words from "Wallflower." Like a slapstick comedy sketch designed to go on for so long it becomes uncomfortable, Stubbs hammered the joke relentlessly, and what was uncomfortable soon became funnier than when it started. He invaded his girlfriend's space as she pulled away in horror with her hair spilling across her smile. The man paraded around the bar with his pint in hand, needling people, spreading joy, elevating everyone's mood to a higher state. Stubbs even danced. The band kept a strict balance of work and play in those days and seemed to do both at full tilt. Years of relentless touring had taught the introvert to entertain and keep it light.

He soon sat at the table to talk with the kids who had travelled so far to meet him, and he had no other choice but to collect himself. I remember little from the scattered interaction besides him giving us a once-over. He remembered Jason but not me. He offered two comments both related to our clothes.

"What's with the headband, mate? You look like Axl Rose," he asked Jason, smiling with his regular teeth. Stubbs seemed to find his own boldness satisfying. I could tell by a quick shift of his eyes that Jason had been stung. A fleeting feeling of embarrassment draped the table in silence. Though I sometimes thought Jason's confidence needed to be cut down to size, I felt his pain as if I were his conjoined twin. I would've leapt to his defence but was robbed of words. Unlike Axl, who would've retreated to his dressing room for ten years, Jason shrugged it off.

I was wearing a New Model Army shirt that I'd bought at Zillo Festival in Germany. Stubbs pointed at it. I held my breath. Thankfully he seemed to like the band. We talked about them briefly before he broke into song, singing the chorus from New Model Army's "Green and Grey."

He waved his finger about like the conductor of a drunken choir. The night was both a rainy window and a sun-bleached Polaroid. Hearing Stubbs's singing made Jason feel better because it was the Irishman that introduced me to both Leatherface and New Model Army. Stubbs's eyes lit up when we all joined in.

"PEOPLE LIKE ME HAVE SOMETHING TO SING ABOUT."
— "BAKED POTATO," STUBBS

FRANKIE NORMAN WARSAW STUBBS
— LEATHERFACE, JESSE, POPE

Frankie Stubbs was born in 1962 and spent his entire life in Sunderland, England. I've heard him say, "You're born in Sunderland. You fuckin' die in Sunderland." I think the implication being that it felt as if there was no way out at times. That it was a brutal place to have grown up. He describes gangs roaming the streets dressed in outfits inspired by the 1971 film *A Clockwork Orange* and "literally beating the shit out of one another." The two remarks about his hometown paint a vivid picture.

He's been passionate about language, words, and images for as long as he can remember, regardless of his callous surroundings. The first book to cultivate this fascination for vocabulary and vision was Harper Lee's *To Kill a Mockingbird*. He also holds the film adaptation directed by Robert Mulligan in high regard. He admits there might be too many to choose from when speaking of influential authors. But his voice lights up when he mentions Ken Kesey's *One Flew Over the*

Cuckoo's Nest. I can't help but wonder if there might be subtle parallels between the themes of intellectual liberty found in this book and some of Leatherface's songs.

Stubbs would lie in bed in his younger days listening to John Peel's radio show, not unlike the rest of England. It was on those nights that he first fell in love with music, but most of all with punk. Stubbs now jokes the reason he has such a shit life is because of how influential Peel's radio show was. There's something cathartic about listening to the radio with the lights dimmed. How things have changed with the invasion of cellphones. Access to any kind of music, no matter how obscure, at a finger's touch. The mystery abolished. The convenience more of a curse than a blessing. I believe those who discovered new music via the old avenues were given something very special. This was a time of quality over quantity, where passion was passed along in the journey. You were let in on a secret by the faceless broadcaster talking from a small room somewhere out in the deep, dark night. A calming voice drifting from the radio towers out across the waves and skies and into our homes. The pride of discovery is a gift, and patience is a virtue. If there's something I could give the youth of today, it might be this.

You can sense this romantic spirit when talking with Stubbs. On the street you'd never know he was the lead singer of an important band that inspired the lives of so many around the globe. He is respected by his coworkers as a quiet man at the car dealership where he works. People struggle to believe the truth when they find out his history. I have a feeling he wouldn't even mention it if you didn't already know. There's true power in humility. We sometimes forget the waves of emotion and passion that can pour from a single unassuming person.

There's a video from 1998 of Stubbs playing "Pale Moonlight" in a yellow T-shirt. It's a clear window into the man in question and offers more insight than anything I could ever write. If it doesn't move you, then I'm sorry for your loss. I draw comparisons to the haunting footage of Townes Van Zandt playing "Waiting Around to Die" in his house in Texas. Tears stream down the face of the old Black man who sits next to him as the heartbreaking story in Van Zandt's song reveals itself. This video, and Van Zandt's jarring, uncompromising truths, made him arguably one of the world's most revered troubadours. Steve Earle said he'd get up on Bob Dylan's coffee table in his cowboy boots and tell him so. When I watched Stubbs playing "Pale Moonlight" in this video for the first time, my heart was thumping by the end. He can channel the undefinable like few can, and I'd get up on Earle's dining table in my Converse and let him know this. That video is a portrait of human sadness and hope I've only ever heard in a Van Zandt song.

A curious thing happened when Stubbs started collecting the music heard on Peel's radio show. After reading the lyrics to the songs from some of the albums he'd acquired, he felt as if their composers could've spent more time nurturing the ideas they were singing about. It very well could have been in those moments that Stubbs decided to separate himself.

A percentage of this person's musical makeup is grounded with pop sensibility. I also think he just knows a good song when he hears it. One can easily discern this by simply looking at Leatherface's covers: "Eagle" by ABBA, "Candle in the Wind" by Elton John, "In the Ghetto" by Elvis Presley, "True Colors" by Cyndi Lauper, "Talkin' 'Bout a Revolution" by Tracy Chapman, "Message in a Bottle" by the Police, "The Ship Song" by Nick Cave and the Bad Seeds. Stubbs looked beyond the confines of England's industrial, chanting pub rock, the working-class, knuckle-dragging bands he was surrounded by. Not that those bands didn't have their place, but because Stubbs is different. A famous quote from the singer was that he thought his band was doing alright when people with backpacks and large prescription glasses started taking over the front row at their concerts, and the punks and shaved heads found their way to the back.

The friendship between Stubbs and Hammond grew stronger as they spent more time together. It's amusing to think that the two of them wanted to form a band because they both played Gordon Smith guitars. When they met up Stubbs would teach Hammond how to play songs like "Alternative Ulster" by Stiff Little Fingers and other punk classics on the guitar. They could sense the growing connection between their diverse styles of guitar playing. It didn't take long for the two of them to further what they started. Stubbs asked Lainey (because he was too fast of a drummer for H.D.Q.) to come and jam with a new project he'd started with Hammond. Lainey agreed. In these early stages, Stubbs laid down his one condition to them: no singers allowed. The three friends started rehearsing a small set of songs in a garage behind Stubbs's apartment as the final shipyard in Sunderland closed down in 1988. The space stood in dire condition. A hole in the roof allowed the blistering noise of what soon became known as Leatherface's sound to pour out into the streets. The dank timber began to rot and mushrooms sprouted from the ceiling after years of rain pissing down on the shack. Some of the growth was more than a foot thick. The canopy still leaked no matter how much Stubbs patched and poured liquid tar across the roof to seal it. Still the wild mushrooms grew taller and thicker.

Hammond defied Stubbs's rule of no singers and slinked into rehearsal one day with a vocalist at his side. Stubbs stuck to his guns and walked out. After some time, they coerced him back into practising. But it didn't take long before Hammond tried to sneak in another singer without any warning. This time it was a kid in his twenties. Instead of leaving, Stubbs humoured his friend's persistence and obvious desire for vocals. He watched as the kid lay down on the floor of the garage and sang on his back. This angered Stubbs to no end. But it was when he started screaming about goblins and ice caves that Stubbs drew the line and walked out.

They reached the diplomatic agreement that all members would sing and take a stab at writing lyrics. They tracked the instrumentation for their first five-song demo after this treaty was struck. The shells of these songs would later become "Colorado Joe/Leningrad Vlad," "Discipline," and "Cabbage Case." Their agreement to be a collective and collaborate lyrically didn't happen. When the time came to record vocals for the demo, the only one who showed up with any words was

Stubbs: "I became the singer because the lazy bastards couldn't be bothered." Hammond boasted many years later in an interview that Stubbs was the finest lyricist in the U.K.

The name of the band may have never surfaced without the friendship between Stubbs and Hammond. The epiphany happened one night at Stubbs's flat while the two bandmates lay side by side in the middle of the living room floor. They were staring at the chipped plaster on the ceiling, drunk off their legs. With all the brainstorming the two had done together trying to think of a great band name, nothing had emerged from the ether.

On the telly next to where the two friends lay, the iconic film character Leatherface spun around with his chainsaw on the dirt road in the morning sun. The truck sped off with the bloodied girl in the back, leaving him in the dust. The warm sunrise on the screen spilled across the two of them. A revelation came at that moment as Stubbs glanced at his favourite film. But there was something else. He propped up onto his elbow with his frantic eyes searching the bookcase against the wall. Stubbs pulled himself up and stumbled across the living room and slid a book titled *Leatherface* from its place on the shelf. It was published in 1958 by Ernest Dudley and is a story about the ghost of a hanged highwayman who haunts the Dover Road. Stubbs held the novel so Hammond could see the title from where he lay, then nodded toward the telly screen. Hammond smiled mischievously from his place on the floor.

Laurence Bell signed the band to Roughneck Recording Company after hearing their first full-length album, *Cherry Knowle*, and things began to take shape for the group. Speculation mounted among music execs that Leatherface might be a candidate to garner big success in the U.K. with the anticipation of their third LP, *Mush*. Bell can't recall if the band recorded any demos at all in preparation for the album. It seemed to be a perfect storm and was done on the fly. All songs were co-written by Stubbs and Hammond and their prowess as a team came full tilt. Hammond always composed the music for the verses before handing it over to Stubbs to attach a chorus. Stubbs would drop the words on top when the structure was intact. This is how the two of them worked together right through to the end.

With the looming buzz of the release, the band needed a vehicle to tour the record. Stubbs's occupation at the time was a merchandiser of top-grade psilocybin. He sold a quality product at a reasonable price. It didn't take much effort or time to purchase the van with college kids and professors gobbling the 'shrooms up like Dairy Milks. He gifted a generous supply to the team at Roughneck Records. The label suggested the title of the album should be *Mush* sometime later. Perhaps a hero's journey was taken where the name revealed itself.

When you read the lyrics to the songs from this album, it's difficult to imagine they came about simply by default, but maybe that was the world's way of making a little room for Stubbs, because the world has a funny way of doing that for people of tremendous substance.

"YOU'RE WEARING THAT, WEARING THAT BLAND OLD HAT,
YOUR BOXER SHORTS, ARE YOUR MOST INNER THOUGHTS,
A THOUSAND MILES OF OLD HEADLINES, MEMORIES OF HER,
THAT FLOWERHEAD, THAT SOUR GRAPE, THAT UN-ENGLISH STATE,
MEANS YOU DO, LIKE TO WAIT, VIOLENT AND DISNEY-LIKE."

– "SOUR GRAPES," STUBBS

BELLY OF THE BEAST

I woke to the sound of blistering guitars and my head caving in. *What is happening?* I covered my ears as if I were under attack. But the song also sounded amazing. The chorus dragged me from whatever vestige of sleep I clung to.

"YOUUUUUUUUUUUU WERE HAPPIER, DREAMING TOO." Stubbs's voice was like a war cry. With my eyes pried open, I must have looked like the *Clockwork Orange* image. I bolted upright to find Jason laughing his ass off, falling against the wall, holding a CD case.

"Fuck, dude!" I shouted over the music.

The bastard had placed a speaker on either side of my head and let it rip. I slumped down and listened, half wasted from the night before. *How could this song have never made it onto an album?* Two rare discography discs emerged in 1998. The song "Dreaming" came from

Discography Part Two. It was originally released on a 7" with a cover of ABBA's "Eagle" on the other side. It was fucking awesome.

What a way to start the day. We sat in Lainey's room and listened to the rest of the disc, laughing about Stubbs's hick teeth from the night before. The afternoon would bring the anticipated Leatherface rehearsal Burdon had invited us to. Optimism was radiating. I spent the rest of the morning rolling around the chorus of "Dreaming" in my soupy brain.

We reached the jam space later that afternoon, oblivious to the landmark's musical legacy. Leatherface's rehearsal room was dubbed "Frankie's Bunker" back in 1999. It was one of the many rooms inside the building that was known to the local community as the Bunker. It looked as if it could have been any rehearsal space anywhere in the world. Little did we know it was the newest location of what had been a DIY punk rock institution in the town for decades.

Unemployment among youth had been at an all-time high during the '80s in Sunderland. Because of how expensive rehearsal spaces were at that time, young punks relentlessly searched for a secret hideout to get wild in. A man named Andy Gibson helped form the Sunderland Musicians Collective and secured necessary funding to lease a garage in south Hendon. Positive local press helped prevent the initiative from getting shut down for ongoing noise violations. In 1982 the collective was offered an upstairs room at Green Terrace School in Sunderland. The new location was painted camouflage, with draped fishing nets that had been found at the docks. The name was born out of the new décor.

Some of the first gigs in this space boasted anarcho-punk bands such as Poison Girls. This was a diverse, non-profit organization run by co-operative rules. Every kind of band under the punk umbrella played there, from new wave to Oi!. Popular zines such as *Acts of Defiance* started advertising the growing shows and inspired the opening of similar venues in neighbouring towns. They raised money for social causes, like striking miners. A regular police presence was felt outside the Bunker. But authorities left them alone. At least they knew where the anarchists were on any given night.

The roof of the building next door blew off in 1983 and landed on top of the Bunker, damaging it irreparably. This led them to the new location that is now at 29 Stockton Road. The turn of the century almost saw the end of the beloved space when cuts were made to the funding by the government. It had been the collective's lifeblood for so long. Even a generous donation from John Peel couldn't keep it open. Kenny Sanger and Adrian Woodland, who both played in many bands in the Bunker's early days bought the building, and the music community that the Bunker helped create continues to thrive. It is now the home of a record label, rehearsal space, and a recording studio. It's also the base of Little Rocket Records, owned by Graeme Philliskirk.

It was in the Bunker that Philliskirk witnessed the rise of Leatherface. His pride peaked as their third LP loomed on the horizon. He remembers friends stumbling back there at three a.m. and Stubbs playing excerpts of songs from what would later be known as *Mush*. There was a real buzz while the tight-knit circle hunkered in the dim light to listen. Little did they know the true scope of what those songs would become. He describes the record as one that from front to back "will rip your fucking head off. That by the time the album was done, you'd want to listen to it again because you were left dumbfounded."

In 2017, the Bunker celebrated its thirty-fifth year as a Sunderland staple.

Through the door to Frankie's Bunker we could see Stubbs, Lainey, Evans, and Burdon. My heart beat fast and my mouth felt dry as I hesitated in the doorway to the musty room. It was like walking into a fine China shop with my hands buried in my pockets. I paused, listening to the fluorescent bulbs fizzle above, unsure if I should enter. My eyes scanned a trophy-like display of empty Carling cans on a cabinet in the corner: they'd won many tournaments. Each wall was painted with a different mistint. I was curious to know what lyrics were scribed on the papers scattered across the floor as I glanced down at their filing cabinet. After failing to look natural standing in the corner, we sat on a sagging loveseat against the wall.

The four of them talked low and joked in a much different manner than the night before. I pulled a beer from a plastic bag and cracked it, falling into full observation mode. When I ran into Burdon twenty-two years later, he said to me, "Wait, you were sitting on the sofa right? You didn't make a peep, mate!" Stubbs held his trademark Gordon Smith guitar. He strummed a few notes. The amp hissed.

The band was rehearsing for the release of their upcoming album that would later be titled *Horsebox*. I had been secretly hoping they'd perform a private show for us but came to accept this wouldn't be the case. The thought of a new record was exhilarating enough. There was never a time when I didn't want to hear a new song.

The tune started with the familiar palm muted notes that had become the band's trademark sound. Lainey came in hard with a mid-tempo beat after a few measures. It was difficult to figure out whether Stubbs was growling or whispering when he started singing. Maybe both. A gift given only to him and Tom Waits.

We knew it was coming. We could hear it building. The verse of "Sour Grapes" opened wide into its chorus on that damp afternoon in Sunderland. There's nothing that resonates more with me than a heavy, contemplative heart full of sincerity. It sounded like the sun behind the clouds. It sounded like tears. Like memory. It was a poem and instantly nostalgic.

"Days and days, days and days," Stubbs sang.

The song came pounding with mesmerizing melancholy. My heart thumped as I sipped my beer, my clammy hand gripping the can. My other balled into a fist. Then came the peace that they always bring. I looked around at the tough-looking people around me. It didn't add up. Some things just aren't what they seem in this life. It was okay. Everything was okay.

A vision came to me as this new song was being built. I'd heard Leatherface for the first time in Darrell's basement in a suburb of Toronto with Jason sitting next to me. And now, we found ourselves years later on the other side of the ocean together in the practice space of the band that had altered the course of our existence.

I thought back to the connections and friendships that sparked the night they played in Buffalo. Leatherface's words and music had drawn us in like a magnetic field. What was an ordinary rehearsal for the band that afternoon was sacred to us. We found ourselves in the belly of the beast after all the miles and years. I could feel a power drifting in the dank room. It was so much larger than us. They let us in to their world, their lair, and their creative process. I wouldn't have believed what gifts the future held if shown from the start, and there was no one there to witness it besides Jason and me.

The experiences of our journey began to unfold around us in what seemed to be an expanding, complex web. What I know about life is that you'll begin to see what you're truly looking for as long as you keep searching. It's a universal order. Adventure, romanticism, and inspiration were revealing themselves to us.

In Frankie's Bunker with all the Carling cans, scattered lyric sheets, and the cracking snare drum, with the promise of things to come, where Stubbs sang "days and days," my heart drifted into the night like the sombre note of a strummed Gordon Smith.

"IN THE PALM OF MY HAND I HOLD THESE GRAINS OF SAND.
AND IF I CLING TO YOU TIGHT WILL YOU BE THERE.
YOU SMOKE DOPE EVERY DAY WHILE I DRINK MY NIGHTS AWAY.
AND IF I CLOSE MY EYES TIGHT YOU'LL STILL BE THERE."

— "HOODLUM," STUBBS

AUSTIN LUCAS — GUIDED CRADLE, RUNE,
TWENTY THIRD CHAPTER

Bloomington, Indiana–born musician Austin Lucas watched as the arcane, three-piece British punk band took the stage inside San Francisco's Bottom of the Hill. They noticed something unnerving about the band's appearance as Leatherface paced about, setting up their gear. Lucas realized the dark purple circles surrounding their eyes weren't from sleep deprivation as the dim stage lights may have first suggested — a common look among hard-living touring bands. They looked closer and realized that each member of Leatherface had a pair of black eyes. That wasn't all. The group all had bruised and broken noses as well. It would seem the "English thug" stereotype that preceded them came as effortlessly as Lainey pulling off his shirt in preparation for their set.

The shock of Leatherface's presence settled into the waiting crowd as Stubbs and Burdon plugged in their instruments and tuned. Lucas's eyes wandered away from the beat-up band to their merch booth, where a monstrous person stood dressed in full clown regalia towering over the table of records and shirts.

Had Lucas known in those few minutes that within two years the clown, Chris "Big Rock" Schaefer, would go on to be one of Lucas's roommates, I'm sure they would have smiled harder than they already were. Lucas wondered who in the holy fuck these people were and how they'd come to look as if they'd clawed their way out of a bar brawl. All questions disappeared as Leatherface's music erupted from the stage. Watching and listening, Lucas's previous perceptions about the band were challenged. This could've been a turning point in their punk rock tastes.

Austin Lucas would find their true voice and carve a deep path in the Americana and alt-country genre later in life. But thirty years of punk and hardcore roots are hard to shake and appear to be the backbone of everything they stand for. The end of the '90s was a time that Lucas holds dear because it represented the last of the punk rock shows with enough urgency for music to be a *true* driving force in their life. It was during this closing door of time that Lucas witnessed the true capabilities of Leatherface onstage. Lucas feels there are a few select punk and hardcore bands in the world whose live performances are crucial to understanding their true potential. They feel passionately that Leatherface was one of these acts, and it may have even been to their detriment. Leatherface's live delivery was so powerful at times that to go back and listen to the records didn't seem to do them justice.

Lucas refers to the sound they heard that night on Potrero Hill as nothing short of a force of nature. The band's presence was ominous, and the clown brought levity. The music came screaming right down the middle. This was Lucas's first real introduction to Leatherface even though they were familiar with the band's catalogue. You can't look away when it happens like that. You can't deny Leatherface's authenticity or their ability to do what they did. You can only listen and say to yourself, "Fuck my life, this is good."

Lucas and Schaefer had both expatriated from the U.S. to the Czech Republic around the same time. The two of them found themselves in a serendipitous moment sitting together in Lucas's brother's bar, the Blind Eye, in Prague. Schaefer knew Lucas's brother Noah well. Big Rock sat in his usual chair, where a sign was drilled into the bar that read, "This seat is reserved for Big Rock. He's bigger and cooler than you." It was a declaration of how adored Schaefer was and an indication of how much time he spent there. "He was an important-ass person in my friend group, and in multiple avenues, and all through the circles of my life. He was tied in."

It was in the Blind Eye that Lucas learned what Schaefer did when he wasn't sitting on his favourite stool. Lucas was gobsmacked when the big man mentioned nonchalantly that he was the tour manager for MDC, Adolescents, Dead Kennedys, and others. But when Schaefer mentioned Leatherface, he talked about them as if they were his home. Though much of his time was dedicated to touring with some of the most popular punk musicians from around the world, Leatherface remained the band he worked with most. Lucas also expressed his appreciation for them, recalling the pivotal moment back in San Francisco at Bottom of the Hill. Big Rock lit up like a set of stage lights. "You were at that show?" he asked Lucas.

"Yeah, that was my first time seeing them, they all had black eyes and broken noses!"

"I was the guy in the clown suit at the merch table," Big Rock said. Lucas couldn't believe it. They thought in those moments how wonderful and hilarious life's twists and turns can be. It wasn't long before the two friends moved in together and found Leatherface sleeping on their floor whenever the band rolled through the Czech Republic. Lucas befriended the members after some time. They felt an instant connection with Burdon, but they couldn't get close to Stubbs. Lucas explains that at that time Stubbs seemed like a pit bull who'd been beaten up, and they maintained a safe distance from the singer. Lucas recalls sitting in a restaurant listening to an argument between his brother Noah and Stubbs about the Clash. Stubbs called Strummer a "posh boy" as he argued against Noah's love for them. Lucas began to worry that the brothers would have to fight Leatherface right there in the restaurant because of how heated the dispute became. Lucky for everyone involved the situation diffused itself.

Having a row was not uncommon between the members of Leatherface according to Duncan Redmonds, who remembers one of these interactions being so loud the police thought a fist fight was happening in the apartment. There was also the cold winter night when Rosie (Leatherface road crew) sleepwalked out of Redmonds's flat in nothing but his underwear. Still asleep, Rosie thankfully found his way back in and snuggled up shivering with Stubbs, causing another great calamity. Redmonds recalls thinking how only Leatherface (sometimes referred to by the nickname "The Boat") could row in their sleep.

Lucas says, "Being Chris's friend was fun. He was extremely generous. He liked to give. He liked to facilitate fun. He didn't care much about money and looked at money more as something that couldn't buy life experience. He was a ridiculous human who didn't have much in the way of shame, which is something I adore about people, and a quality I strive for. I've also never seen another person pound white-wine spritzers, vodka, and ecstasy like him. And just keep on doing it for days. That dude was a fucking machine when it came to partying. I think that is something the members of Leatherface related to and actually respected. They could still be up at ten a.m. slugging beers, talking about heading to the bar, and I'd be like, 'Okay, I'm good now.'"

Lucas bought Big Rock a set of floaties for his arms when they lived together because his favourite pastime was getting drunk and soaking in the tub. Lucas never worried about him drowning though because he was too large for such a thing to happen. Years after Lucas moved back to the States however, Schaefer passed from carbon monoxide asphyxiation one tragic night after falling asleep in the tub in his apartment in Prague.

When Graeme Philliskirk, the newest bassist in Leatherface, asked Big Rock who his favourite band of all time to work with was, he replied, "Leatherface." When Philliskirk asked who the worst band he'd worked with was, he also replied, "Leatherface." The band buried their friend Chris "Big Rock" Schaefer in his jean jacket and red and white Leatherface jersey. Schaefer had managed to lose a considerable amount of weight and turn an unhealthy lifestyle around before his death. Philliskirk was so surprised when he saw him, he felt he needed a new nickname. Schaefer would be known as "Little Rocket" from that day forward.

Lucas wouldn't have discovered Leatherface in quite the same way without Chuck Ragan's involvement. In 1998, Lucas's metallic-crust band, Twenty Third Chapter, played in Gainesville at a club called the Hardback Cafe. Ragan, Wollard, As Friends Rust, and many others from the Gainesville music scene attended the show. Lucas made an impression on the crowd. Lucas knew of Hot Water Music at the time but wasn't exactly sold on their sound. Ragan approached them and introduced himself after Lucas's set to tell them he loved the show. Ragan liked Lucas's band so much that he wanted to swap merch. Lucas agreed to the trade, thinking they might give the Hot Water Music swag to their partner at the time, who was the only emo fan in the relationship. Ragan sent Lucas the care package full of music. Lucas's split with their partner meant they would now feel obligated to listen to the albums. Turns out Hot Water Music was so good they went on to be one of Lucas's favourite bands, and their pen-pal relationship with Ragan flourished into a friendship.

It was around this time that Lucas relocated across the country to San Francisco. Ragan sent them a message letting them know that Hot Water Music would be passing through town shortly after Lucas had settled into their new home. Ragan said they'd be playing at Bottom of the Hill with this incredible band from the U.K.

"Leatherface was the embodiment of everything I wanted Hüsker Dü to turn into, and where I wanted Hüsker Dü to go. And like

Motörhead, Leatherface had that sweet spot too. It's catchy but not too catchy, the guitar playing's really smart. The writing is cool. It's this area that's like, 'I refuse to sell out entirely, and I'm just going to be really good at this thing, and if you like it, fuckin' rad, let's get on board, if you don't, well sorry, bye.' Some bands, they just have that chi where they collect all their energy from their spirit and they blast it out into the crowd, and Leatherface is a band that could always do that. They were an enormous rock 'n' roll machine, and there's nothing else quite like it. They were a band that never stopped impressing me, and they always made me feel things, even made me cry, made me feel emotions that other bands just couldn't."

I DON'T KNOW FOR HOW LONG

The beer felt cold in my hand. The threat of rain loomed from the layers of cloud overhead. Drops soon fell to the concrete between the white hopscotch lines painted in the Sunderland schoolyard. Dark circles formed as they hit. The tree branches swayed above.

When I cracked the can it sounded like the air brakes on a lorry releasing. I popped a smoke between my lips and lit it fast before realizing I'd put it in backwards. My face winced at the rotten taste of toxic fumes from the smoldering filter. I placed the cigarette beside my shoe, hoping Jason didn't notice how awkward I was. We each brought a carton of Player's Extra Lights with us. The last pack had been squashed because of how dishevelled my backpack was inside. I placed the crumpled cigarette pack on the ground in front of me, knowing we would be there for a while. A second attempt at lighting the smoke proved successful. Both of us were skilled at finding urban hideouts, and the quiet Sunderland schoolyard was our comfort zone.

I remembered a time when Jason and I first started hanging out as we sat smoking in the schoolyard. We'd went off to Darrell's basement as usual. The door opened with a creak. His smiling Jamaican roommate, King, peered through the crack in the door and told us he wasn't home. He sounded like Sylvester Stallone as he spoke. We laughed about his Rocky-esque tone as we walked back down the drive. Not home? He couldn't be at school, I knew that much. I remember feeling worried that he might have gotten a job. We decided to go to the Elmhurst Plaza instead of to the river with the little weed we had between the two of us. For whatever reason, the opposite direction beckoned to us that day. The two of us walked along the lane behind the mall. The drive was up against the unkempt yards of shabby north Toronto bungalows. Ratty bushes spilled over the chain-link fences. We stepped over the muddy puddles, swerved around a green dumpster, and past the fat recycler from the diner where solidified grease hung like icicles from its sides. We came across a section with pipes and ducts running up the grey concrete walls. There was a frosted window with bars over it. We sparked a joint and pulled a few drags from it in our private recess.

"Why did we come *here*?" Jason asked through his mischievous smile.

"Dunno," I said, also finding our choice amusing.

There were a few reasons to go to the Elmhurst Plaza. The 7-Eleven was the only place selling smokes to underage kids then. The guy behind the cash knew me as a minor and would hike the price after looking around through the corner of his eye to make sure no one was watching.

The second reason was the BiWay. Here's what I know about flannel shirts: the best ones aren't hanging on a rack for you to try on, they're pinned up tight and wrapped in plastic. The shirt may or may not fit, but life's a gamble. BiWay was where you could find me if I ever had seven dollars burning a hole in my pocket. It's amazing what riches lie in shoddy places.

The third reason was Mr. T. I reached home one day to learn that Mr. T was at the Elmhurst Plaza filming a movie. Back through the door I went without a word. I hopped on my BMX and pedalled as fast as I could toward the mall. Anticipation grew as the rumour became a reality. Crowds of spectators, film trucks, lights, and crew members were scattered everywhere. There were women with headsets and clipboards facilitating the commotion. I wiggled between some people along the yellow tape and tried to catch sight of him. B.A. Baracus emerged with his gold chains and mohawk to make his rounds along the tape, greeting his fans. If I didn't blurt out "T!" he wouldn't have seen me as he approached. He looked down at me and said in his iconic growl, "Wassup, kiiid."

"Really?" Jason asked.

"Yeah man, T was right over there. It was the best." I took a drag and continued, "I've never been around the back of this shithole." Jason seemed to be enjoying the atmosphere. "It doesn't look like Canada back here though," I said, my imagination already running wild from the high. He glanced around before smiling. I knew he could see it.

"Where are we then?" Jason said, entertaining me. He passed the canoeing spliff. I wadded spit down onto it, pretending like I knew what I was doing. My attempt to look like a seasoned pot smoker was appalling.

"Dunno." I scanned our surroundings. Cough. Something about the colourless brick walls, the overcast sky, and the barred window. "Kinda looks like England," I said, having no idea what England really looked like besides from what I'd seen on *Coronation Street*.

"Hollllllyyy shit, it does," he agreed, his bloodshot eyes widening and taking in the forming vision before him. We became a couple of blokes in an alley behind a pub smoking a joint somewhere in nondescript

England on that tired day in Canada. It felt strange to project the future in that hour, and even stranger when years later we were living it.

There I sat in the back of the school in Sunderland taking in its strange semblance to the lane behind Elmhurst Plaza. The memory of us played in my head while a light rain dampened the ground. I took a long drag from my cigarette. The link between the scene of our youth and the steely skies, the cadence of green trees, and the afternoon buzz had me feeling lit up. One of the greatest things I've heard is the lyric from Stubbs "We whistled to the wind and drank a lot of gin." It's difficult to describe how much these words agree with me. How I accept them unconditionally. The way my imagination leaps to life and awakens my senses, shows me something borrowed from a memory long ago. I'm reminded of how good it feels to be in the moment and take it in. I believe those words are about time and peace. It's about showing up and paying attention. It implies that a good, long conversation was had. It implores us to live our lives despite what that may look like to others. It's confident and calming.

The day was easy with good vibes. We were living the lyric, and we both could feel it. I felt close to the Irishman that day. We talked and joked about our friends, our voices full of love and appreciation.

The band that Jason and I were in had run its course. It had been some time since we played music together, and we were full of new clarity after watching Leatherface write their songs. "Days and days," Jason sang low. Drip. Drop. Cigarette smoke wafted from between our fingers. Our words rolled through the afternoon as we wondered what Scotland would bring the next day.

"Chris, should we start something when we get back?" he suggested at the height of a pleasant buzz and the crest of his inspiration. I liked the thought. I loved Jason's songs and believed in him.

"Heck yeah," I agreed taking a swig, already imagining what the band would sound like. Jason would have some things to say when we got back home. "It would be cool if we did some heavier stuff, then some mellow, acoustic stuff . . . mixed in."

"Yeah, totally," he said, already writing a song in his head. Songwriters do that. Their heads are full of words, hearts are full of melody.

"Like, if we played live, we could do a real fast one, and then we could all lay off and you play an acoustic song. Freak people out a bit."

"Oh yeah." He agreed. I knew he liked the idea. We both sat in silence thinking about the possibility.

"What are we going to call it?" I asked, jumping the gun. When in Rome. I needed to hear the name. Knowing would help me visualize what the songs would sound like. Jason knew I wanted to daydream. I could sense a band name was already floating around in his brain. I became dreamier with the more beer I drank.

"I always thought Wendigo would be a good name," he said, smiling, knowing the suggestion sounded a little cheesy, but gambling that I'd appreciate the poetic aspect. Wendigo is a mythological spirit from folklore of the Algonquin-speaking First Nations in Canada. It reminded me of Farley Mowat, who I liked very much. I could also recall an animated commercial break that told the story on TVO back in the day. I loved the watercolour images in it as a kid.

"Mmmm . . . too cryptic? Might sound weird to those who don't know what a Wendigo is."

"What about Long Time Coming?" he suggested after some time.
"Yup, I like that."

Now I could hear the songs. I knew what his voice would sound like and what words he would choose. We drank long into the day, feeling the anticipation of our Scotland-bound journey the following morning. Our asses hurt from the hard concrete, and our throats were wrecked from the smokes.

If there's a thing in this world as beautiful as the leaves waving in the wind or the raindrops hanging in a bobbing cobweb in the corner of an eavestrough, it's the great promise of friends starting a band together. It's like starting a gang and saying, "I don't know for how long, but I'll try and stay by your side." And that's better than nothing. Even if it's only for a short while, there's reassurance that we won't go it alone. We'll make something together, and for better or worse, it will be remembered.

"WE CLIMB HILLS ALL THE TIME, THERE ARE HILLS IN OUR MINDS.
AND THIS I DON'T MIND BUT THE HILLS IN OUR MINDS
CANNOT BE MEASURED IN MILES AND IT'S CATCHER IN THE RYE.
FEED THE FISHERMAN LIES BEAT A BIBLIOPHILE.
IT'S AN EVEN COLDER CLIMATE.
THERE WAS RHYTHM AND RHYME.
THE RHYTHM DIES BUT THE RHYME IS ALIVE.
THE RHYME IS ALIVE, THE RHYME'S ALIVE."

- "SHIPYARDS," STUBBS

EDINBURGH

From the sidewalk where we stood smoking outside the pub, I could just see the tip of Arthur's Seat beyond the city like an inverted, moss-covered horse jaw. Accommodations still hadn't been sorted as the first signs of dusk backlit the Scottish town known as Dùn Èideann. Drinking pints was about the height of our accomplishments since arriving.

"What about up there?" I asked, gesturing with my cigarette. Jason turned to look. Running parallel to the city was the imposing peak called Arthur's Seat in Holyrood Park. The long ridge watches over Edinburgh and offers an incredible view in all directions. One of the many myths of Scotland claims that the hill is actually a sleeping dragon. A more foreboding aspect involves seventeen neatly arranged mini-coffins that were discovered somewhere up on the hill. Tiny wooden figures dressed in rags were found inside. We set off weaving among the streets with our packs hoisted over our shoulders.

Things always appear closer than they are. It took us about forty-five minutes to make it to the entrance of Holyrood Park, where we could see the base of the hill. Our reluctance was showing itself in the form of silence. Beyond a parking lot stretched the grass where the grounds begun. We walked through a sparse grove of leafy trees for about a hundred yards of level ground before stepping across the flat rocks that had been built up into a little bridge over a watery ditch. It was a daunting sensation looking up at the hefty black silhouette rising from the ground. Its edges seemed to have no end. I wondered if finding a spot to camp at the bottom might have been the wiser decision. A broad trail of flattened grass beyond the trees led us to the beginning of the incline. Different elevations of the hill were stacked like shipping containers that seemed to rise from behind one another, a giant's staircase to the sky. We began the long climb with each trepidatious step, oblivious to the extinct volcano beneath our feet. It had been dormant for 350 million years. The volcanic rock makes up of a group of rolling hills, Arthur's Seat being the main peak. It's approximately a mile east of the city centre and rises to a height of roughly 820 feet.

We walked through the grass, the narrowing path giving way to uneven terrain. The light was fading all around us. *Here we go, as sketchy as this is.* The journey had started with nervous laughter echoing in the night as we mocked our own naïveté. Only twenty minutes had passed before the back of my legs burned and our breathing got heavier. The path ahead of us became difficult to see as the shadows grew long. Knowing only in the moment whether our route turned, dipped, or rose slowed the pace considerably. The trail widened up the incline where thick foliage spilled over on either side. The hill shot up toward the sky in the distance before us. The hike became laborious as the straps from my heavy pack dug into my bony shoulders. The muscles in my thighs were tightening, my knee like a rusty hinge. We stopped to catch our breath and drank some water. A half-hour into the climb, Jason looked more tired than I've ever seen him.

A point was reached where the city couldn't be seen. We had found ourselves in a concave depression with walls of bushes on either side. The darkness enveloping the surroundings was alarming. I was really beginning to feel that attempting the trek with the sun going down had been a poor judgment call. Anything could have happened out there. The recess where we stood would've made for an ideal place to get axed. Guilt washed over me.

I couldn't help but to think of a story told to me at camp when I was a kid about the Goat Man. It involved a miner who'd been trapped from the waist down beneath a landslide of rocks. In a bid for survival, the man killed a passing goat. He amputated his legs to free himself from the boulders before he sawed the goat's off and attached the animal's in place of his. The beast has been rumoured to roam the Niagara Escarpment in Ontario to this day. I had visions of hooves digging into the stones as it clomped across our path. White eyes poised to kill. Spittle foaming at the corner of its mouth as it growled.

I looked ahead at Jason panting. Even the fit Irishman wasn't accustomed to this sort of workout. We stepped up a rocky path in the middle of the landscape with a low, whistling breeze skimming across the terra.

"Wait, Chris, hold up a minute," Jason huffed after a stretch of straight trudging. His energy level had plummeted. Having three pints inside us wasn't helping. He sat down on his bag with his elbows on his knees and his head lowered.

"Christ," he said between breaths. "Ahhhhhhhh, how high is this thing?!" he screamed into the night, his voice echoing far and wide. He followed his complaint with a hardy laugh and cough. It all seemed absurd. The only thought pushing me forward was how mystifying it would be waking up on top. After we rested for some time, we hauled up our bags again. We stumbled across a wide section of mud that we didn't see coming. Our shoes splashed and slipped through the shallow mire. A decision was made to head off the path and climb the steep, dry bluff beside us. The two of us scaled the grassy slope with some effort. Certain ridges demanded we bend and pull at the landscape with our hands to get over. I turned to look behind us. The sweeping, rolling landscape looked like a sea of black waves.

We climbed in silence for the better part of an hour, listening only to our footsteps in the dirt and the hiss of wind. The city could almost be seen in its entirety. A view unlike anything I'd ever witnessed revealed itself. I was glowing like the lights below. The land began to level at what felt like the three-quarter mark of the climb. I felt nervous, tired, and eager. We intersected with a forged path of narrow stone steps that led to the final ridge.

"Jay, we're higher than we've ever been in Darrell's basement!" I yelled into the night.

I felt the victorious moment approaching as I clambered my way up the final inches of the summit with my Converse pushing through the crumbling stones like a young punk climbing his way onstage for the first time.

We dropped our packs and bodies into the grass with a series of thuds, our hearts racing. Jason and I stood when we'd caught our breath and took in the vista for the first time. Edinburgh sprawled below us like a wide-lens photograph of a thousand flickering candles, like an alien landscape dissipating into the darkness beyond. Like an unholy tangled mess of Christmas lights had been tossed to the ground. "Holllleeeyy shit!" I yelled. A draft whistled like a bagpipe drone down the slope of the peak. That's when someone called out to us. The hair on my neck stood straight up as the voice cut through the night.

"Hey!"

The two of us almost jumped off the ridge in fright. We turned fast to see where the voice had come from. A silhouetted figure approached through the grass. Thud, thud, thud.

Whoa, who is that?! My heart sped up. *It's the fuckin' Goat Man.*

"Hello," he spoke again. I began unzipping the pocket where I kept the Leatherman.

"Hello," Jason said with caution in his voice.

"How're you doin'?" the man said, drawing nearer. I scanned his legs looking for fur. His voice sounded friendly, and he held a can of beer in his hand. I relaxed a little when I spotted it. A moment of silence followed. The two of us were dumbfounded.

"Tired," I replied. Everyone laughed.

"Where ya from?"

"Canada, Toronto . . ." The person moved closer to have a look at our faces, his hair and windbreaker whipping in the wind.

"Stellar, have you come to rediscover yer roots?"

"IIIIII guess sooo," Jason replied, amused and charmed by the question.

"Welcome home then," he replied. The man walked toward Jason and hugged him, then walked over and hugged me.

"Come have a beer." He gestured for us to follow him up the slope where more figures stood far off in the moonlight.

We thought it might be best to hike down to just below the summit on the city side to block the heavier gusts rising up the opposite ridge. Setting up camp in the darkness on the side of a blustery cliff felt like an impossible task, but we managed to get the tent up and sturdy after some wrangling. I reached up, pretending to pluck the round yellow globe above us from its resting place in the deep indigo sky. The chorus of "I Want the Moon" will forever be the sound of hope to me since the fated afternoon in Darrell's room. There's something about Stubbs's voice in that chorus that urges us to leave behind everything unnecessary in life. That we all could find, "a peaceful place to call home." From the gloomy depths of Rexdale to the windswept peaks of Edinburgh, it was a wonderful life.

We laid out our things, pried our eyes from the incredible view, then crawled into our dome and zipped up the city below. The two of us talked and recalled the party we found when finally reaching the peak.

The next morning we woke up on "Archer's Seat," as William Maitland called it, the implication that it was the "height of arrows." I lay there recounting our steps up the side of the 800-foot hill in the middle of the night. I unzipped the tent anticipating the view. A moody morning sky of wide white paint strokes streaked across the grey. I was awestruck as I climbed into the cold air and laced up my Converse in the damp grass. My legs were stiff. My head was groggy. I sat and smoked a cigarette and pulled my hood up while staring down at Edinburgh below. Cathedrals looked like black toothpicks. The whole city a monochrome maze of hatched streets. I was exhausted and shivering, but the vista left me reeling.

Jason's head emerged with an already lit cigarette. He was lying on his stomach. "Little Bones, what the hell is happening?" he said half asleep. He looked like a smoking turtle with only his head poking out from the round tent behind him. This amused me to no end. We looked out in silence with the frosty sighs pushing through the air.

It was mornings like this on our journey that I couldn't get warm. The damp was invasive. The sun had lost its way. Not since the fleeting day back at Zillo Festival in Germany could it be found anywhere. I tried to keep my testiness at bay. It was difficult between the chill in my bones and my empty stomach.

We brought our valuables with us and trudged back down through the sweeping landscape. It was hard to believe we'd climbed the hill in near darkness. We followed a visible and direct path, saying hello to morning hikers heading up. They offered polite greetings and cautious looks.

Jason and I explored the sights in Edinburgh's Old Town. From where we stood, St. Giles' Cathedral looked like a satanic fortress in the overcast light. I walked around observing the statues outside, the Gothic windows, and the carved stone saints standing guard above the arched entrance. A man in a white furry hat and blue kilt filled the cool air with the sounds of the Highlands as he played the bagpipes. Students acting out "life" scenarios for a drama class on a street corner near the square mesmerized us for an undetermined amount of time.

"What is this?" I asked.

"Dunno, it's like some sort of Alcoholics Anonymous thing. It's bumming me out."

"I know, right." But still we watched.

We found Jacob's Ladder after exploring some more, a pathway winding up through the volcanic rock that connects the Old Town to the New Town. The pathway's name was taken from the biblical story of Jacob and his dream of a rope ladder that led to heaven. The endless treading on cobblestone and the trek up to Arthur's Seat and back were taking a toll on my feet and doing nothing for my irritated state.

We decided that the best plan of action would be to gather as many supplies as we could manage, climb back up to our campsite, and stay put until more provisions were needed. I loved Edinburgh but wasn't interested in sightseeing. Something about that hill beckoned to me.

We bought bread, cheese, Scottish candy bars, toilet paper, and as many Tennent's lagers as we could fit in a bag. I felt a shift in mood knowing we could just relax and read once we got back to the site. Early evening was approaching yet again as we made our way through the streets to slug our way back up the trails, panting and cursing as dusk lit the sky. It felt so comforting to eat, bundle up, and find a spot in the grass to watch the light fade. A warm tone above signalled the first sight of the sun since Germany. I knew what Jason was thinking.

"Man, that New Model Army show was great, huh?" I asked.

"Oh yeah, so good. That new song was one of the best things I've ever heard."

"Right?" I agreed.

We had seen them play at Zillo Festival in Germany a few days before arriving in Britain. Lead singer Justin Sullivan asked the crowd to take in the sunset before they played an intense new song called "You Weren't There."

"Before we start this one, I want everyone to turn around and have a look at what's happening out there on the horizon," Sullivan had said, almost as if he'd planned the moment all along. The crowd turned to look. Rays of pink and orange light blasted above the trees behind us. "We're all here together," he said, his voice like a dissonant commentary to the waning blaze.

On a freezing night years before, Jason and I sat huddled in his Chevrolet Tracker. It was an amusing automobile for such a hefty person to drive. He always snickered as he wedged himself in, trying to get comfortable. The whole thing rocked as he did. I always feared the Tracker would roll over if we sped around turns, ever since I noticed the warning sticker on the dashboard about this.

We could have been in a parking lot in Woodbridge or the back of a venue somewhere in Detroit. The frost was reaching up the windows like skeleton hands. The heater made a sound but didn't seem to work. Those were the times when we'd talk. Those were the times we'd play each other new music, with the snow falling outside the window of the Tracker.

I could sense Jason looking at me through the corner of his eye as New Model Army played. He knew I would make it known if I liked something, and he was drawn to this about me. The music was dark, brooding, and driving. Justin Sullivan sang about hometown politics in "Better Than Them." The song pulls you into the dim pubs of his world, where rivalry and class will see many nights end with broken beer bottles in hand. The song has always sounded like a Francis Ford

Coppola film to me. Jason wanted me to listen to words because he knew I was someone that paid attention. He knew how to hook me. Those lyrics turned to cinema in my mind. On many dark nights we sat in parking lots, nursing beers, smoking, keeping warm — listening to films.

I thought about the Tracker while we ate cheese sandwiches by the tent and talked.

"I've been thinkin', Jay," I started.

"What," he said while chewing, looking at me. I took another bite, knowing it would irritate him having to wait. "What?" he asked again.

"I was thinkin'... that ..." Chew. "Maybe you should ..." Chew. "You should put out a solo album," I suggested.

"Hmmpph." He entertained me on the pretense that it involved him and a solo album. He also became suspicious.

"Yeah, you should change your name though."

"What do you mean?" he asked annoyed, but also enjoying the "piss" coming his way.

"You should change it to ... Blue Jay Dwyer."

"Shut the fuck up," he said, smiling.

"Yeah, you could wear like a '70s powder-blue suit with a big white collar. That would be cool, right? You could have coiffed hair. Oh riiiiight, you can't grow hair anymore. Well, there's wigs for that kind of thing."

"Shut your goddamn pie hole, MacDonald."

"You could do that ditty that you always used to do, how'd it go?" Then I sang while snapping my fingers: "It was a brisk winter morning and the birdies were chirping in their funny little birdie way." I tried to sound like Dean Martin. His serious undertone cracked before he started laughing.

Then we got to drinking. The wind moved the tent and bent the grass across my legs. The view of Edinburgh faded before its orange lights flickered back to life and blew our mind. A heavy darkness draped itself across the hillside. The sky was a giant ocean. I tried to suppress a lurking apprehension. The twinkling scene below comforted me, but my attention would veer to the shadows of my peripheral vision at the sound of a twig snapping or a rustle. I would crane my neck around, expecting to see someone up on the ridge. My imagination conjured a translucent figure looking down at us. But only the fast-moving clouds beyond the looming ledge could be seen.

We drank many cans to the sounds of the churning gusts flooding the landscape. The night grew tense and the hour late. I kept a close eye on the tent in fear of it setting sail. I could see it taking off and tumbling down the hill in my mind's eye. Tennent's, at 4%, will only get you so far when trying to drown a growing disquiet. Half-drunk, cold, and stiff, we cut our losses. We crawled into our dome to sleep.

Jason nodded off quickly and began to snore. His chest heaved and his presence in the confined space was intrusive. Rest came only in slivers and my mind wandered. I drifted in and out below a thin veil of consciousness for hours. It was as if my eyes were slightly open but my mind was under lock. The slumber was reminiscent of our night in King's Cross station, where the lights washed away any true sleep and the skittering of rats stole our souls.

I understood the sombre history of Edinburgh, and I could feel its past while exploring the streets earlier. The distant howl droned until finally I fell under. For how long, I don't know. What I do know is that I woke later in the dark with the wind lashing at our tent as if a great, invisible hand were grabbing at it. Nylon flapped around my head. A relentless hiss created a disorienting space within my mind. I conjured noises that may or may not have been real. My limbs felt like wood. My ears were alert to every sparse sound that could be movement.

Thud.

My eyes shot open, recognizing what could be a footstep near the tent.

Whoa. My heart leapt. I could feel it pounding low in the bottom of my throat.

There's something outside other than the wind. Holy fuck.

A squall ripped at the walls of the tent. My body tightened.

Jesus Christ. This was a bad idea. How in the world is that fucker beside me sleeping? I thought as Jason grunted.

I could hear grass being pressed down close by.

Really? Yes. Holy Christ. Is it the guy who greeted us? He knows where the tent was set up. It's the fuckin' Goat Man.

Something else other than the "whisssssha" of nylon. Sounds within a sound.

Thud. Thud.

I could see the hooves in the grass as it crept closer in the night.

I need to unzip and look. But I couldn't. A jog, a faster succession of steps. I reached up and held the zipper between my fingers, but I couldn't open it.

THUD.

Yo. This is not fun.

I lay there paralyzed for what seemed like forever, reunited with the dread I felt before arriving in Europe. All deserted anxieties came back. You can run, but you can't hide, this became clear. There was no choice but to lie still and listen. I waited through the endless night for morning to come.

The weather calmed after a long period of drifting between consciousness and nervous slumber. The black gave way to splinters of light. My arms and chest relaxed. My mind stopped running laps. Only then did I manage to truly sleep.

I woke later to a warmth blanketing the outside of the tent and a calmer breeze. Relief came through me as I pulled my sleeping bag from my face, the footsteps still fresh in my head.

"Tell me I can wear my T-shirt today. Tell me," I called in hopes that the sun was out.

"Ahaha, maybeee . . . ?" Jason said from outside the tent, the uptick in his voice was promising. I could picture him squinting at the sky.

I crawled out and scanned the ground for signs of hoofprints. There was flattened grass that made my heart skip, but it could've been from us. It was hard to tell. My eyes felt battered. My head felt like it might crack open like an egg and ooze out my round yellow brain.

"Goddamn," I groaned. Jason laughed.

"Need to cool it on the Tennent's, they'll kill you."

"I was up all night . . . I could hear footsteps all around the tent."

"You're tripping out, MacDonald, you're losing it."

"Well, you wouldn't have heard anything, not with snoring like that. Sounded like you were dying. Are you? I hope so."

"Shut your hole, MacDonald. Or I'll kill you."

"Are you twelve?"

"Have another Tennent's, you little prick."

That's when I wanted him to be more earnest. That's when I wanted him not to make everything into a joke. His dismissiveness irked me.

A warm draft blew across the hill. At first glance the sky was overcast, but hints of peach and blue lay beyond the translucent whisps. I carried the dread through the morning.

The sun came out in all its glory and warmed our hearts and the grass along the hill. The victory gave me mountains of energy, and I hiked down the hill with a vise attached to my head. No word of a lie, it was the worst hangover I've lived through. It was like riding a bike with bare feet on steel pedals kind of awful. But I set this aside. I was only concerned with how long the sun would be out and finding coffee. The entire trek down had me thinking about the footsteps. I made a promise with myself that I'd be walking down the hill for good if we had to endure another night of heavy wind. I would sooner sleep in Waverley station.

I managed to get back up the hill with a warm coffee. The steam rose like a ghost into the cool morning air as I held my Styrofoam cup with both hands, the beads of condensation cool on my lips. My sense of humour returned as did the colour in my fingers. Something about the scene reminded of the 1989 commercial for Fleischmann's Margarine. We see a rugged-looking dad in a yellow raincoat in the commercial. He climbs high up the rocks to take in the view of the raging sea below. "In my old life, I was too busy, too important to get away. I had it all. Then I saw I was still missing out. I changed a lot. Meet the new and improved me. I'm more careful of what I eat, and when I use margarine, I use Fleischmann's." There's a full tub of margarine with him on his hike. He places it on a rock along with some tomatoes and grapes. He then spreads the margarine on the bread with a small bowie knife. The camera pans way back as he says, "You know, life is about making changes, not compromises." I thought that he was lucky my brother Rob didn't sharpen that knife for him.

How much funnier would the commercial have been if he kept cutting his fingers? "Whoops, that's okay," he would reassure the viewers, spreading blood and butter together. The passenger with the soup-strainer moustache and knit sweater would be peeping out from behind a rock looking very, very concerned.

As a kid I wanted to be the Fleischmann's guy. I didn't have a tub of margarine, or tomatoes, or grapes with me in Edinburgh, but I had a warm coffee and a croissant. My view was comparable except for the raging sea in the commercial. A strange sense of pride came over me. *I'm the Fleischmann's guy.* A rugged smile carved itself across my face.

The buttery morning light warmed the landscape. My head cleared and I began to feel human again. We went our separate ways to explore. I climbed back to the top of the ridge and headed across the slope on the opposite side. The scene entranced me as much as the city view did. The meadow stretched forever, and a bright white light shone from beyond the next ridge like an explosion.

I walked along the sepia-drenched land for a long while, through the pink carpets of wild mountain thyme. Volcanic peaks breached from the dirt. I stared out into the great beyond, listening to the earth from the top of a larger lookout.

I found a spot to lie as I made my way back up. What had looked like a brooding sky for days and days had finally composed itself. I felt peace watching the smoke-like clouds drift across the pale blue panorama. My eyes closed to the sound of the breeze sliding up the hill and the warmth on my face. The wind at higher elevations seems to have a different depth to it. It's full-bodied and sounds more like the ocean. When I woke later, I watched a web between two tall blades of grass move in the air. The thread was so fine that it was almost invisible from certain angles but would catch the light, becoming gold and iridescent. Drops of dew gleamed inside. There was a tiny insect caught in the silk, its fight to escape futile. The spider emerged from the web's shadowed corner and advanced after many minutes. It made me think of how helpless we are to time. How impending it is.

There's something about being alone in these sorts of situations. Isolation brings that feeling of exclusiveness. As Stubbs would say: "Everything under the sun must be for everyone." And he's right. But sometimes it can feel like it's yours alone. My mind cleared itself of the intense worry I had felt the night before. My thoughts shifted to all of the strange and beautiful things happening around me.

I realized that the idea of abandonment was possible. An eye opened as my mind wandered further. I thought about my early days of punk when we would climb into the rafters of the bridge near my high school to find that secret hideout. Where once a great clang signalled an afternoon of death and power, the earth now breathed easy. Nostalgia was in the air, or maybe it was déjà vu that I was feeling as I looked at the field stretching before me.

Everything was changing. Up on that hill a clarity appeared. It showed me the path of revolt was inside myself. That I had to follow it deep inside to find true autonomy. Where something as simple as discovering a field to lie in for a few moments would find me governed by no other. Peace was my new unrest. Not allowing my old anger to flourish was my new upheaval. Nature was my revolution. Punk was all around just as it always was, just with a different face.

The next day was very much the same. In the fields we lay, letting it sink in. Living it. Turning off the machine. We whiled away the long afternoon watching the sun glide from one end of the sky to the other before evening splashed across the land like a great black wave. The city below lit the belly of the sky with a tangerine glow, burning like coals in a fire. Cold beer and cigarettes, flicking ashes in the grass. The long whine of night.

A mysterious shadowy figure had welcomed us on our first night in Scotland, though I now felt as if the true reception came from the land itself. There was a fine thread binding me to the sleeping dragon below. I felt the tug as we said goodbye to the hill and descended.

I watched in a melancholy daze as the crowds of people down in Waverley station drifted by like shoals of fish, weaving among each other, disappearing into the sea. All of it fleeting. What's that old saying, people come, people go? Announcements above. Yellow digital lights on the train schedule board. Suitcase wheels machine-gunning across tiles. Everyone moving toward something.

We were peering over a map when I noticed a blade of grass on my pack that had come down from Arthur's Seat with me. I tucked it in the top pocket. I unravelled the plastic wrap from a day-old cheese sandwich and took a big bite. Jason looked at me like a father about to swipe his disobedient kid in the head. We couldn't figure out whether to see the Isle of Skye or Glasgow next. We sat back on the bench, trying to decide what our next move would be, when Jason said, "Look at this crank," nodding to an older business-type lady. I glanced before playing along.

"You mean Louise?"

"Yeah, she smokes two packs a day."

"Oh yeah. She hates the world for sure."

She eyed us so we looked down. Then she stopped and was standing right in front of us.

"Excuse me, are you two travelling by train?" she asked. We looked up as she stared down.

"Yes, we'll be taking a train," I responded.

"Well, you can have these if you like?" She held two Scottish rail passes toward us.

"We were just going to buy a couple of tickets," Jason told her.

"They're unlimited, for a week," she said. I reached up and she placed them in my hand. "Go on, take them, I don't need them anymore." She gave a sweet smile.

"Are you sure?" I asked. "That's so nice of you, really?"

"Sure, have fun then, lads," she replied with kindness in her voice. The woman walked away in a hurry.

"No shiiiit," I said. "Well, where should we go?"

"Inverness?" Jason suggested, oblivious to just how alien things would soon get.

"DO YOU UNDERSTAND WHAT IT'S LIKE, TO BE A LAUGHINGSTOCK IN LIFE?
DO YOU UNDERSTAND WHAT IT'S LIKE OR WHO YOU ARE"

— "BOWL OF FLIES," STUBBS

DAVEY QUINN — TILTWHEEL

"One of the things about punk rock is you can walk up to a band you've went to see and either punch them in the face or give them a hug, especially in San Diego." Seeing as Davey Quinn's punched two of the members of Leatherface and broken both their noses, the sentiment is as brash as it is real.

Quinn received a package of albums once in the mail while DJing at local college radio station KTSW out of San Marcos, Texas. One record was Keith Morris's new band, Bug Lamp. The other was Leatherface's *Mush*. He remembers loving both. But his thought at the time was that the only good punk being made in the '90s was coming out of England. Quinn used to run three different radio shows on Sundays: a generic local show, a heavy metal show, and a punk show that he'd taken over from someone else. He'd bring a twelve-pack with him to keep him company for the nine hours that, as Quinn puts it, he "talked to the sky." Quinn didn't believe anyone was out there on the receiving end, only his voice and his tunes drifting out into the stifling Texas heat. He even put Leatherface songs on the local show because he wanted to hear more of them, and it reached a point where he was playing *Mush* all the time. Three years later an epiphany struck.

Quinn was pulling off the highway to escape a horrific traffic jam that had forced him to take an alternate route back home. He was waiting at a lengthy light after exiting the freeway, the kind where two or three cycles pass before you get through. Leatherface's "Bowl of Flies" was blasting from the speaker connected to a twenty-foot length of wire that he'd toss into the back of the van. It was in those pivotal minutes of waiting his turn to go through the intersection that he realized how good Leatherface was. Quinn found himself staring into space as the light turned green. He could see clearly as his mind's eye took over. An understanding came over him as the van began to roll through the light. He said to himself out loud, "This is my favourite record of all time."

"I've gone through deaths in the family, trauma, great shit, success, and fucking victories over work, life, and love, which I don't remember that much detail about, but I remember the exact feeling, it was literally like warming up a little, I don't want to sound like Julia Roberts or something . . . I warmed up a little bit, thinking this is the greatest record I've ever heard. And I'm not a person like that, I don't judge whether a Whopper is better than a Big Mac, they're both garbage. I don't have that contest mentality."

It was after that reckoning in his van that he began to listen to the album with a new set of ears. He'd discovered the subtleties and layers within. It became an examination into why he felt the way he did that afternoon at the traffic light.

The California punk learned later that Leatherface would be touring the United States with Hot Water Music. His excitement grew at this news. Quinn somehow managed to get Stubbs's contact through a Japanese Leatherface fan site and emailed the singer on a whim. It was a direct inquiry that read, "I see you will be coming through the

U.S. on tour. Do you need a sound guy?" The email was as blunt and forthright as Stubbs's reply: "Yes we do."

It had been a few months without any correspondence though. Quinn took a deep breath as he wrote a follow-up email, hoping his job as sound technician was still happening. Stubbs wrote back apologizing for the silence. Turns out the tour manager had already booked Quinn's plane ticket with a list of dates starting in Denver, as well as a pay schedule, though Quinn admits he was prepared to work for free. Leatherface and their new sound tech had a beer in the parking lot when Quinn picked the band up at Denver International Airport. He knew he was dealing with some very thirsty and unpretentious people. What followed would be a long journey of shenanigans and friendship where something as simple as an email somehow led to countless tours, both as sound tech and with Quinn's band, Tiltwheel, as a supporting act.

Quinn bears a permanent reminder of their time together from one particular show in Pomona, California. It was at the height of their U.S. tour. The band played with the Anniversary (Vagrant Records), who couldn't sound any less like Leatherface. Each act welcomed the diversity though and enjoyed one another's company. Both artists played great sets and were celebrating their victory afterward. What followed was an unforgettable, crude chain of events. To everyone's bewilderment, Stubbs decided to jump headfirst into a nearby trash bin while caught in the throes of life on the road and punk rock intoxication. Groans of agony echoed from inside. As the singer emerged they could see his face was bruised and bleeding. His nose was also broken.

A light went off in Quinn's head as he channelled his dormant English hoodlum. He suggested Stubbs shouldn't be the only one with a broken nose, proving that if punk rock is anything, it's loyal. The crew agreed that they should all have busted noses as well. Quinn wound up and threw a hook at Lainey while rolling in the van on the way back to the hotel. Stubbs felt he didn't hit him hard enough with his first shot. Quinn connected hard on the second punch and successfully broke Lainey's nose.

They piled back in the van the next day on a royal tear and headed to the bar to meet Eva, the booking agent, for the first time. She wondered what she was getting herself into as the ragtag band fell through the door. The quest for absolute loyalty continued. Quinn tried his best to get Lainey to reciprocate the beating after many drinks. Lainey wouldn't budge. It's been said that Lainey's patience could've been the drummer's greatest virtue, until he'd reach a certain point, that is. Then it's over. You're done like the dishes. Lainey's temper rose to the point where he'd had enough of the nagging and hammered Quinn just to get him to shut up. Blood sprayed across the barroom floor. Eva couldn't believe the horror and began to laugh at the gross display. Davey Burdon was next in line. But his bandmates didn't have the heart to hit him like that. It didn't feel right, what with Burdon being so young and innocent. None of them could be convinced to go through with it. That's when Quinn stepped up and did what he had to do. Lil' Davey Burdon had his nose broken by his own sound tech. The punch left great black rings around his baby blues.

They stopped once in Ashland, Oregon, to rest one night after driving in from L.A. The band headed up through the mountains to stay at a cheap motel that Quinn knew of. There was a bar in the motel's parking lot where an open mic was already in full swing. Most of Leatherface headed to their rooms to sleep. Quinn was thirsty and eager to play guitar as he made his way over to the twinkling lights. Lainey tagged along.

The bartender had never heard an English accent so thick. Quinn became the translator after Lainey's failed attempt to pronounce "Budweiser." This sparked an idea in Quinn's mischievous mind. The two musicians went on to get, as Quinn puts it, "absolutely mangled." This involved many more Budweisers. Sneaky Davey Quinn had signed the drummer up to sing a song for the open mic when Lainey wasn't paying attention. The confused drummer rose from his seat and headed toward the stage when the host called his name. Quinn was already laughing his ass off behind him. Lainey wasn't quite sure what he was supposed to do once onstage. Drunk and timid, he asked the crowd, "What am I here for?"

"Tell a joke!" people shouted. Lainey composed himself and delivered his best joke after some consideration. By the sounds of it though, Lainey can't quite hit the funny bone as hard as he can hit the snare. Quinn let Lainey sweat for a minute before heading up onstage to help his friend out, translating the joke into plain old American English.

Quinn holds his memories with Leatherface near and dear to his heart. He feels that he learned the true meaning of "yes" and "no" from the band. These are words that are sometimes convoluted where he comes from in the state of California. His implication is that the members of Leatherface are very real. They say what they feel and don't mince words. They have the power to bring you into their life and change it for good. Quinn met the most beautiful redhead he's ever seen while on tour with the band and married her. "If you spend enough time with them, you'll see a little darkness along the way, but you'll leave with something very important." Quinn is someone who has written songs for most of his life. He's been on a long pursuit to convey his ideas and feelings with words and music. He understands the power of self-expression. When Quinn says, "You could write a song about how you feel about Leatherface," you get the impression this could be the highest of compliments to pass between humans.

"THE SCIENCE OF FINANCE, WE GIVE IT TO THE MINISTRY.
WHILE YOU SELL FLOWERS, FLOWERS ON THE STREET.
AND WHEN YOUR ONLY HAPPINESS IS YOUR CHARITY.
AND YOUR ONLY WARMTH, IS COMMUNAL SONG."

— "SCHEME OF THINGS," STUBBS

INVERNESS

If ever you find yourself in Inverness (Inbhir Nis) entertaining a handwritten sign in the window of a random pub boasting two-for-one Jack Daniel's shots, I would say you're entitled to make your own mistakes. Speaking from experience, I urge you to please do the right thing. Choosing to guzzle the American whisky in the heart of the Scottish Highlands was a regret I've had to endure. We got ripped fast, and it wasn't long before we were reminiscing and talking about music.

"What do you think the best Leatherface cover is?" I slurred, feeling downright mischievous.

"MMmmmm . . . I don't know," Jason said while I dumped a swig of beer down the hatch. "You stink," he added.

"I know, it's brutal. Um, I would have to go with 'Eagle,' the ABBA cover, hands down, best fucking cover song I've ever heard. Like, nothing comes close," I replied, contorting my hand into an eagle claw. Jason pondered my suggestion for quite some time.

"'Hops and Barley,' final answer."

He took a gulp, licked his lips, and smiled.

```
"DEFINE WHAT YOU MEAN.
DEFINE WHAT YOU SAY.
DEFINE YOUR MIND,
AND DO THE RIGHT THING."

- "DO THE RIGHT THING," STUBBS
```

SEAN FORBES — WAT TYLER, ROUGH TRADE RECORDS

"Leatherface is a difficult one for me; I'll approach it as honestly as I can." It's an important sentiment coming from Sean Forbes. Maybe it's because he's seldom serious when being interviewed: on Vice's *Record Shop Dude*, I've watched him hold up an album to the viewers and say as little as "pompous nonsense," or "good punk," or "shit punk," then toss it on a pile. Maybe it's because Leatherface fits in the narrow margin of music to truly move this person, which I gather is not an easy task.

Forbes ("Fat Bob") has worked as a buyer (and moaner) at the hallowed record shop Rough Trade West for thirty-five years. The doors opened in 1976, and in 1978 the independent store gave birth to a successful record label that signed the Smiths. "This is the job I've always wanted. I'm stuck with very little wage and no prospects, so it's absolutely perfect for my lifestyle of going nowhere."

Leatherface led me to Forbes's music many moons ago. Wat Tyler (Lookout! Records) was a band steeped in political discourse and rich with elaborate, inside jokes that emerged out of the earlier anarcho-punk band 4 Minute Warning. I could sense the depth of Forbes's humour shining through even then, although admittedly, my brain wasn't attuned to this level of complexity. There was something complementary about the two bands. Perhaps it was how lyrically clever they both were. I wasn't surprised when one of the first things Forbes said to me when I had the pleasure of interacting with him was, "The lyrics are what made Leatherface special. However, their best song was 'Hops and Barley,' so they couldn't have been that special." I believe Leatherface's version of Wat Tyler's "Hops and Barley" is as iconic as Wat Tyler's version of Leatherface's "Not Superstitious." I'd even argue it's the best interpretation of a Leatherface song ever recorded. Vice versa for "Hops and Barley," which Stubbs says he bought from Wat Tyler for six quid.

Then there's Hard Skin, which may or may not be an Oi! parody. You'll have to ask him yourself because I don't want to. What *is* true is that Forbes has lived and witnessed the original Oi! bands that influenced the whole movement. Hard Skin's first record, *Hard Nuts and Hard Cunts*, was a staple at the tattoo shop I worked at in the early 2000s. I could never figure out if they were serious, and that in itself might be the point. The motto on the cover alone, "the new wave of close shave," suggests they like having a little fun.

Snuff played their final show in August 1991 at Kilburn National Ballroom in London, a notorious venue that's hosted everyone from Johnny Cash to David Bowie. Redmonds, Crighton, and Wells found themselves without a gig after the show's epic end. The departure of Steven "The Eagle" Charlton from Leatherface after the release of *Mush* left them yet again without a bassist. "He was told by his girlfriend that he wasn't going on tour anymore" is how Forbes puts it. Here's where the plot thickens. All three members of Snuff applied for the position of Leatherface's new bass player unbeknownst to the others.

Forbes later attended a Leatherface show with Redmonds at Camden's Underworld where they ran into Wells. When Leatherface emerged onstage to play their first show back with a new bass player, a look of surprise, envy, and pride fell across their faces when they saw their former bandmate Andy Crighton onstage with the group they loved so much. Only then did the truth emerge about how they all applied for the position in secret. Forbes says the situation was priceless. Knowing his thirst for humour, I can easily imagine him enjoying the moment. It's no surprise that, being a proper bass player, Crighton got the gig. Redmonds remembers telling Stubbs to look after Crighton. Stubbs said the same thing to Redmonds when Snuff got back together again a few years later.

"Sunderland is what makes them special. If you've ever been there, you know you want to get out, and [that's] probably why they toured so much. Hammond and Stubbs are what made Leatherface special. They were a perfect fit musically, but not the best fit personally. Lainey is what made Leatherface special. His relentless drive on the drums is what pushed them forward. The lyrics are what made them special . . ."

It was Leatherface's first gig in London when Forbes met Stubbs. Meantime Records had tasked Forbes with organizing the show, which was at the Old White Horse in Brixton with a band called F.U.A.L. He wishes this night would have been a light bulb moment for him, but it wasn't. The big man laments how he could have seen Leatherface's first ever set in London instead of working the door, which he referred to as "fighting the crusties for 2.50 quid." Fat Bob hints at what could only resemble pride at having been there in the very beginning.

Leatherface's loyal following grew fast amongst this tight-knit music community. Forbes describes Wat Tyler's initial tours with Leatherface in 1989 as "thirty days of brutal, psychological warfare." While the two bands were on the road with Snuff they played a game. The rules seemed simple: whoever stayed up the latest and said "Leatherface" won. Leatherface remained a final thought on at least one band member's mind every night along their journey.

"I rarely listen to Leatherface. It's just filled with too much sadness, to tell you the truth. Such a waste of life and all of their lives cut short. Andy, the man who would ask to borrow five pounds from you, as he was skint, yet still offered to buy you a drink with that money. A real diamond. Lainey, absolute solid citizen of a man. A gentle thug. Dickie Hammond, the man who wrote the line, 'Spent all day in the fucking pub,'cause I'm a cunt' for Hard Skin. Last time I saw him he was climbing over the barrier at Rebellion to stage-dive. Luckily, he was stopped, as he would have killed people if he had. I miss all of them in different ways. We shared time together, touring and laughing and arguing. How Leatherface put up with Wat Tyler, I'll never know. Everyone thinks *Mush* is the classic, but if I ever listen to Leatherface it's always 'Do the Right Thing.' It has it all. Great musicianship, soul, heartfelt lyrics, and hooks galore."

Jason and I argued about Leatherface's cover songs before agreeing that choosing between "Eagle" and "Hops and Barley"was too difficult. It wasn't long before we worked ourselves into a frenzy and started getting cut eye from the barkeep.

We fell into the night singing "Eagle" at the sky. The street lights flickered to life as darkness fell. Our voices seemed to echo while we walked through what felt like a film set. An aerial view of the neighbourhood glowing auburn at the bottom of the long hill could be seen from where we were. That's when we noticed someone coming down the sidewalk as we lit our cigarettes. A lanky man clutching his coat tight across his body shuffled toward us from across the road. His ragged, loose pants swayed. He muttered as fast as he walked and got too close much too fast. "Awright, ye git a light fur mah ciggy? Ah hae bin trying to fin' yin forever." His accent was as thick as Atlantic fog. A burp came from beyond the wiry white whiskers.

"What?" Jason asked.

He jabbered under his breath looking nervous, eyes glazed and distant. "Ye takin' the pish?"

"Huh, sorry?"

"YE TAKIN' THE PISH?" he shouted, showing his haggard teeth. I stepped back and looked to Jason to translate.

The man pulled a knife from inside his jacket, the blade gleaming in the yellow light.

The steel flashed along with our lives. Everything slowed in the Inverness night. I noticed the streetlights hovering like UFOs with their pale tractor beams shining down. The branches of the black trees beyond waved their feathered tentacles. My brain went black.

"Look, we don't want any trouble. We're from Canada on a holiday," Jason blurted out, cutting the tension.

He looked at us through his narrowed eyes. "Cnada?" he asked, burping again.

I sensed optimism in the man.

"Yeah, Canada . . ."

"Ahhh Cnada. Why didn't you say so." His temper cooled. The high-alert scene eased. He then asked, "Wanna buy some cocaine?" We stood dumbfounded.

"Uh, we're not in the market for that right now, thank you, though," Jason told him.

He mumbled something before he turned and walked away after slipping the shank into his coat. The clapping of his shoes faded as he drifted from sight. I took what seemed to be the first breath in minutes with everything quiet again. No words could be found as we looked at each other. His presence was enveloped by the last far-off tractor beam.

We sat, trying to digest what had happened, shaken, limbs buzzing. Then we both began to laugh. It was all we could do and the only thing that made sense. I looked at the little pink scars on my hand, remembering how I'd stabbed myself so many times with the Leatherman on the train.

We both felt lucky to be Canadian in that moment. It was a strange sensation to think we may not have made it to the Isle of Skye if we'd answered incorrectly.

We passed an illuminated telephone booth as we carried on. The red metal box, glowing and vacant, looked so lonely in the Inverness night. There was a little gold crown above the door.

"I'm gonna call Chad," Jason said, turning sideways and sliding through its doors, digging for change. After a minute he was connected with our friend from back home.

"Holy shit Chad, you're not gonna believe this," he said into the receiver with a head full of swill, happy to be alive.

I stepped away and sat on the curb. While they talked, I fished a smoke from my pack and stared down the empty street that sliced the suburban landscape in two. There wasn't a soul to be seen. I kept looking back to where the old man had disappeared, expecting him to return. A feeling of embarrassment came over me. My cheeks got hot when I considered my failure to act in a moment of emergency. I remembered thinking at the beginning of the trip how it was going to be my job to keep us from danger. The scene of the stranger almost shanking us replayed in my mind. My jittery hands lit the cigarette

Jason threw his head back in laughter, delighted to have saved the day. Fucking Irishman. I turned back to the view of the houses below where someone else came into view. A pair of skinny legs crossed from the sidewalk to the middle of the road, making their way up the hill toward us. I watched as the figure inched closer in the night. The only voice to be heard was, "We almost got stabbed" and "Chad, we slept on a mountain!"

I crushed the butt under my shoe then leaned back on my hands. Skinny legs crossed over each other and looked as if they might belong to a female.

I lit another because of my nerves. Smoke wafted up as I waited patiently. I *needed* to see the face on the lone walker closing in on me. My curiosity burned like the little red heater between my fingers. The person darkened as they reached the crest of the hill, just before the angle of the slope changed. Their legs looked like a pair of french fries stepping through the night. As they reached the top of the incline, their red shoes came into view as the lighting changed again. The rosy footwear gave the impression that their french fry legs were dipped in ketchup. They were smoking as well, leaving trails of dissipating filigree behind them. Whoever it was didn't seem intimidated by the stranger sitting on the curb looking back at them. The telephone booth rocked and rattled behind me.

Closer. Closer.

A young woman, I presumed, trying not to stare.

She took a drag under the streetlamp. Dusty blond hair, wiry thin.

Laughter from behind.

Fries and ketchup.

Eyes locked. How weird.

Her pace slowed as she closed in on the final ten feet.

Her expression searched.

I could see her clearer now. Seven feet away. Familiar. *Where do I know this face? I've seen her before.* She stopped and took another drag with her head tilted to one side. I tried to steady my hand as I raised my cigarette to my lips. The haze cleared before she stepped forward and spoke. What came out of her mouth was what I least expected to hear. Her voice was like a bullet whizzing by my head in the still air of the deserted street. I can still hear it today.

"Chrissss?"

Huh? Who is that!? Oh my gaaawdd. What's her name again? Yes. Uh Tanya, fuck, Tan . . . Tammy.

"Tammy?"

She faced me head on. I jumped to my feet. We both stood speechless trying to comprehend the bizarre situation. I somehow knew Tammy through a friend back home.

"What the fuck?" I said, bewildered. I wanted to reach out and touch her, make sure she wasn't a mirage. It felt too surreal to be true. *But how?* They say the world is a tiny place, but that small? "What are you doing ... here?" I said, walking closer. We hugged. Awkward. Her skeletal, weightless frame leaned into me. She was real.

"What are *you* doing here?" she asked in return.

"I ... We almost got stabbed ..." I started, then turned to Jason, who dropped the phone back on the cradle and fell from the booth. He looked at the enclosure like he might wrestle it.

"Really? Are you okay?"

"Uh, yeah," I said. "I think so ..."

"Hello," Jason said, putting on the cordial tone he would use when greeting the opposite sex. She pointed to him, smiling.

"Wait, Jayyyy, right?"

"Tammy?" he asked, before cackling. It's like he'd known the night's ridiculousness was far from over. It became clear she was wasted as we spoke.

"Seriously, what are you doing in the middle of Inverness, Scotland?" I prodded.

"Well, I met this GUUY," she said, her voice trailing off. "We've been partying." She puffed off the cigarette, exhaling out of the side of her mouth. "For days."

"Days, huh?"

"Days and days. Been doin' a lot of blow, actually ..."

"Oh, cool ..."

"Yuuup, looots of blow." She sniffed as her eyes darted to the side. Another moment when laughter was our only response.

Her departure warped our minds further than her arrival did. She staggered across the road and yelled over her shoulder, "Seeeeeya, dudes! Been a slice!"

"Wait, Tammy. I love you," Jason called out.

She blew a kiss then mumbled something before turning to walk. "What did she say?"

"I dunno."

"Maybe her boyfriend was our man with the shank back there."

We watched her go tripping into the haze of the tractor beam that swallowed her as well. We're all just stumbling through obscurity, looking for something, a meaning, or just someone to talk to, searching for the secret, waiting for the sound, killing time beneath the moon.

ISLE OF SKYE

They say that visiting the Isle of Skye can be an awakening experience. I often wonder if others have come to Skye the way we did, where the journey to the island went missing along the way, as if we'd travelled through an intangible tunnel cloaked in mist. Time seemed non-existent. I became lucid only as the landscape revealed itself, like opening my eyes from a long sleep.

Perhaps I was experiencing the aftershock of two-for-one Jack Daniel's shots from the night before. The Tennessee sour mash is known for causing similar side effects.

My eyes followed the immense slope of lush, ragged umbrage into the unknown. Large raindrops fell at a slow, even pace. A row of white houses seemed illuminated in the grey afternoon. My memory hears only the boats rocking in the harbour and our footsteps on the gravel.

This is what I'd been waiting for.

Kyleakin (Caol Àcain) is a village on the east coast of Skye. It sits across the water from the mainland town of Kyle of Lochalsh. Kyleakin is the home of Castle Moil (Caisteal Maol) built in the fifteenth century, and the ruins of which are still visible.

Our accommodations were not far from the harbour. The road led us along the water's edge for a short time, then up into the landscape. There was a boat with flaking powder-blue paint that had "Stoirm" written in an arc on the stern. Low, rolling mountains stretched through the entire panorama across Loch Alsh. They receded behind Castle Moil, almost as if giants had pounded the earth over the centuries. We made our way around the bend where a small cottage came into view. Leafy hedges bordered the gardens. Window boxes of flowers were on either side of the door. We walked under the arbour and knocked.

A kind woman led us to our room. Inside was warm and dry with bunk beds full of clean blankets. It was reassuring to know we wouldn't be sleeping in a tent on a gusty cliffside. The woman was soft-spoken. Her eyes told me that she had spent her life smiling. They flashed and crinkled before she handed us the key. I switched on the lamp beside the bed, its glow pooling across the quilt. I've never been in a spot more secret than that room.

The wind and water is all you'll hear in Skye at times. The atmosphere is hypnotizing. But there are other sounds too. The door to the pub had the throaty croak of a bird. Inside we caught the murmurs of Gaelic in low light. Talisker came like a torch to the damp, helping to alleviate the stiffness in my knee. On days like that one, it bent about as well as a healthy tree branch. We sipped without words. Only a slight smile from the server who brought steaming steak pie. I set my empty whisky glass on the table with a knock. Full belly. Mended once more. Echoes thumped in the evening along the dock. Tide lapping below. Our aching feet slid through the pebbles as we walked the seaside lane past the warm light spilling from the windows of the houses. Gusts in from the loch. Shhhhh. Crack! Up in the void beyond the village. We sat on the stone wall and stared at the black waves rolling in. The moon cut the clouds like a scythe. Like cigarette smoke, my thoughts slid away. The boats groaned in the deep Atlantic as a bell dinged distant in the pitch. We buried our cold hands, retreated up the hill toward our secret hideout to lie down, disappearing into books. Plaid sheets. Silence.

Morning brought a walk close to Castle Moil. The structure stood like a jagged tooth against a white sky, a fortress now fallen and battered by time, as all things must be.

The looming blue-grey clouds folded over the rising hills. Ghost-like fog slid down, weaving around the rust-coloured rocks piercing the knotted growth and moss. Wet shoes. Big steps. *Take it in. Take it in.* Time slipped away back at our sitting spot in the bay. My mind erased and became a hollow drum, new again under the spell of the water. Only a passenger reflecting light now. I read the engraved poem that curved around and around in the granite, the one that seared itself into me: "but a broken finger-joint in this scarred figure that has emerged out of formlessness into the now that is burning like an orange sunfall over Skye." Shivers up my spine. Back to the cabin where we vanished into books again and kept calm by the lamp. Sleep.

I awoke and slipped into the morning. Walked the route parallel to the great hill reaching at the low sky. I felt the tug of my lineage. Skye felt like a new home, or like an old home, like I was a son who'd disappeared then returned with his head down.

The taste of Talisker, sweet, smoke, ash in the afternoon. She will light up the darkened heart. Oh, how she will light up the darkened heart. We ate dinner, content to say very little. Deeper, heavy skies and heavier still. Skye introduced poetry into my life the same way Leatherface did, indirect yet absolute. They both showed me there was more than meets the eye. Skye is not just some place on earth and Leatherface is not just a punk band. "Beauty is poetry. Poetry is lonely. Simplicity is beauty. And beauty is more than skin deep." We slept in a womb at the edge of the world, where outside Skye's zephyr whistled. Where the weightless hands of pixies tapped at the window, silhouetted in the rainy night.

GLASGOW

It felt like we hadn't spoken in days. We shook off the trance that Skye had left us in to the sound of people, honking cars, clanging trains, the smell of exhaust and desperation. Jason and I hauled our packs over our shoulders and moved fast. It was imperative that we made tracks to the hostel so we could still have time to explore. Tomorrow would find us on a ferry to Belfast. *What would the night deliver to us?* I wondered.

What hooked us was Men at Work's "Down Under" thumping from inside the club. Jason sang along outside. We learned that the large bouncer, Tommy, was from Saskatchewan. We laughed along with him for a few minutes at the door before he waved us by. Tommy called over his shoulder as we headed in, "If you can't get laid in there, shoot yourselves."

The tunes matched the vibe. Red strobe lights. Dark as all hell. But it felt exhilarating to hear loud music. Two young women danced nearby and we made eye contact. It wasn't long before we were yelling to each other. We sang and drank well past midnight. Kirsten invited us to stay at her house after talking for a time. She said it would be more comfortable than the hostel.

We stood with everyone gathered in the early hour commotion outside the club, smoking and joking. Jason staggered off to talk with some tough-looking blokes in a neighbouring circle. He was louder than usual. I could hear his baritone from many feet away. It always sounded like he'd swallowed a megaphone when he was in that state. I was drunk myself, but I kept a close eye on him. We both knew he could rip my head clean from my shoulders, but I think I had a keener sensitivity to my surroundings. I told Kirsten and her friend about Tammy in Inverness. I still couldn't for the life of me wrap my head around how we'd crossed paths. They were smitten with my story.

"That's so weird," Kirsten said between puffs. I liked how she held her cigarette movie-star-style, elbow tucked at the waist, smoke balanced between two straight fingers held in a backward peace sign. "What do you think it means?"

"Man . . . I really don't know." More laughter.

"I dunno either, maybe it means you should marry 'er. Shouldn't have let her get away," Kirsten teased. Big smile, taking the piss.

That's when a woman with a high ponytail and an Adidas jacket approached. She was chewing gum and snapped a pink bubble in front of us. Her sharp, black-mascara-lined eyes stared straight at me.

"Is that your man over there, standin' with them?"

"What, that one?" I asked.

"Aye, you better go and get him, those lads are raring to chib him."

I didn't understand, but knew something bad might happen if I wasn't quick, so I searched our new friends' faces for clearer understanding.

"Chib, like knife him," Kirsten said, motioning with a stabbing gesture and eyes full of urgency. She put a hand on my shoulder and pushed.

A warmth rose in my body. Jason bellowed again. I looked over. The lads around him weren't returning his blithesome demeanour. Golf shirts and uneasy glances. Smoking. Staring at their shoes. Pacing. *Fuck me.* The one who looked really pissed off by Jason's presence had his hand inside his jacket pocket. *Oh no.* Something gripped my chest as the heat climbed higher. *I don't want to do this right now.* The man with the knife in Inverness flashed in my mind. *Ye takin' the pish!*

Fear couldn't get in the way. I kept my eyes locked on the one that looked mad at Jason as I closed in. The guy's jaw clenched. A lump formed in my throat. A dull thud deep inside. He turned so that his pocketed hand was facing toward their circle. *It's so no one will see him pull out whatever he's concealing. Jesus.*

I sped to my friend. His laughter boomed as I neared the crowd. The dude's jaw bulged as if he had a rock in the side of his cheek. My body was stiff and moving mechanically. I lumbered in and swung an arm around his shoulder and U-turned Jason.

"Time to go," I said low.

"Ahhh c'mon, whuudya doin', I was just making friends," he said. By friends he meant he was just about to get into it.

"We have to go to Kirsten's now, it's getting late, fucko." By mentioning her name, I knew he wouldn't argue. By calling him a "fucko," I switched his brain back to humour. He forgot all about his "friends" as we walked away. I looked back at their sharp eyes. My chest thumped in unison with our steps. Another chibbing dodged for the time being. I let out a breath into the air.

"You're the fucko, MacDonald," he said before cackling like a rummy. "I fuckin' love you, man."

We found ourselves stumbling from a cab in front of a sprawl of brown brick suburban Glasgow townhouses. I sat down by myself to examine my new surroundings once inside. The only thing in my field of vision besides the television was a row of portraits in small plastic gold frames. I sat on the sofa alone. I took in the terrible selection of VHS tapes below the telly, weighing my choices, thinking about the near "chibbings." *Are we going to make it out of the U.K. alive?*

The Disney classic *Dumbo* looked to me like the best option. I inserted the ancient video into the player after crawling across the carpet in the dark. I figured out how to work the remote with slow, wasted agility. On the bright screen was the elephant feeling sorry for itself for being born with a flaw. *What a shitty movie. I'd rather get chibbed than watch this piece of shit.* I watched for about twenty minutes with an expression a bit like the static I woke to later on.

We rose in a fury with Jason stomping down the stairs. Heavy man on carpeted steps. Thud, thud, thud. The sound scared me awake and made me think of Arthur's Seat.

"We're late, let's go," he said, with a smile. Kirsten had already called us a cab. *Oh god.* I peeled myself like a melted Dairy Milk from her rose-patterned sofa. I saw her sitting on the stairs looking misty and tired. She seemed like a kind person, and smiled with something sympathetic in her expression. During the chaos I told her I watched *Dumbo* before I went to bed, which made her laugh. They hugged and whispered before we left.

After picking up our gear from the hostel, we caught the next available train and rumbled out of Glasgow. Two hours later we pulled into the ferry terminal in Stranraer. I woke hours later to some rowdy football boys arguing about Australia. I slipped out through the door and listened to the banshee-like howls over the North Channel in the heavy blue of night. We sailed across the deep black sea. Goodbye, Scotland. You're a beast, and I'll love you forever.

"I'VE SEEN PEOPLE TURN TO GOD,
THEIR DISCIPLINE IS PRAISING THE LORD.
I'VE SEEN PEOPLE GO OFF TO WAR,
GETTING DISCIPLINE AND NEEDING MORE.
I'VE SEEN PEOPLE JUNK UP IN THE STREET,
THEIR DISCIPLINE IS NEEDLE SPEAK.
I'VE SEEN MANY THINGS IN MY TIME,
I HAVEN'T SEEN WATER TURN TO WINE."

– "DISCIPLINE," STUBBS

JDM — 2005

"If you can be bothered . . ."

This was Stubbs's glib response to John Di Marco's initial email to
the Sunderland musician. He'd written the singer in a fit of inspiration
to ask what he thought about putting together a Leatherface tribute
album. JDM suggested releasing the album on his independent record
label, Rubber Factory Records.

Documenting is to believe that something should be remembered.
Some create because they want to document, while others document
the creators. Our friend JDM has a strong archival impulse. He acts
on his instincts while the rest of us flail about trying to make things.
I believe his foresight is synced with mortality — he knows that time
is short. That it all must be captured and remembered. Like a bottle
of smoke.

Hidden within the walls of his lair lies the evidence. Those who are
lucky enough to have seen this place know what I'm talking about. It's

as if JDM bought the house to safeguard the bookcases crammed with literature, stacks of punk records, zines, cassette tapes, CDs. For me, it's paradise. The computer's storage contains thousands of photographs and forgotten recordings. I find this to be an endearing quality as most of us move forward with reckless abandon.

JDM grew up in Woodbridge and went to King City Secondary School with Jason and Cactus. It was in these crucial years he heard the music that impacted him forever. Our friend first heard a song from *Mush* that Jason played for him. JDM believed Leatherface could be the greatest rock 'n' roll band in the world from that day on.

Leatherface reached that inevitable stage in their existence when "life" seemed to shadow their music following 2004's *Dog Disco*. There came a myriad of personal reasons, and the band soon fell into a state of hiatus and even obscurity. The steam in the machine had slowed after many years of pounding the pavement. Fans thought that they were witnessing the final days of the group they loved so much.

It was JDM's clairvoyance that led him to put together *A Tribute to Leatherface*. He jumps at any chance to promote his friends and the music he believes in. But I also feel that his intuition told him that it was time for something to happen during these years of silence from the band. You do what you can when you care deeply about something. JDM went out on a limb into the future not knowing how the project would be received.

The album took three years to complete. He pushed through the many moments during its creation when giving up seemed imminent. The 2008 double disc boasts forty-one tracks and thirty-five artists from around the globe. Fans worldwide celebrated the release and the album garnered well-deserved positive praise.

I entertain the idea that Leatherface could then see a broader scope into their importance. This cult classic band had clearly grown into something bigger over the years. The album is a letter to them that simply reads, "Do you know what you mean to us?" Maybe it would help turn the engine over once more. JDM made a prodigious effort to show his appreciation and love. It's more than most do. I'm proud of him because of this.

BELFAST, NORTHERN IRELAND

What remained of the daylight glinted off the round chrome handle running the length of the bar. A mirror behind the bottles reflected a pint glass in every hand in the room, as well as a few Budweisers. The place was alive with chatter. The bartender dried his hands on a towel and leaned over the wood toward me with a toothpick in his teeth. His tweed cap shadowed his eyes.

It was in this Belfast pub tucked in a shadowed alley that we had our first taste of authentic Irish-poured Guinness. I recall it being the best beer I'd ever tasted, but this could've been because we were so happy to have made it to Ireland. I sat at the bar while Jason mingled. The man sitting next to me talked about politics. I listened and nodded my head, acknowledging his points, adding little to the conversation. He talked about injustice. The real kind. The kind that's difficult to comprehend because I live a charmed life. His words were whispered and impassioned. I paid close attention and kept the barkeep busy pouring black gold. The pub closed early and we sat on the curb in the narrow lane watching the silhouettes of people disappear into the sewer grate smoke.

Belfast has experienced a seemingly endless conflict between its Catholic and Protestant citizens, also respectively called Nationalist/ Republican and Unionist/Loyalist. The most recent of these civil wars raged from the '60s through the late '90s and was at its worst between 1970 and 1972, but the strain still could be felt in 1999.

In the late '60s, a period of heightened violence known as the Troubles led to "peace walls," which still act as barriers to reinforce residential segregation within the city. A study identified ninety-seven separate walls and barriers within the city limits in 2017. The city was sectioned into three areas when we were there in 1999 — neutral, Protestant, and Catholic. It's hard to understand the scope of darkness this city has experienced until you're there.

There seemed to be an absence of police cars in the city. I only saw armoured vehicles rolling slow and heavy through the streets. They looked like tanks, but also like trucks, and were clad in matte grey steel. Our decision to get into the heart of things may not have been the wisest, but we needed to see some of what happened out there. We devised a route that would take us along Shankill Road, through the peace barrier, and onto Falls Road. Rumour had it that IRA headquarters could be found somewhere on lower Falls Road.

Falls Road is a densely populated district dominated by Irish Catholics, but Shankill Road remained Protestant and Unionist. The two have often found themselves in a long and terrifying conflict. This was an aggressive civil war of street fighting, sniper attacks, firebombs, terrorism, passion, and unrest. Thousands of innocent lives were lost and many more were wounded in the discord. To explain it beyond that is not my place. A simple web search will give you mountains of accurate information needed to fully understand just how intense, complicated, and horrific it really was.

Peace was declared in 1998. But in 1999 this history of bloodshed was evident everywhere, written all over the walls.

The name of the road alone is scary — Shankill. Its name derives from the Irish word Seanchill, meaning "old church." I can't help but think of knives when I hear it.

I was an outsider looking in. Was I supposed to see it all as I did? You could just feel it in the air. It's in the woman's face outside the market. Her smile is tolerant, but she knows things you know nothing about. She'll tell you this in a single glance before looking down. But perhaps she could just sense my discomfort. It's in the mannerisms of the men gathered on the corner who have perfected seeing you without looking at you at all. Don't kid yourself. My eyes were drawn to the brutalist aspects of my surroundings. I like to think that there was more than the barrack-style townhouses that seemed to be everywhere. Maybe that's all I saw because I was so uneasy so early into our exploration.

One side of Shankill Road was lined with quiet mom-and-pop shops. Any of them could've been bombed at some point. We walked next to a rusted chain-link fence bordering a field of grass and weeds. In the distance was a row of brown brick buildings. That's where we spotted our first mural.

We stood looking through the diamonds in the fence across the abandoned flatland with the cool skies above. The mural depicted three people in balaclavas dressed all in black. Two of them stood next to a door with guns held tight to their chests. The other figure stood to the side, waiting with a hammer raised above their head. I stared at this painting for a long time with the weight of its message coming down hard. A truck broke the silence with a loud clang as it revved around the corner, its back wheels jumping the curb. We carried on. More murals of crests of Loyalist paramilitary group the Ulster Defence Association and the more secretive Red Hand Commando. Loyalist slogans and warnings revealed themselves to us farther up the road, some in plain sight, others peeking out from side streets. All I could do was stare at the images. We came across a memorial for residents and locals killed in conflict somewhere along the way. There were flower crosses, portraits, lists of the deceased.

I'd spent many nights with Jason talking Irish politics, and he was fiery about the subject. It couldn't be avoided when he'd get into it. But no amount of what my friend taught me could have prepared me for the day we walked Shankill Road. These wounds were still fresh. An ominous reminder of what transpired crept through the tired streets.

A tattoo parlour came into view in the strip of shops across the road. It was a welcoming sight of safety to Jason and me. We headed toward the studio in hopes of reprieve. Maybe we'd make a friend. The door opened into a dim room with music playing in the background. The smell of Dettol and green soap was comforting in that second, but I could already tell it wasn't a good idea for us to be in there by the look of the burly dude standing behind the counter. Two or three others in the back stopped what they were doing to look at us. When I smiled and nodded the gesture wasn't returned. One of them stepped closer with a stony expression. I glanced up to see Ulster Volunteer Force tattoo designs on the walls. *Holy shit.* It was impossible to appear relaxed while scanning the Loyalist flash. The big one with the ginger beard crossed his thick arms. The coldest stare came bearing down on us. This memory is vivid. Perhaps we'd found ourselves in a locals-only establishment. I only knew our presence wasn't welcome. The two of us stood there for an uncomfortable amount of time before making sure not to bang the door as we retreated. Our eyes were wide as we looked at each other in disbelief. I glanced back expecting to see the red beard swinging at us with a bat.

The exact location of the Cupar Way peace wall was unclear. We decided to ask a man walking by with an armful of grocery bags. "Excuse me, sir, could you tell us the way to Falls Road?"

"Oh. Sure thing, lads, it's just a few streets that way." His voice was friendly, and he answered us without hesitation. But it's what he said next that gave me goosebumps. "Be careful, boys," he warned while turning away.

We followed his directions through the streets. What I thought at first was an outdoor football stadium emerging from behind the neighbourhood rooftops was actually the barrier's fenced top. The streets brought us to a small walkway leading onto the road along the peace line. Belfast is about six miles at its widest point, but it's been said there are nearly twenty miles of dividing walls and other obstacles within the city limits. The structures were only meant to be temporary. We walked parallel to it on the other side of the street looking up in trepidation. Graffiti littered the lower half closest to the sidewalk.

The militant steel cladding reached upwards of forty feet, three times higher than the Berlin Wall. The barrier was at its highest point near the gate that allowed access to the Catholic neighbourhoods. These sections of metal fencing grasped at the sky. Floodlights pointed downward from the metal frame. Razor wire crowned the top like a tangle of thorns. We continued on, slow and calculated. The feeling was comparable to stumbling away from a fist fight when your legs have turned to jelly. Like making an exit from a store you've just shoplifted from.

This time spent passing through the barrier was very tense. I could imagine the kind of violence that must have occurred for a structure of its magnitude to be built. A carnal, last-ditch effort for survival. It was difficult coming to terms with knowing people could hurt each other like that, as I imagined them tearing each other apart. I guess we all build walls. It's hard to know whether they keep the peace or slowly make it worse. Often it's easier to hide behind them than to face what's on the other side. The barrier's impending presence coupled with the thick, political tension in the air reminded me of "Not Superstitious," and had me humming the song in an attempt to remain calm. "You're not a politician and without a thought you'd build a fort to defend what you are. You're not religious and without Catholicism you would turn to God to save your soul."

I looked down at the scuffed white toes of my Converse carrying me through the dense obstruction. No words were spoken for some time. We'd made it far enough away with our kneecaps intact that I relaxed. It was farther into the Catholic area that we found ourselves lost again. We asked a woman walking her dog, "Excuse me, could you tell us the way to Falls Road, please?"

"It's just a few streets that way, boys. Should find it soon," she said, smiling before her expression changed. "Be careful, lads." It was the second admonition within twenty minutes. There was an unfamiliar flicker of worry in Jason's eyes.

Within several minutes we were on Falls Road, its name derived from the Irish túath na bhFál, meaning "territory of the enclosures." There were so many murals it was hard to take it all in. I remember some of them were for other countries with similar struggles. Large IRA letters on a telephone pole reminded us of where we were. Everything felt severe. The energy was off-kilter and disorienting. Although I'm glad we experienced this, our exploration didn't feel right. I felt like I had no place even looking or trying to understand. The word "tourist" wasn't sitting well with me at all. We spotted the famous mural of Bobby Sands, a member of the IRA who died on a hunger strike while imprisoned at the HM Prison Maze in Northern Ireland. There were memorials, crosses, flowers — at some point the difference between a graveyard and a neighbourhood became difficult to decipher. Reminders were everywhere. I stopped and stared into a brick alley at the ragged white letters spray-painted across the wall. The writing was urgent and full of pain about a child killed by rubber bullets.

We reached what could have been lower Falls Road and stood at the intersection, leaning against a railing, smoking. I spotted a tower with cameras pointed in every direction. No stone unturned.

"Look at that up there," I said in a low voice.

"Holy shit. That's nuts."

"Someone's watching us for sure."

"Take a pic for me, MacDonald," Jason said, teasing.

"I'd rather not, thanks."

On the corner of the intersection was what appeared to be an IRA support shop. Jason was already on his way over to it and I had no choice but to follow. I felt leery trailing behind my friend through the door. The inside looked as if it could have been any old dusty gift shop in Niagara Falls full of snow globes, T-shirts, mugs, and key chains — the only difference was that everything in this shop was IRA themed.

An older woman greeted us with a wide smile full of translucent grey-blue teeth. Her eyes were glazed and vacant as she leaned in, pointing to the soldier in a balaclava holding a rifle on the T-shirt rack. Above the image it read "Provisional Irish Republican Army" and below "Will do what it takes."

"That's me," she said, tapping the soldier with a gangly finger. Her smile drifted from her face like a flag in a dying wind. Her eyes looked through us at something far away.

An older man standing next to us at the cash turned in our direction. He knew right away we weren't local. After talking, we learned his name was Joseph. He expressed his disappointment that we'd come all the way to Ireland only to "waste our time in the city." Joseph said we had to see the northwest coast to experience the island properly. There was a bus station an hour out of Belfast where we could catch a ride to Donegal. He offered to drive us to the hostel and collect our bags, then take us to the station. We were unsure whether to accept this invitation, as we weren't accustomed to such generosity. But also, I could sense an urgency beyond his smile, which made me wary. Jason and I searched each other's eyes to see what the other was thinking. It felt as if Joseph didn't want us in Belfast any longer, almost like he was trying to warn us, or protect us without actually saying it. Maybe he was just a kind person. We agreed with reluctance, and walked out of the IRA store with Joseph and a little bell ringing behind us. The three of us headed to his car parked around the corner. *What if he was delivering us directly to the IRA?* The closing door sounded so final. He started the engine. I bit my lip with my heart revving. Tension rose as the dusty blue station wagon weaved among the streets.

"ARE YOU THE LITTLE GIRL WHO'LL GROW UP TO SAVE THE WORLD?
OR ARE YOU THE LITTLE BOY WHO CARRIES ON THE EVIL MEN DO?"

— "EVIL THAT MEN DO," STUBBS

SERGIE LOOBKOFF — SAMIAM

Guitarist Sergie Loobkoff was swimming in two extra-large Leatherface shirts as he hugged Leighton Evans and Davey Burdon inside their tour van. Loobkoff felt he'd made a true connection with the two youngsters out on the road, but the time had come to embrace the bittersweet moment of final farewells. The heartfelt mood was ripped away from them as the door of the van jolted open and slid across the rails with a loud bang. I imagine the jarring seconds similar to having the sheets torn from you while sleeping. Waiting outside the door was an angry Frankie Stubbs. The vibe inside the van spiralled downwards as Stubbs demanded that Loobkoff get out of the van.

Loobkoff hadn't seen this side of Stubbs throughout their tour together. He smiled at the singer because he thought it must be a joke. That's when Stubbs lunged forward and grabbed him by his baggy, layered Leatherface shirts and rag-dolled Loobkoff from the van. Loobkoff admits to the foolhardy pride and temper that he and his brother were born with. He says he wasn't scared of Stubbs even with the surprise attack. Loobkoff thought of Stubbs as a drunken, sad old man in those moments, someone whose introverted behaviour had perplexed Loobkoff while on tour. Burdon and Evans watched with timid bewilderment from inside the van. Loobkoff broke free from Stubbs's clutches, stared him in the eye, and yelled, "Motherfucker, what the fuck do you think you're doing?"

"Ah nevvvvver liked you," Stubbs spat back. The statement confused Loobkoff. The two of them had gotten along until that point. Stubbs swung at Loobkoff, not with a fist but with what can only be described as an "eagle claw," hooking Loobkoff hard in the nose with two talon-like fingers and surprising force. The guitar player says the vicious rake left him reeling with pain. Loobkoff pulled himself together with his hand over his wincing face. That's when Lainey emerged from the shadows and corralled Loobkoff like a cowboy would a steer. The intimidating drummer dragged him down the ramp into the parking lot below. Stubbs and Lainey believed that Loobkoff had said something disrespectful about their deceased friend and bass player, Andy Crighton. It happened in the hours after the final show of the tour. Loobkoff saw Stubbs talking with Samiam singer Jason Beebout as he sat on top of Loobkoff's amp. Unbeknownst to Loobkoff, Stubbs and Beebout were talking about Crighton. Loobkoff walked over and told Beebout to get off the amp in a joking manner. Loobkoff thinks that Stubbs interpreted the interruption as a sign of disrespect.

Loobkoff searched Lainey's eyes in the underground and pleaded that he would never have done anything to insult Crighton. The Samiam guitarist now describes Crighton as one of the sweetest, most beloved people to walk the earth. "He really was the nicest human. He would have taken his shirt off in a rainstorm and put it over your head to keep you dry kind of nice." The guitarist's desperate appeal seemed to have an effect on Lainey, who turned around without saying a word and walked back up the ramp, jumped in the van, and slammed the door. Seconds later the vehicle sped off.

Crighton's death was still fresh and it's easy to imagine a dark cloud hanging over Leatherface in this time. Their loyalty to their circle of friends is like a deep river. Like the fictional Leatherface, they felt their family had been threatened. It's clear that Crighton was loved and missed by all.

Loobkoff can remember when Samiam toured with Snuff before Crighton joined Leatherface. They ended up at some guy named Pat's house in Minneapolis looking through his extensive record collection. There was one LP that Loobkoff was drawn to as he flipped through the stack. He pulled it out and examined Leatherface's *Mush*. Loobkoff had never heard of them, but something about the album was calling him. Redmonds walked over and said, "Mate, that's the shite right there." He didn't have a chance to listen to the record before having to pile back in the van with the members of Snuff and hit the road. Loobkoff noticed the same cassette tape lying on the van's dashboard. All three members of Snuff began to hype the album in an exaggerated, comedic display as if selling a product on the telly. Then they slid it into the dashboard.

None of the intricacies of Leatherface's music hit Loobkoff at first listen. His only thought was that they were trying to rip off Motörhead. He could feel himself looking for something negative to say about what he was hearing because at the time he believed his musical tastes were more refined than those of his peers. Loobkoff knew deep down it wasn't this way. You can only fight it for so long before Leatherface's inexplicable draw begins to take you over. Loobkoff lost the fight when Samiam invited Leatherface to play a handful of shows with them.

The unfortunate altercation between Stubbs and Loobkoff doesn't define how Loobkoff feels about them today. "I think about them just like you think about them, a band that I've loved for a long time." Loobkoff admits with pride that he's loved Leatherface for thirty years, even after getting eagle-clawed in the face by Stubbs. I feel Loobkoff is setting his ego aside and paying a high compliment, considering how easily bad blood comes in such a volatile industry.

When I told Stubbs about it over a few glasses of red wine he broke into a theatrical, improv song recounting the infamous eagle-claw incident.

```
"LIKE A TIMEBOMB ABOUT TO GO OFF.
ONCE BITTEN IS NOT ENOUGH.
GETTING TOO CLOSE IS SOMETHING TO DO.
A FASCINATING PAST TIME IT IS TOO.
AMATEUR DRAMATIC.
DIVORCED FROM THE PRAGMATIC.
AN INHERENT LACK OF STYLE.
ROTUND AND ROBUST.
UNBRIDLED LUST.
PARALYSED AND BLINKERED.
NO COMMON SENSE."

- "FAT, EARTHY, FLIRT," STUBBS
```

DONEGAL

The bus driver gave us a quirky look when we asked him to bring us as far north as possible. "Go on then, get comfortable," he said. I could have sworn I saw a smirk as he turned back to the wheel when we walked by.

The fabric seats inside the dim interior were decorated with festive party patterns, and reminded me of how some things in life are universal. The familiarity was comforting. The bus hissed and squeaked as the driver pulled the door closed then swerved into the street.

"Did all of that actually just happen?" I asked.

"Did what just happen?"

"Like, all of it. Did we get run out of Belfast? Or did Joseph genuinely want us to experience the north? Something felt off about the way it went down."

"I don't know, Chris. He was a nice old guy. Maybe he just didn't want us to see all the ugly shit, and wanted us to see the beauty instead, that there's more to it if we look harder," Jason replied with a nervous smile on his face. He rubbed the top of his head. "Yeah."

"Maybe. It was just weird how eager he was."

"I know what you're saying. Remember all that I've told you? Shit's real. Very real."

"Did we look suspicious?"

"Maybe something was about to happen that he didn't want us to be a part of. I don't know."

I sat back in my seat.

The bus rolled through Derry, another city beaten by the Troubles, where we peered out at more murals akin to those we saw in Belfast. More sad history.

The dark swaying silence of the bus moving farther into the country was uncomfortable, but also welcoming. As I began to drift, I couldn't help but replay the recent events. I'd wake intermittently in panic before falling under again.

When I opened my eyes sometime later, a great concern had amassed inside me. The window next to me began to rattle and jangle my nerves with every bump. There was only blackness and raindrops outside the tinted windows.

"How long we been goin' for?" I asked in a daze.

"A few hours ..." Jason replied in a baritone voice.

My mind created a scenario where Joseph was the delivery person for the IRA. He'd pick up suspicious folk and bring them to the station. The bus driver would then take them to the IRA's clandestine interrogation facility out on the coast. Even though we'd asked the driver to bring us as far north as possible, we could have been anywhere. The thought made my palms sweat. I pulled myself up and looked over my headrest and surveyed my surroundings. It was reassuring to know that at least we wouldn't go down alone. There were ten people riding with us who were sleeping or reading.

The bus shifted gears, slowed, and made a final squeak before stopping for good on the shoulder. With a "pssssshhhhh," the door opened.

The rain could be heard outside. The driver said over his seat, "Here you go, boys, most northern point." I was relieved to not listen to the shaking window anymore.

We thanked him as we stepped down into the dirt. He dragged our packs from inside the compartment below. The driver hiked up his pants while he stomped back up the steps with his wallet chain dangling behind him. He nodded as he got comfortable but didn't make eye contact as the door swung closed. The bus swerved back onto the road with its red tail lights bobbing, getting smaller and smaller. They disappeared far away for good. Our exact location was unknown, and the reality of our situation sunk in. We were alone out in the pitch black of the Irish seaboard with only the falling rain and the sound of the pounding waves. It took a minute for our eyes and brains to adjust to this new scene. This new predicament. We pulled our hoods up, hauled up our packs, and started walking just like we always did. My mind's eye could see people in balaclavas emerging from the night with guns pointed. I buried the thought. Tiny lights glowed in the distance where the bus had disappeared. Like cavemen, we made our way toward the fire. With my Converse splashing through puddles, I was regretting the decision to come way out there. But there was also relief to be out of Belfast.

"Where in the fuck *are* we?" I said, kicking the gravel.

"Northern Ireland, my friend," Jason said, laughing. I could tell he felt relieved as well.

"You don't say now?" I yelled in a terrible Irish accent.

More laughter.

"I don't know, MacDonald. Guess we'll find out."

I muttered, "This is nuts. Seriously."

"I know, what the fuck, we're on this deserted rainy road in the middle of God-knows-where," his voice seemed to echo. The two of us walked forward into the unknown, somewhere along the wild Atlantic coast of northwest Ireland.

With every step our hope grew brighter. A structure came into view. Out on a misty spit, pointing to the ocean was a long, two-storey building that looked like a mirage. This ghost-like structure dissipated behind us as we walked on. The only sounds to be heard were the ocean and the dirt crunching beneath our shoes. A gradual hill led us down to a row of pale buildings close to the road's edge. They emerged slowly in the night, and we could see it was a tiny village. The two of us reached the safety of the glow we'd spotted from so far back. A circular sign hung above. *Yes . . . is that . . . what I think it is? . . . A pub.*

"You kidding me right now?"

"A pub? Out here?"

We pulled the wooden door open and stepped into a small, warm room. The sound of fiddles was low. People huddled at the bar turned to look our way. They greeted us with friendly faces as we pulled our wet hoods back and slid our packs off. My heavy jeans were plastered to my thighs. Rain squished between my toes. The server started setting cutlery and placing glasses of water down on a table near the back. She seemed happy to know we'd come all the way from Canada, and sped off to pour some pints of Guinness. I could feel my spirit lift after having just rolled in from the cold to find an inviting table. Only a few hours had passed since being scared shitless in the heart of Belfast. It felt perplexing to be offered such comforts away from such sombre vibes. I peeled off my wet sweatshirt. My hands were pale blue. Our exact location had yet to be determined. Jason asked the server when she returned.

"Soooooo," he started with a smile, looking up at her as she placed the beer on the table. "Where are we exactly?" The three of us were amused at our obliviousness. We'd ended up in a place called Bunbeg located in County Donegal. Bunbeg was the smallest village in Gweedore and is the anglicised version of An Bun Beag, which means "the small river mouth." It took a second before we pronounced it correctly.

"Perfect," Jason replied, sounding as if we'd planned the trek to Bunbeg all along. We both raised our glasses. She smiled and welcomed us.

If there was a pub, then things felt better than they were, always, that's how it was on our journey. And especially in the middle of an uncertain and soggy Donegal night. Spending six pounds on a pint to warm up and get our bearings seemed sensible to me, although funds were dwindling quickly at this point. It was best not to think about it.

Something very curious began to unfold as we took in our surroundings. The door opened and in walked a younger crowd. They made themselves at home and ordered drinks. They seemed out of place in the quiet countryside.

"Seems weird, no?"

"What?" Jason asked, before diving into his Guinness.

"Young people in the middle of nowhere."

"I guess. More pressing matters, MacDonald. Where will we stay tonight?"

"I vote for the beach if the rain stops."

"And if it doesn't?" I took a sip and thought long and hard but had no real response.

"I dunno. I mean, too bad this pub wasn't open twenty-four hours." Jason pulled out his *Europe on a Shoestring* book and started flipping through it. The ocean ran parallel to the road we came in on as far as we could discern. I was praying for the rain to let up.

"Was that a hotel back there, the long white one? Probably expensive if it was," I said.

"Dunno, am looking now."

The door opened again. A small group of young women entered this time. Jason pulled his eyes from the pages. I stared over my pint glass.

"Seriously though, seems *weird*, no?" I asked again.

"What?"

"Pretty women, in the middle of nowhere."

"Pretty women can't live in the middle of nowhere?"

"Well, of course they can, just, there's nothing fucking around here."

We whispered about Belfast, blown away at what we'd seen and felt there. Jason shook his head in disbelief. We talked about the burly guy from the tattoo shop who looked as if he was going to gut us on the spot. The lady in the IRA support store's chilling declaration still rang in our heads. I mouthed, "That's me." In mid-conversation the door opened again, and more people entered the pub.

There's something strange happening, I know it, I thought.

The sleepy snug in the rainy Donegal night soon was alive. I tried to read the faces of the locals sitting at the bar as the newest group walked in. They didn't appear to think anything of it. The fiddle music swooned. The youthful shouts grew louder and some people danced. *But where did they come from?* The crowd was soon spilling into our corner of the pub. I stood to talk with a girl standing close to our table, needing to solve the mystery.

"Excuse me," I said. She smiled as she turned. "I'm wondering, where has everyone come from?" I tried not to face her directly so she wouldn't smell my bad breath. I realized the words sounded obtuse, but continued, "It just seems that there are only a few houses here, from what I can see . . ."

She giggled. "Where ya from?"

"Canada." She gestured for me to follow her through the front door. Her long straight hair swayed as I trailed her outside. The young woman walked into the road and pointed her arm like an arrow.

"What am I looking for?" I asked, feeling dumb.

"We're 'eaded down there. Everyone from Dublin and Belfast comes up here to party, there's a nightclub down the way." I looked but couldn't see anything.

"A club, really? I don't see anything."

"Yeah, you can't see it from here, but if you follow this road, then make a left and follow it. Ten-minute walk," she replied, amused that I had no idea what was happening.

"But why is it way out here?"

"Dunno, juss is!"

"Wow."

We headed in and I slid back into my chair at the table. She sipped her drink and looked out of the corner of her eye at us, waiting for me to fill Jason in on the strange new discovery. I could tell she was listening.

"What's happening, MacDonald?" Jason asked in a low voice. He said things in a very serious manner that could also sound like a joke. A strange gift, given only to him.

"You're not going to believe it."

"Tell me."

"There's a club over there."

"A what?"

"A club, a dance club."

He was delighted. Once again, the adventure had taken another unexpected turn. She smiled wide and turned back to her friends.

"I guess I know where we're headed tonight. This place may not be open twenty-four hours, but that might be if worse comes to worse," he said before hauling from his beer. Then with an "ahhhhh," he wiped his thin lips against the back of his hand. It was the sound of a satisfied explorer who'd discovered the risk and adventure he'd pined for. He too had become a Fleischmann's man.

The fiddle whined from major to minor in the background, reeling and rollicking like the land outside, moody like the pensive, vaulted sky. Like the howl of a seaside gale sliding through the cracks of a stone wall. Like the sharp squeak of a saw through timber. An older man's shoe started thumping the floor in time with the music. It wasn't a stomp, but it was louder than a tap and he pushed down with just the right amount of force to be heard. I pictured the floorboards beneath his stool, faded with wear. His carved, leathery face had seen a few days on the water, seen some sun and salt. He was wise. I entertained the idea that he could beat you to a pulp but would rather tell you a story and buy you a drink. His charcoal tweed cap sat above his red cheeks and angled smile. I got the impression that his woolen sweater was a permanent fixture. The young woman twirled, with her hair fanning like the wing of a bird. Her smile flashed as she spun. In that moment I wanted to stay forever. We ordered two more pints in a drunkard's attempt to do exactly that.

GRAEME PHILLISKIRK — LEATHERFACE, MEDICTATION, LITTLE ROCKET RECORDS, BULLTACO, RUGRAT

"People are like spiders, they build a web, they never go any further."

Graeme Philliskirk tells me this as he looks from the window of the new recording studio down into Sunderland's streets. "I see people's little lives built around an area, some of them no bigger than forty feet; they'll go to work and come back and not move anywhere around it. I think we wanted to move further than that. We weren't just spiders, happy having a web, being happy where we were, having the same views. We wanted to learn more about what was out there. We wanted to get out and weren't frightened to stare it in the face. It's very much a northeastern thing, it's this utter despair of having nothing, and nothing to look forward to, nothing in your life, living in a fuckin' shithole, but also having the ability to rise above it and see the good things. And to want more, and actually see the happiness around you as well. There's that mad collective of emotions that you're constantly faced with, but it's also having the brawn for standing up for what you believe in. There's another side to it as well, when these sensitivities come into it. I think Frankie's like that, and I'm like that as well. At times we feel a little embarrassed to have to acknowledge that as well, because when we were growing up you were told to shut the fuck up, or you'd get fuckin' smacked, or the big guys would give you a beating because you had something slightly different to say. There was, and is still, a lot of that going on here today. And sometimes there is that sort of 'Do I dare say that? Will people understand what I'm trying to say? Is it too sensitive, what I'm trying to say? I'm supposed to be as tough as nails living here.'"

Philliskirk was born and raised in Sunderland. He speaks of his home with an underlying romanticism when he isn't describing the northeast coast as a hard fucking place to live. "Whenever I smell the sea, it's home. Almost like a drawing, or a calling."

The newest bassist to join the cult of Leatherface prefers to describe the weather from other people's perspectives. He illustrates it from the viewpoint of folks he's known who've lived amongst harsher Icelandic climates. These people compare the northeast of Sunderland to a wind that cuts you like a frozen sword. As exaggerated as it may sound, the rumours are true. The extreme temperatures are a direct result of the contrasting air masses colliding over the country and above the northeast, where the wind is sent from the Arctic. Some people might be referring to the cold streets of Sunderland when talking about how you might get your head stoved in if you're not careful. But they're also talking about its temperature.

He was born into a family of shipbuilders. Philliskirk's father was a forceful individual with no grey areas, who at times turned to the drink. This sombre way of life that led men away from their sensitivities seems to be a common story where he lives. He remembers the launching of . ships into the River Wear after the town worked tirelessly to construct the enormous hulls. These were moments of immense pride and community. For a fleeting day the weights were shed and everything felt lighter. The town doesn't seem to be able to offer much in the way of opportunity, but it's a home to people, real, hard-working people who share a strong sense of togetherness.

Philliskirk was raised with conflict already embedded into his life because the boy's aunt was Black and living in a predominantly white, working-class town. An interracial family wasn't always welcome in a place like Sunderland in the mid-'80s. He grew up throwing haymakers at anyone who crossed his aunt and his cousins. But it wasn't only for their safety that he fought. There was a boxing club not far from where Philliskirk and his mates lived. Training helped prepare you to to defend yourself on Friday nights.

Philliskirk's other aunt was an anarchist and a punk who exposed the boy to her record collection at an early age. She gave him the keys to the kingdom to listen to records when she wasn't there. He was the only family member allowed access to her room. Philliskirk remembers being mesmerized by Killing Joke's first album as he held it in his hands. Something about the cover art reminded him of Belfast and Derry. The violence and strife the Irish were experiencing was also relatable to life in Sunderland. He placed it on the record player, turned up the volume, and was changed forever. The song "Requiem" would hook just about any young, impressionable kid. His aunt could see the twinkle in his eye and continued feeding him this alternative lifestyle. Philliskirk was desperate to celebrate on New Year's Eve but was still too young to hit the pubs with his mates. He took refuge by the radio instead, listening to a concert broadcast live from Belfast. The headliner was Stiff Little Fingers. The opening act was some band nobody had heard of. They called themselves U2. He held his cassette deck to the radio and recorded the entire show front to back. Across the airwaves his young, hungry ears could hear the audience going "absolutely fucking mental." He listened to the recording he'd made over and over again with his heart racing until a new path formed and a splinter of hope shone through the clouds of coal dust.

Philliskirk said yes when his teacher Mr. Peacock asked him if he wanted to take part in music lessons after school. Mr. Peacock brought in an acoustic guitar case, set it down, unbuckled the latches, lifted the lid, and pulled out the six-string instrument. Philliskirk admits that he didn't even know what it was at first. His mind exploded in disbelief as his teacher gave the guitar a strum. The teenager continued with his lessons and learned how to play well enough. His immediate family couldn't afford something as luxurious as a guitar in those days. Philliskirk's father couldn't hide his disapproval when his grandad bought him one. But the kid didn't let the unfortunate circumstance sway him in the slightest. He was determined to play music, plain and simple.

There was no hope on the horizon with Thatcher in power. His family had little money and Sunderland was going through a harsh period of economic collapse. Like Leighton Evans, Philliskirk's athletic build should have been a green light into a life of football, but his family wasn't middle class enough to be accepted. Many people tried their best to help get him in, but his family was shunned. He left school with disparity setting in and turned to selling drugs as a last resort. This involvement led to Philliskirk's involvement in one of the largest drug busts the town had ever seen. Philliskirk states he would have spent many years behind bars if it weren't for two friends who took the rap. If you were born in Sunderland, you turned to football, mining, drugs, or music.

As the years went by his musicianship improved. It was no surprise when Philliskirk found himself hanging around the town's historical punk rock hub, the Bunker, with all that his aunt had armed him with. He talks about this time in his life as electric. There were gangs of musicians coming and going, and he describes the Bunker's vibe as a collective of musicians in those days. The exception was H.D.Q., who had a solid lineup in place and were making waves with their sound. The young punk would catch glimpses of the revered Dickie Hammond as well as Frankie Stubbs and began to know their faces well. Running into one another seemed inevitable when they all drank at the same pub. Philliskirk noticed something strange happening during all of this. He was seeing Stubbs, Hammond, and Laing all playing together and thought for a short while that Stubbs had joined H.D.Q. What he was actually witnessing was Leatherface rising from the ashes of H.D.Q.

There were a few different factors that led to Philliskirk and Stubbs becoming closer mates. One of them being the British National Party's rise in popularity. The two friends attended rallies and fought the opposition together because they both had zero tolerance for racism. Their trust and friendship strengthened in the aftermath of the street battles. A love for John Peel also brought them together. They recognize that without Peel's influence, the lot of them wouldn't have gravitated toward one another as they did. It's pretty cool to think that John Peel brought them hope and the idea of community. He rallied the people together to form bands and make music. Those bands would then bring more people together when they played shows and toured. The wheel kept turning.

Philliskirk can remember Leatherface's drive to get out of the grips of Sunderland as they went searching "further afield." He could feel that this band that he'd grown close to might go on to do something very special. He could see them about to break free from the confining walls of their hometown, which was no easy feat. In the beginning stages, he would watch them rehearse in the Bunker. Philliskirk remembers what hit him the hardest in those days was Lainey's drumming. It was clear the band had a backbone strong enough to leave a lasting impression. A snare hit so hard it would demand that people listen. What Philliskirk saw was a band that built themselves around a rock named Andrew Laing. He then started hearing Stubbs's and Hammond's "Dag Nasty-style" guitars as their sound progressed. Not until later did he hear the complexities of Stubbs's voice and all that he had to say. Once these elements started to sink into people, some hated them, and some loved them and those that loved them couldn't get enough. He watched the band come to life like a brewing storm.

Years passed and Philliskirk decided to move to Manchester for a stint. When he returned, he learned that Burdon, Leatherface's bass player of six years, was moving on to pursue his own endeavours with his project Former Cell Mates. The bass player torch needed to be passed on yet again. Burdon told Philliskirk that he couldn't think of a better person to fill the shoes. All eyes were on Philliskirk as the candidate. Hammond pushed for it as well. Stubbs and Philliskirk ended up at the Ivy House, where it seems the answers to all Leatherface's conundrums lay at the bottom of a pint glass. The two friends sealed the deal after lifting a few. Philliskirk set to studying YouTube videos of Crighton's bass playing, who had also been Philliskirk's dear friend. He tried hard to decipher his mindset and all that was happening in the songs. When he speaks of Crighton his voice softens and settles into a warm tone full of honesty, "If there was ever a proper fuckin' bass player, it was Andy fuckin' Crighton."

It was at Out of Spite DIY music festival in Leeds that Philliskirk played his first gig with Leatherface as the headlining act. To fill these boots was a daunting task for the strongest of players. He had to earn his place in the band. When the hardcore German fans hissed, "Who the fuck are you?" he stood his ground as the newcomer. It wasn't until the second tour back through Germany that his presence was accepted. He also had to learn how to hang on for dear life when the band was at its fiercest. Philliskirk describes playing live with Leatherface as a series of disorienting vignettes where real time would somehow slow. He compares the sensation to being brought under water. Only when the music came flooding back did he feel like he could get through the remainder of the sets unscathed. To this day, Philliskirk and Burdon don't talk about Leatherface as *their* band, but rather as this esoteric "thing" that chose them to move it forward through the ages.

I left the Bunbeg pub only after being dragged from my chair. With our damp packs, we followed the young woman's directions into the night. The fiddle faded with every step we took away from the pub, until only our shoes on the blacktop and the white noise of the Atlantic could be heard. The rain had finally stopped. A decision was made to head toward the water.

We stepped into the tall, wet grass at the side of the road and made our way into the dunes. It left drops on my hands as we passed through. Our shoes slid into the soft sand and we trudged forward onto a sprawling beach. The silver-dime moon left a receding shimmering path across the ocean. Streaks of fast-moving clouds passed overhead.

Once the tent was up, I asked, "You seen the pegs?"

"Should be in the tent bag, no?"

"Nope. Not in there."

"You must have left them in Edinburgh, MacDonald."

"Me, eh?"

"Well, it wasn't me, so must've been you. Don't worry, it's not gonna blow away."

After changing into dry pants, we covered our packs with sleeping bags, creating the illusion of two people sleeping inside. Oldest trick in the book. Nobody could be seen across the barren landscape. "Later, Ron, later, Debbie!" I yelled as we made our way back up the slope.

We headed left past small houses perched in the dark, chimneys puffing wood smoke into the sky. Lovely. The club droned as we rounded the bend, its sign revealing itself as we drew closer. It read "Millennium," in black letters on a white board. *How weird, out here, of all places.* I could make out "Psycho Killer" by Talking Heads coming from inside as we ventured closer. We stood outside, wondering what the hours were. I asked the great big guy with a meaty head and a clunky tribal tattoo how late they were open. The cut-off was one a.m.

Red and blue laser beams grazed across a sea of moving bodies. I stood in complete disbelief of the raging dance club out in the middle of Donegal. There was something dream-like about it, as if we were in a bad horror movie. We ordered drinks from the bar with our skint funds and took in the bouncing heads from the railing on the second floor.

Dudes in dress shirts leaning over a stand-up table gave us taunting looks. *What else is new?*

A pretty voice cut through the bass as we took it in. "Hey, there you are!"

I turned to find the woman with the long hair from the pub, her eyes twinkling.

"Hey!"

"You found it!"

"Yeah!"

"So anyways, what are you doin' out here?"

"Sorry?"

"Whaaaaat are youu doin waaay out here, in Donegal?"

"Oh, listening to ABBA," I said, as "Dancing Queen" now bumped in the background.

"You like ABBA?" she asked, smiling.

"Oh yes," I said in a serious tone.

She smiled and leaned in. "You don't look like the type. I can't tell whether you actually do."

"I do," I said into her ear. "Ever hear their song 'Eagle'?"

"No. Is it good?"

"Oh man, it'll get its claws into you for sure."

I was telling the truth. I think of my childhood living room when I hear them. There's a strange memory lingering in me. It involves me watching *Road Warrior* with the sound off and ABBA playing in the background on the stereo. The dust-covered man with gnarly teeth in goggles and his flying machine are the images I see when I listen to ABBA. I told my new friend about my bizarre recollection. She seemed charmed.

"You have the most beautiful accent," she told me.

"You don't get out much, huh?" I asked. "Besides, I'm not the one with the beautiful accent." I didn't want to say goodbye when she had to leave.

I woke to a tenuous light filtering through the nylon with the sound of the tide in the distance. For a long while I lay there with my head resting on my flattened sweater. It was a rare occasion to feel comfortable. My mind was weighted from the night before. But I also felt as airy as the seabirds above.

I picked sand from my lip and from the insides of my ears. It was caked on my foul socks. Life was beautiful and gritty. I thought of the dusty man with the flying machine from *Road Warrior* again and how he lived just fine with it. *Fuck, I love that movie.* That cool dog, that car, that kid with the big mullet who screams all the time. I unzipped the tent and crawled into the golden earth like a vampire creeping from its tomb. The high-definition beach radiated in stark contrast to the night before, when we pitched the tent in a sea of blue and black. White and yellow houses were perched along the green, rocky coast stretching toward the ocean. Our camp was located in a horseshoe of land with spits on either side. Bunbeg was revealing its true self to us.

Jagged rocks climbed from the water not far from shore. Waves washed around a white boulder smoothed from the tides. A driftwood log bobbed like a femur bone. Silhouetted birds flew in a straight ragged stitch through the husk of a pale blue sky along the horizon. Shark-tooth sailboats protruded from the ocean's jaws in the distance. I knew we'd gambled by setting up camp where we did, but was glad we had. I went on a search for coffee and breakfast, enjoying the walk alone.

The truth is I enjoyed being hungover with Jason more than I did being drunk with him. I don't know what that was about. It was just when we felt most connected. There was a perfect balance between delirium and reality in that space. Morning brought with it a self-awareness. We understood the importance of enjoying every moment when possible. We also could sense it wouldn't last forever. All of it, maybe even the things we couldn't admit. Leatherface's "Bowl of Flies" was always on my mind, its meaning, its brazen poetic reminder. When the Irishman finally got himself upright, we tromped across the beach barefoot toward the glistening water. My pants were falling off and covered with golden specks. We stood ten feet apart and relieved ourselves in the waves. With the ocean wind on our bare skin, we sang at the top of our lungs: "Lighted cigarettes, burn out of time. Like a rainforest, but not metaphoric. In fact like a piss in the Atlantic!"

We spent most of the day separate from each other. I walked for a long time over the bullwhip kelp washed up in the sand and examining tiny crabs the tide had left behind. While I was sitting on a rock listening to the ocean, a family came along with a little boy that played close by. The kid threw stones into the water. His laughter sailed into the air.

I thought about how we came to be on the beach. The point where the bus driver dropped us off, to be exact. We had asked him to let us out at the northernmost tip of his route. But I started to wonder if he had other intentions. I think he let us off a ways from the little pub on purpose. His idea would be to first instill in us the feeling of being lost, knowing we would head in the direction of the lights. He knew we would stumble on Millennium, where all the young people would be. I remember that smirk he gave us as he turned back toward the steering wheel.

The day came and went by like the clouds. The tide crashed while the dusk faded again to black, as did our moods. Seabirds could still be heard in the distance through the night. What a triumph. But I had a nagging feeling that something wasn't quite right. There were fewer and fewer words being spoken between us. The only lights for miles were the houses in the distance, the moon above, and the heaters from our smokes. Before long, they all went away.

"IS THERE A LITTLE BIT OF LIGHT, LITTLE BIT OF HOPE?"

– "DIEGO GARCIA," STUBBS

WRONGBAR, TORONTO — FEBRUARY 22, 2010

Leatherface reunited following the lengthy hiatus after 2004's *Dog Disco*, only this round with Hammond on lead guitar for the first time in a decade. The band added a few select Ontario dates when booking their tour through the United States. They couldn't pass up the opportunity to play two nights in Toronto, marking their first Canadian appearance. The first show would be for the public at Wrongbar. The second would be an invite-only event held at Bovine Sex Club.

Philliskirk reached out to Cactus with an exciting offer. He wanted to know if Cactus's band Sinkin' Ships would be the supporting act for the scheduled North American tour. This was the opportunity Cactus had waited all his life for, and it felt like a dream come true. But complications prevented Sinkin' Ships from joining them for the entire tour. The band instead signed on for the Ontario dates Leatherface had booked. Jason's group, Summer of '92, was also added to the Toronto bill.

Philliskirk sent Cactus several packages. He'd become a friend and the keeper of the sacred merchandise. Cactus hauled the shipment inside his apartment on the day it arrived. He stared at the delivery, unsure of whether he should look inside one of the boxes. I can imagine his eyes scanning the packages through his glasses while walking nervously back and forth. Curiosity pushed him to the brink before opening one of them to see what treasures lay within. Inside was Leatherface's long-awaited latest release, *The Stormy Petrel.*

Our prickly friend was presented with another dilemma more troublesome than the first — the searing question of whether he should listen to the album or not. He paced, smoked, and argued with himself. Cactus flipped the album around and pored over the song titles, longing to hear it. Undecided, he picked up the phone and called his bandmate Mark Harpur. He called JDM when he hung up with Harpur.

"Yeah, it's right here, a whole box of 'em," Cactus said into the phone. "I don't know . . . Should I? I don't know." Laugh. "I want to . . ."

He caved and ripped off the plastic and popped the disc from its cover. The anticipation became almost too much to bear. Hammond was back in the band, and he was one of Cactus's biggest influences. He rolled a joint and poured himself a drink. He positioned the speakers so that one was on either side of his head when he lay down between them. It was the same way Jason had arranged them around me on that morning at Lainey's house back in 1999. It was an effective way to listen to the band.

He puffed and listened. On the opening track, he heard Stubbs and Hammond on guitar together again. He got goosebumps as he wondered if he was the first person in Canada to hear this new record. Anticipation rose when the reality set in of how he'd be opening for his heroes in his hometown after all that time. Cactus stood tall with confidence. He chewed up the rest of his joint, washed it down with some Jack Daniel's, and flexed into the mirror.

Summer of '92 took a moment before their set began. Dressed in his tweed cap and Carling jersey, Jason spoke into the mic: "Most of you know how much this means to me." The quiet sentiment fell beneath the noise in the place. I caught it though.

Our hangouts had become rarer and rarer since returning from our trip eleven years before the Wrongbar show. We formed Long Time Coming when we'd come back and even managed to record a few songs. It was a fun year playing music together again before the project fizzled out. At some point, our interactions happened only in passing.

Friendship is like a castle, a far-off tower in the landscape. The bricks will hold if you build it with your heart and protect it. The monument will stand strong with the passing moon. Some fall to ruin though. As neglected as they sometimes become, their remains still bear the effort of their builders. Very few disappear without a trace.

The show was very emotional for me. There were friends in the room that I've shared significant and heartbreaking moments with. But our greetings had become reserved and withdrawn somewhere along the line. Old grudges die hard. There were other friends, ones who when we hugged it was like we were brothers with a light of understanding blasting between us.

Jason's reflective songs that night brought up emotions I hadn't acknowledged in a long while. I could hear the pain that his voice almost always carried when he sang. I thought how great it was for him to be opening for Leatherface. I felt proud of him. It was impossible not to think about all the days we had spent together on our journey, back when we were at our finest. I understood that things had come to be as they should in the dark of the bar. That time had crept upon us. It struck me hard how people weave in and out of each other's lives. Our trip changed the two of us on a level that was difficult to comprehend. It set in place something we both chased down different roads for years to come. Jason drove across Canada to Yellowknife, writing dark folk songs about the prairies. I followed the sun down the California coast searching for the ocean and any sign of Kerouac. We knew a considerable part of our makeup could be traced back to movement. It was the gold we both discovered. The truth is, we were born into this love of exploration together. One thing I didn't want to admit was how much I grew in his presence. And what I didn't acknowledge for many years was how he'd showed up to see a lot of this, even if it was just so he didn't feel alone. It seemed so abstruse that we'd disconnected and went separate ways after such a transformative experience with one another. Wasn't it supposed to be the opposite? Every so often I take a walk out into that field and stand where our fort stood and listen to its song in the wind.

I welcomed the relief as Sinkin' Ships took the stage. Cactus told me that all his hard work throughout the years came to fruition that night. He summed up the show as a homecoming, and I can't say I disagree. Almost everyone we knew was in the room.

Sinkin' Ships ripped through their set with fierceness. Knowing your heroes are watching will do that to a band. A shirtless Harpur moved full of bravado across the stage. Allan commanded the crowd's attention with her attitude and huge vocals. Hawco pulled his bass up high and strummed every note in perfect time with Farr on drums. Cactus's guitar playing has always been relentless. He held a wide stance with his head down and thrashed through his shining moments. He wore a look of awareness and contentment that was telling of his arrival.

Dickie Hammond and Frankie Stubbs stood side by side under the lights of the stage, a sight we thought we'd never see with our own eyes. Both were dressed in black button-up shirts to mark the occasion. Cactus must have felt so stoked when he saw Philliskirk sling his bass over a Sinkin' Ships shirt. The crowd yelled. The walls were electric. I will always remember the quick smile that Stubbs and Hammond exchanged before starting. Hammond then lowered his chin, and was ready to play. Stubbs looked bright-eyed out into the sea before him, leaned into the microphone, and said, "Let's just get this shit started."

The crowd cheered as Stubbs paced in a circle, embracing the nervous energy in the room, making sure his band was ready. "Isn't Life Just Sweet?" started with its slow build of dueling arpeggiated guitar chords. The bass pedal pumped with the high hats. It was beautiful hearing those two guitars reunited onstage again, like a modern sequel to "Wallflower." It reminded me of how February's snowbanks would soon be rivers as spring's tempered air returned. The drums ascended in a perfect build with Philliskirk's bass. The eager crowd beckoned. Stubbs and Hammond rocked their heads side to side along to the melody. Patience was key in that moment of deliberate restraint.

We could feel the power we'd pined for during the intro of "My World's End." Someone stood close to the side of the stage with their head down, arms crossed, eyes closed tight and absorbing all the energy like a medium at a séance. Stubbs lunged at the mic. The person looked up to put a face to the wolf growling from the PA. Their head banged with a clenched jaw, feeling every phrase and every pounding beat.

They transitioned seamlessly into "I Want the Moon," into that vehicle revving its engine onstage. Fingers shot like arrows from the crowd leaning helplessly against the weight of the bulldozer pushing us forward. It was all so uncompromising as Stubbs roared the words to the verse. You could see every muscle in his body flex. The veins in his neck bulged. A wave of ghost-like chants rose to the rafters as Wrongbar became a Sunderland football stadium. The floor shook beneath the weight and flux of the dancing hundreds. The scene jittered like a found footage-style horror movie. JDM stood with one foot on the stage, pointing as high as he could reach and blew a kiss.

You know the lightning's in the bottle when you see Stubbs gyrate his shoulders while singing. That's how you know he's got it. His eyes rolled back as his head bobbled around during the song's close. Screams of excitement erupted. He reached for his beer on top of his amp and downed a celebratory swig, living, breathing, embracing, knowing someday it might be gone.

I heard the familiar stop . . .

And start again of "Not a Day Goes By." I saw my youth like a fireball of light and warmth inside me. I was young again, walking down Islington Avenue with the sensation that my life had just changed forever. I heard the voice calling from the tomb way down inside me as I moved into the whirlwind.

I grabbed hold of the monitor and pulled myself from the churning bodies below. Not since the Misfits show when Jason rescued me from Michale Graves had I considered stage-diving again. The beating I'd endured at the Opera House flickered through my mind in the seconds that I stood headbanging. Jason was in the front row, pressed up tight. I remembered what it felt like being slammed onto the floor. I remembered the violence.

Like a split geode with crystals cloaked inside its unadorned exterior, some things aren't what they seem. Here is a punk band that addressed the human experience with sincerity, understanding, and compassion despite a harsh upbringing in North East England. As aggressive as it may appear, their music speaks of something deeper — the pursuit of an alternate awareness. An unwavering truth we owe to ourselves. We were all in Frankie Stubbs's home that night, where it gets dark at times, but where the fire will always warm you.

This memory of the Misfits was washed away as quick as it came. In its place came pacification. I stepped forward and leapt toward the crowd across the blanket of reaching hands. Leatherface was once again the greatest rock 'n' roll band in the world.

"Springtime" brought budding concessions. Controlled feedback rang like an electrified Tibetan singing bowl. Our friends gathered under the lights feeling a warm embrace in the terse, melancholic vocals. Stubbs smiled into the frenzied crowd after he sang the first line of the verse. Philliskirk's hand pounded the bass strings. Fists punched the air above. Beer cans sailed like grenades. There wasn't a still soul to be seen. Stubbs danced his jig and sang out his signature "cha cha." The gesture meant that things were right in the world.

Stubbs wrote "Springtime" while the band was touring hard. They'd always maintained a humour that has seen them through the darkest hours. This levity became their lighthouse. But life out there in the wild is volatile. Playing in a band that's toured as often as Leatherface did is not for the faint of heart. It's when friends become family and relationships strengthen amidst dysfunction. But the constant pressures of the road and the need to entertain will break anyone down. Their mantra began to crack under the weight. Bad blood was seeping in. Within this growing friction between bandmates, the line appeared: "There's a little bit of springtime." He remembered better days when they all felt happier. Stubbs put the words down without so much as a scratched-out line.

The night at Wrongbar brought some wounded hearts into the building, but the pain was relieved. Leatherface stitched the openings, just as they did long ago: "There's a little bit of springtime in the back of mind, that remembers things, perhaps as they should've been, rather than lies, rather than the cruelty, that sometimes we were guilty of and as everybody knows, we were only young and really couldn't have known. We were very young."

We knew these lyrics better than we knew our own families. We understood the message perhaps too well. A part of me thinks we'd let our friendships falter so that we could feel the true meaning of what was being said, to feel human again. Those lyrics were a warning, but instead, we let many things that could have been get away. Now we truly understood. Now we sang it to our younger selves.

The healing message was temporary; Frankie Stubbs is a medic. It takes a special power to bring symmetry among people, to cut the weights and reunite a fractured community. Three minutes and eighteen seconds of morphine.

The name of their newest album, *The Stormy Petrel*, is fitting on many levels. Its title refers to the Sunderland hero and local lifeboat volunteer Joseph Ray Hodgson, nicknamed "The Stormy Petrel," who risked his life on many occasions to save others from the cruel North Sea. He saved individuals as well as entire crews of ships. In the end Hodgson died a poor man despite his fame.

Leatherface is the underdog you find yourself rooting for. The challenger with fewer wins, but more heart than all of them. Theirs is a story full of struggle, tragedy, sadness, and ultimate triumph, and these songs were full of conviction and renewed strength.

Davey Quinn witnessed first-hand the magic of this show as sound technician that night. Quinn saw something that evening he's never seen during a Leatherface set, let alone any concert. He noticed two men in a loving embrace so tender that Quinn described the couple as being one person. They gazed into each other's eyes with more love than he's ever seen. It was magnetic watching them sing along to every word coming from the stage. He couldn't look away.

The lights darkened during the breakdown in "Diego Garcia." One guitar weaved around the other's trained feedback. "Is there a little bit of light? Is there little bit of hope?" Stubbs's voice was like a ditch full of sincerity. Hammond tilted his head back and closed his eyes, his face illuminated by the only light in the venue. It was a biblical moment suspended in time.

"WHEN IT STARTS TO GET DARKER
AND THE RAIN CLOUDS ARE WINNING.
I KNOW THEY HAVE WON,
WHEN THE FOGHORN COMES.
THE SEAGULLS SOUND LIKE THEY'RE IN MY ROOM.
THERE'S A FLY ON THE ARM OF THE CHAIR THAT I'M SITTING."

— "MY WORLD'S END," STUBBS

STOIRM

It was the seventh week of our journey, and it was taking its toll. We stumbled on a bed and breakfast on the outskirts of Bunbeg where we rested after our campout on the beach. A steaming bath washed the grit from our bodies. The comfy bed filled us with fleeting strength. We made friends with a pony in the field. But our souls were tired. The damp Atlantic air cut like a hatchet at our limbs. We walked slowly along the road, making our way to the neighbouring town, where we'd secured a campsite. It could have been Derrybeg, but I can't say for sure. I only knew that it was where we'd be catching the bus back to Dublin. The sky grew eerily overcast and looked as if the clouds could burst at any minute. There was apprehension about the grim weather, with no other option but to sleep in the rain if need be. An impending 7:15 a.m. wake-up the next morning was also a source of unease. The only bus leaving Gweedore back to Dublin was at eight a.m. We'd miss our flight home if we weren't on it. I felt wary of Jason's mood, which was a little

227

like the looming sky. We hadn't been tethered to any sort of schedule for the whole trip, and the seriousness of our situation was weighing in. I feared that if there was a pub in the village, the temptation would be too great to have one last blast before returning home. It was while we walked this road that I decided I'd be staying in for the night. I was feeling homesick in that hour. The thought of another beer made me grimace.

"I'm stayin' in the tent tonight and reading," I said, exhausted, letting him know where I stood.

"Hmmmmph," he replied. "Probably a good idea."

His agreement reassured me. However, I don't like when people tell me what I want to hear.

The village emerged at the end of the road. The bus stop was located outside a café on the corner. There was a small restaurant across the street. That's when I saw the pub. Like a siren, it sang to us its sweet Irish song. We headed up the hill and found our campsite only one block from the bus stop. The location was promising. It wasn't much of a campground as it was a grassy courtyard surrounded by tall trees and bushes.

There was a small rectangular building to one side of the site. As we got closer, I realized it was a washroom. This lone lavatory's presence surprised me because of how out of place it seemed. I examined the red spray-painted clown face with x's for eyes and a dripping smile on the building's exterior.

This could come in handy, actually. Having shelter would be ideal if the weather turned. The tent went up in silence as I monitored the sky. We explored the village when we finished setting up camp. I remember being so hungry that day. We walked into the café to find the place full of smiling kids eating doughnuts. They were loud and had chocolate and sprinkles all over their faces. It was a glorious sight. I ordered a chocolate-glazed to go.

It surprised me when outside Jason revealed his true feelings about doughnuts. The kids in the background screamed in delight. His irritability cut through his smile.

"You're disgusting, MacDonald," he said, as I bit into mine.

"Whaaaat, you don't like doughnuts?" I asked, taken aback. "You should try one, look how happy *they* are," I said, thumbing over my shoulder.

"They're all out of their tree on sugar."

"They're loving life. You should try it sometime."

We assessed our surroundings before killing time back at the tent, reading and keeping an eye on the weather. It hadn't gotten any worse, which lifted my spirits. We headed to the restaurant near the main intersection at dinner time. I pulled open the door and walked into a room that had wraparound windows, checkered tablecloths, and a vintage menu board.

I ordered a steak pie and garlic cheesy fries. I had become addicted to this new french fry phenomenon since arriving in the U.K. The closer we were to getting on the plane, the more I ate, like a squirrel storing up for winter. Jason looked at me with increasing vexation and bewilderment as I shovelled my dinner in. The pie tasted so delicious on that moody day in Gweedore. The flaky pastry cracked and caved, the steaming gravy pouring out.

I tend to say "mmm" after every bite when I eat something delicious. Its uncontrollable. I suppose I could stop if I put some effort into it, but it's difficult. Sometimes the "mmms" are a little longer, sometimes shorter, sometimes in a different octave. This "John Candy–ism" was getting under Jason's skin fast.

We smoked cigarettes outside the tent in the grass as night fell across the land. It seemed like both of us were staying put when we settled into the tent. My plan of attack was to read as much as I could, and sleep well. Morning would be upon us.

Jason's restlessness began to mount. By the way he shifted his body, I could tell he couldn't get comfortable. The edge of page scraped across my chest as I read. I could even hear myself swallow. Jason farted loud and terrible. It sounded like a goblin yelling. The leaves rustled outside in the wind.

"Dude, serious? That smells like the worst thing in the world," I said.

Then, my fears from the afternoon became real.

"I know, that's why I'm going to the pub," he said, pulling himself up without making eye contact. "You stayin' here?" his voice gruff, the smell worse.

"Just leave me in your stench? Seriously though, Jay, think it's a good idea? I mean, the bus is so early."

"It'll be fine, and you'll survive," he replied in a heavy voice that suggested I should mind my boundaries. "You stayin'?" The utter absence of enthusiasm suggested he didn't want me to come and that he'd only asked so things would appear normal. But there was tension. For a moment I considered going along to make sure he would make it back. But I couldn't risk putting the morning in jeopardy by getting drunk. And also, the thought of having another drop of alcohol made me want to die. I decided to take the reins.

"Uhh ... Nahhh, just going to read ... Try not to be late," I said, sounding like a worried mother, which irritated him further.

"Suit yourself."

I listened to the thudding of his footsteps slowly disappearing into the wind as he walked down the grassy slope, out into the dark.

BOVINE SEX CLUB, TORONTO – FEBRUARY 2010

I try to think about this night as little as possible. Some of which is denial, because to witness a catastrophe like it makes you examine the part of yourself that was so sure those you've venerated don't experience deficiency. Realizing you're going to fail creeps in like a thief. Knowing there's a price to pay for putting it on the line is a thought better left ignored.

The show was an unadvertised and invite-only event at the Bovine Sex Club in mid-February 2010 that followed the incredible set at Wrongbar a few nights before. There was so much promise in the air. I often wonder if we knew how lucky we were to have had such an intimate show happening for us. "Springtime" is about hindsight. With all we've learned from the song, I wish we would've tried harder not to let something so special fall to ruin. Maybe it was out of our hands, it's hard to know. There were a few colliding factors that led to the night's downfall. As much of a Toronto staple as Bovine is, I would have opted for another venue away from Queen Street. There's speculation that some members of the band found themselves pressured by the adrenalized fans to consume more than usual because there was no green room where they could collect themselves. Impulse got the best of the group and spurred the devil rumoured to be at the heels of Leatherface for decades.

They attempted to compose themselves once onstage. Stubbs fiddled "Alternative Ulster" on his guitar in a bid for lightness. The gesture worked momentarily before they crashed into their set. But the evening's energy was altered when a storm cloud crept across the stage as the songs played on. We knew something was wrong because Stubbs wouldn't dance. But it was when he stopped singing altogether, leaving the band to play on as best they could without the aid of vocals to guide them, that we knew the end was near. It looked to me as if the frontman was testing the band to see if they could make it out alive without him. His eyes cut through the pink lights. We looked at each other with nervous glances, then down at our shoes. I knew in that moment it might be the last time I'd get to see Leatherface perform. I couldn't believe it was falling apart. Another thought hit me: it could be the last time I'd hear the Sunderland troubadour ever sing live again. As their song "Pale Moonlight" derailed in those painful seconds, Frankie Stubbs pulled off his guitar, stepped offstage, and shoved through the front door out into the cold night. He didn't stop walking until he reached the heart of Parkdale.

I wondered if Jason was going to come back as I lay with my flashlight poring over my book, trying to suppress my growing concern. The hour felt late by Gweedore's standards, and still there was no sign of my friend. My watch now read 12:31 a.m. The bushes next to the tent brushed against one another. I thought about the night up on Arthur's Seat again and felt a pang of fear come through me. My mind easily conjured sounds and images that didn't exist.

Goat Man.

12:46.

What the fuck, where is he? At the pub, of course. I don't know why he couldn't have stayed . . .

We'd seen a lot together, and many days on our trip were spent in solitude. But this was the first night we'd been separated. The division made everything feel off-kilter. I turned out the flashlight, closed my eyes, and tried not to think about it. But still my mind raced.

1:16 a.m. came quickly.

The wind picked up.

Did he need a Guinness that bad? Was he that pissed off at me for eating doughnuts? He should have tried some. Would have calmed him down, made him smile like those kids. God those kids looked happy. Love them. Fuck. Should I walk down to the pub? Yes. I'm going. Fuck, I don't want to. I know he's there. It can't still be open. What if he said something stupid? He does that. Guy rubs people the wrong way. He almost got chibbed the other night, good thing I was there. He spouts off sometimes, and if the wrong person felt threatened . . . He's a brawler and an asshole. Can't believe he HAD to go to the pub. He better come back. I gotta go down there. We need to get on that bus at eight a.m. for fuck sakes.

1:42 a.m.

Where. In. The. Holy. Fuck. Is. That. Round. Bastard. I'm gonna murder him, the prick. I can't believe it. Somebody's got him. I'm gonna let that idiot have it good. Punch him like a thunderbolt right in his belly.

Seriously, where is he?

The night crawled like a panther stalking its prey. My nerves were jangling like a tambourine. In the strange space between sleep and consciousness I saw Jason dead on the beach. I heard a chainsaw, I saw Leatherface's eyes like abysmal bird nests.

"NIGHTS TURNING INTO THE DAYS AND WE DIDN'T NOTICE THE CHANGE.
NO I DIDN'T THINK YOU WERE WRONG AND I CAN STILL SING YOUR
FAVOURITE SONG."

— "NOT A DAY GOES BY," STUBBS

GOODBYE, DICKIE

Hammond was dying. His friends and family knew this, and it was only a matter of time before goodbyes would have to be faced. Philliskirk could only gallop alongside his buddy, careening toward the imminent destination that lay on the horizon. Through all the hardship that happens when a friend is dealing with addiction, they maintained the Sunderland humour that surfaces when dark times arrive. There was also no other alternative. They would often joke about Hammond's destructive state at inappropriate times, creating much discomfort for whoever was in earshot. The friends were out of choices; they did what they knew how to do to get through it.

Philliskirk and Montreal native Hugo Mudie (the Sainte Catherines, Yesterday's Ring) had become close pals over the years and entertained the idea of putting together a side project. When they decided to have Hammond play guitar, it may have been a subconscious attempt at documenting the remainder of his talent before the future fell upon them.

The result of these efforts was Medictation, the finest of all the side projects that emerged from Leatherface, in my opinion. Like Lainey said about the tree, "it needs strong roots to grow." Leatherface is that stoic, craggy willow swaying in the grey light and Medictation is the branch strong enough to hold the tire swing. Hammond's signature guitar shines on *Warm Places*. You can almost feel the peace in his heart. Mudie's vocals channel Stubbs in a way that I've never heard anyone else do, yet with his own unique vision full of earnest power.

There was talk of the friends going to play the Fest, in Gainesville, Florida, once the group was established. This however felt like an unsafe venture for Hammond as time drew nearer. Hammond was eager to get to Florida and into the action. When he asked Philliskirk about attending, Hammond was told that he shouldn't come out of concern for his declining health. It was a bid to save his friend's life. Philliskirk told Hammond candidly, "I don't think you're going to make it back if you come along." Hammond was so upset and disappointed that he cried before storming out of the room.

It was Saturday night at the Fest in Gainesville. Philliskirk, Davey Quinn, and Hammond's partner, Siobhan McCollum, were watching Mudie perform onstage. From the back of the room Philliskirk could see a silver chain bouncing around Mudie's neck. The crowd cheered as the band collapsed into a swell of distortion and cymbals as the last song of the night came to a close. It was during this finale that Mudie reached up and took hold of the silver necklace, ripped it from his neck, and threw the chain into the crowd. Philliskirk watched as it sailed to the back of the room. He reached up and caught it somehow. Philliskirk opened his fist and stared down at the cross as the last notes from the guitar fell beneath the humming of amps, leaving nothing but the sound of people in the room. He looked toward his friends standing near the bar while they stared back in shock. Philliskirk thought their stunned expressions were because he'd been the one to catch the cross. But he could see tears streaming from Quinn's and McCollum's eyes. He stood confused, looking down at the phone in Quinn's hand. He knew then that their friend Dickie Hammond had left them. Despite Quinn's abstinence from alcohol, he turned and ordered three shots. Philliskirk made his way to the bar where McCollum said through the tears, "We've just had a phone call."

"I know. He's died, hasn't he?" Philliskirk asked.

"Yeah," she replied and burst further into sadness.

Philliskirk wrapped his arms around his friends as the server slid three shots across the bar.

"I don't know what to say, but I'm going to have a drink," Quinn said, broken-hearted. The three of them raised their glasses because it was all they could do in that moment. Mudie fell to tears as well after learning the tragic news. Philliskirk realized he was still clutching the chain and silver cross tightly as the four of them tried to comprehend the end of their friend's life.

A BEAUTIFUL SENTIMENT
BY SIOBHAN MCCOLLUM

Dickie loved having a plodge in the sea at the beach. He loved walking in the strongest winds that blow on the northeastern coast of England. He was proud of his sons. He didn't understand rock, paper, scissors. His jukebox choices would shock you. He loved peanut butter and he always insisted on the peanut butter option on the menu. He would steal one of my expensive socks with each visit as insurance that I would return. He spent mornings "on the bags" collecting bagged donations for a charity when he wasn't on tour. He was a terrible housekeeper but made a great cup of tea. He cried easily at songs and movies. He gave the very best hugs. I fell head over heels into the most beautiful trouble I've ever been in. And I'm better for it.

BZZZZZZZZZZZZZZzzzzzzzziiiiiiiiiiiiiRRRRRIIIIIIIIP. A large, shaved head breathing hot whisky breath came through the tent flaps. My heart stopped. I thought a chainsaw blade was deep inside in my shoulder. That's when I snapped out of the cinematic vision in my head.

Jason grunted as he squeezed into his sleeping bag, like he was trying to fit into his old Chevrolet Tracker. He was on autopilot, his eyes half shut. The drunkard's ragged stubble looked like stitches in the moonlight. I could tell by his breathing, and his stench, that he was more drunk than he'd ever been.

YOU PIECE OF SHIT.

Even if I could've, I didn't dare say a word. He'd rip my jugular out if I did. He was snoring as soon as he got settled. My heart skipped like a frightened bird. It took great concentration to control my breathing. There would be no chance of sleeping. I thought I'd lay awake until 6:30 or 7:00. Then my body shut down.

I heard the sounds from far away, but they didn't register. My eyes opened to the din of loud static. There was a moment of confusion before reality flooded in. Outside was a torrential, gale-force rain-storm. Wind lashed at the dome, pushing the sopping nylon across my head. It sounded like a Wendigo howling. *Mother of God.* I could hear the bushes whipping next to us. CRACK. BOOM! Thunder filled the earth below with shocking bass that rumbled the ground and rattled my ribcage. I scrambled upright, peeling and pushing the tent away from my body.

Everything was soaked.

7:25. FUCK.

"Jay, get up."

Snore. Choke. Thunder. BOOM.

I unzipped the tent and clamoured into the watery grass, my hands slipping in the mud. It was the most ominous sky I'd ever seen. The clouds looked like the nose of a great mothership hovering over the village, its size and mass not of this world. The disquieting scene stunned me. The surrounding ash trees bent as if invisible archers were drawing arrows behind them. I could feel the tension of their trunks inside my body as I imagined bones splintering. The boughs shook like pom-poms and hissed like snakes as the wind slipped between them. The door to the lavatory building was a banging firecracker behind me. I pulled our packs onto the lawn. The tent lifted from its place and folded over the sleeping mound with no pegs to ground it.

"JAY!"

I forced the dome down and shook his bagged feet. I held the entrance open with my elbows and yelled again. He opened one eye like an ox.

"GET UP."

He rose, slow and dazed as the tent curled over him again, trying to eat him, twirling him up like a crocodile in a death roll. *Jesus Christ.* The rain came down hard like bullets. He emerged, pulling at the grass, then dropped halfway out. The tent looked like a boulder that had crushed his legs. The Goat Man.

I held the structure steady enough for him to writhe free of its clutches. He stood bewildered in the yard, cowering and vulnerable, sheltering his bare arms from the rain.

The Irishman released a painful cry into the fury of the morning as he fell to his knees with his hands on his thighs, broken, surrendered in battle. I thought about the song he'd sung me so many years ago near Dangerous Dan's in those moments of desperation, the one with the chorus about how it would be a good day to die.

The tent rolled across the grass like a strange animal. My hand gripped its bat-like wing as it tried to escape through the bushes toward the sky. I hauled it across the lawn. *Not today, pal. Not today. I'm getting on that bus.*

"THE BATHROOM!" I called like a sergeant with rain beading down my face. I lumbered across the grass with my head down. I was relieved he was alive.

Trying to pull a half-pitched tent through a regular-sized doorway is frustrating. I couldn't think well enough to pull the rods free and flatten it. Common sense had blown away in the storm as I fought, twisted, and wrangled the wiry, webbed bird through the opening. In the corner of my eye, I saw Jason put his hand on the door frame behind me, bracing himself and looking at the ground. His face was rumpled with sickness. Water from the tent dripped into little lakes across the floor. I pushed past the Irishman and tromped through the rain, grabbed both backpacks, and dragged them across the lawn and into the lavatory. My hands were freezing. Jason staggered toward the toilet. Everything was dripping. My untied Converse slipped and I went tripping over one of the packs and stumbled to the floor, rolling in the puddles.

"Fuck you!" I yelled, my voice booming. The fluorescent bulbs fizzled in their cage above.

A horrible resonance erupted from the stall as I lay on my back. It was the sound of Bushmills rushing upstream. It was the sound of pure pain. It was guttural, burbling, violent, wet, and reminiscent of a war cry from a vintage kung fu movie.

It was a scream-barf. Then came the gasping. And the spitting.

"Arsehole," I said, picking myself up from the floor. I dismantled the tent in a fever and rolled it up like a thick nylon joint. I ignored the parts that didn't fit as I punched it into the bag — zip, stuff, zip, stuff.

That's when I noticed a crimson circle on the pocket of my backpack. I reached inside, then pulled my Leatherman into the light. The stainless steel was streaked with what looked like blood. My mouth was bone dry and tasted a bit like mould.

The Irishman retched with more reverberation than the first time. It felt like the world's end as I smelled the knife. *Ketchup*. I shoved it back in. The sky cracked. BOOM. Sheets of rain sliced through the doorway.

Jason composed himself after several minutes, washed his face, and pulled his sweater on. I'll be surprised if I ever see another human look like that again. Only minutes remained to board the bus. We lugged our packs up and braced for the weather. Jason slipped down on one knee in the mud. We made it down the slope to the street where the rain pelted and smacked the pavement. I glanced back at the campsite as we rounded the corner. The red clown with X eyes grinned at me through the watery light on the lavatory's brick exterior. The bus's lights and the clown were the only colour to be seen in the dismal streets. The mothership cloud was over us now. The driver was loading bags as we hobbled toward him like a pair of hobos. He looked up at the sorry sight approaching him.

"Christ almiiiighty," I heard him mutter as we grew close. "You going to Dublin?" he shouted, his glasses fogged, cheeks glossy wet.

"Yessir."

"C'mon, give me your bags then."

"YOU'RE NOT SUPERSTITIOUS AND WITHOUT CHARM YOU WOULD TOUCH WOOD,
IF YOU THOUGHT IT'D DO GOOD.
YOU'RE NOT THE SPORTING TYPE BUT WITHOUT GRIPE YOU WOULD BET
YOUR LIFE,IF YOU THOUGHT YOU WERE RIGHT."
— "NOT SUPERSTITIOUS," STUBBS

HARD LUCK BAR, TORONTO — JULY 30, 2022

I came to like a train emerging from a tunnel, with the dark slipping away behind me. There's a void I sometimes visit when I perform live. It threw me off because I hadn't descended into the "nothing" in a long time. The crowd looked blurry from my place behind the microphone, like I was peering through a half-drunk beer bottle. I hadn't stepped on a stage in two and half years, not since before the pandemic. Everything seemed foreign yet somehow familiar, as if I'd time-travelled back to a job I'd long since left. Like going through the mechanical motions and leaving it all to faith and muscle memory. I became aware that people were onstage with me, but for the duration of the verse they remained just figures in my periphery. When I broke from my fixed state, I saw JDM standing to my left and warmed at the sight of him. He's always there. When I looked to my right, I struggled to understand that the other person who'd come to sing with me was Frankie Stubbs.

I was convinced he was a mirage. A mischievous smile grew on his face as our eyes locked. He stood with his hands behind his back, like someone observing a painting in a gallery. I grinned and dropped my gaze, finding it all so difficult to believe. As I looked back up, Stubbs's smile widened. An old familiar pang of nervous fear shot through me as I almost lost control of the song. But something inside got serious and made me turn my attention away. Being onstage with Stubbs is something I never could have imagined. I held on tight until the end. The three of us sang "Hoodlum" together, along with one of my close friends, Evan Levy, who played his red Stratocaster. Truth is vital, and at times sings with unexpected grace. Jason told me later that he'd nudged Stubbs to get onstage with me. There are things in life that seem so grand that when they happen it feels as if your spirit is drifting two feet above ground.

There he was, the godfather of modern punk with his foot propped on an empty guitar case at the front of the stage, his left thigh cradling the acoustic's curved body. He didn't look like De Niro in an army jacket anymore. Stubbs had grown older with grace, and with time on his side. The singer wore an octopus-print dress shirt. He had black-rimmed eyeglasses instead of black eyes. He had a grey beard and could've been a busker at any west coast market.

Toronto musician Chuck Coles sang from the acoustic stage to the hungover few braving their first drinks of the day at Pouzza Fest in Montreal. It was four years before the night at Hard Luck happened. He was relieved to see that Stubbs and Philliskirk had found their way after directing Stubbs to the wrong venue. The two Englishmen were now watching him intently as he performed. It's a challenge to not be lured by Coles when he starts singing. He was still reeling from the night before, when he'd met Stubbs for the first time after being asked to open for the Sunderland singer as a part of a Pouzza Fest showcase. Coles remembers telling Stubbs in the minutes before his set how nervous he felt, and how easy it was for Stubbs to offer reassurance. "Son, don't be nervous, you have nothing to worry about."

A year later Coles found himself on tour with Stubbs, singing songs at every kind of venue, from the intimacy of a laundromat to fistfights in the Temple of Boom. He knew he'd made a friend that he wouldn't soon forget. Stubbs asked him to sing at his wedding in Las Vegas, where Frankie married Lynsey Shillaw. It might be wrong for me to speculate, but I think Stubbs sees the same natural talent and humour in Coles as he saw in Hammond.

Stubbs told Coles he wanted to come back to Toronto and be in a room with all his friends, past and present. Everyone worked hard to make a one-off show happen. This left many bookers from neighbouring cities confused as to why they couldn't get a piece of him as well. In that terrible witching hour before the doors open, where I question my existence, where I come close to packing my shit and leaving every time, Stubbs was still and reserved. Coles and I paced the room like nervous dogs in a kennel, wondering if anyone would come to take us home. It was Toronto's first Caribbean Carnival since the pandemic and the streets were jammed with traffic. It was also a long weekend — two factors that would make the average show-goer stay in for the night. Had we made a mistake?

Together we hung a V formation of string lights over the stage. They looked like fifty warm and protective suns hovering in a moody sky. My hope was that they'd ward off any rogue dark clouds that might drift into the club. It was a barrier, a forcefield of sorts. I'm not superstitious, but . . . It was my small and altruistic attempt to right the past.

I was convinced no one was coming while I sat backstage talking with Stubbs. It was going to be a disaster, I was sure of it. "Be careful what you say around this guy, he'll put it all in the book," he told Lynsey. This comment cut. Maybe it was a joke, maybe it wasn't. I was too on edge in that moment to fully comprehend why his remark stung. I was scared on all levels. I finally walked out front prepared to face an empty club. But the room was full of people. The feeling of relief was a grand moment shared between Chuck and me. Many in attendance had wondered whether they'd ever get to see Stubbs perform again as well. We poured toward the stage like kids gathering around their older brother who'd returned home.

He sang and spent some time drinking wine as we watched and listened in awe. Hearing the way his songs transformed from punk into what we heard that night was beautiful. His guitar was strung with flatwound strings, and you could hear the classical sensibility in his playing as he fingerpicked. The songs were delivered with care as we all yelled at the roof beams: "Don't you ever say goodbye!"

With a face like a lit lantern and wit like a knife, Stubbs will be known to his fans as someone whose efforts were as large as the ships that Sunderland built. He came back to Toronto because of his ties here, and because there may have been unfinished business to attend to. Stubbs never wanted to be famous, we know this like we know these streets. That's what is so beautiful. After all this time I still ask myself why it is that I keep coming back, but I've learned from him that some things in life were meant to uphold a sense of mystery.

"LIKE A BUTTERFLY WE'VE A VERY SHORT LIFE.
LIGHT A CIGARETTE, IT'LL BURN OUT BEFORE YOUR EYES."

— "BOWL OF FLIES," STUBBS

ROCKY ROAD TO DUBLIN

So, yeah, the song is true. That was my first thought. The bus no longer seemed to be driving on any kind of road that could've been built in the twentieth century. The vehicle would dip down a steep incline and drop your stomach like a kite in a storm, then veer back up the slope and hit a bump as it reached the crest, sending us inches out of our seats. I looked over at Jason's regretful eyes. He braced himself with one outstretched arm across the window frame and the other along the back of the seat, trying to keep himself as stationary as possible. The bus swung, bobbed, slowed, sped, rocked, and did everything except roll right over. And even if it did, it would've rolled right back up and kept bouncing along. I could tell he was digging deep with all his might not to scream-barf again.

"Don't you dare do in here what you did back there. Don't do that to these people," I scolded. Then I smiled. I took advantage because he couldn't speak. "Don't you confuse this with the *porcelain* bus," I continued.

When we thought the ride couldn't get rockier, it did. I began to laugh. *Could we have left the road?* It sure felt like it. Jason closed his eyes and rested his head against the seat in front, praying to a higher power for the terrible ride to end.

We managed to drive out of the storm, but still the rain came down. The mothership cloud that was going to annihilate the village stayed in Gweedore. Who knows what happened there after we left. The bus swerved from the road, much to Jason's relief. Once I saw everyone getting out of their seats, I realized that we'd stopped for a rest. I could see a table set with tea, sandwich halves, and biscuits, right in the gravel drive. *NIIIICE*, I thought, fixing myself a tea and helping myself to a scone. Jason stepped out of sight around the side of the building to vomit. You could hear him from the snack table. I was thankful it didn't reach the volume and malignancy of the morning's heaving. People glanced in his direction. I tried to reassure them with a smile. He staggered out and fixed himself a tea, his hands shaking like a guy that had a bottle too many of Irish whisky the night before.

"Is he alright, dear?" a sweet old lady asked, her eyes full of compassion.

"Oh yeah, he'll be fine, he's a big boy," I said, smiling.

"He *is* a big boy," she replied before sipping her tea.

The driver turned on the crackling radio for everyone to listen to and set off bumping back through the countryside. I heard the happenings around the greater Donegal area. There's one story in particular I will remember forever.

"This juus breakin'," the radio announcer said through the static. "Mr. William Fullerton of N14 County Donegal has lost his crow. The crow was last seen Sunday. The crow answers to the name Joseph. If you have any information of its whereabouts, it would be greatly appreciated."

Everyone looked at one another with worried expressions. Oh Ireland, how your heart is true. What did I say about stereotypes in the beginning?

I thought about the night before, how wild it had been. Jason's thudding footsteps in the grass echoing in my head. *The idiot came back.* There came a feeling of sheepishness somewhere inside me because I knew I hadn't given my friend the benefit of the doubt. I'd convinced myself that he was going to fuck everything up for the next morning before he left. He returned even though he was out of his mind. Guilt crept through me as I thought about how I should've gone searching for him. I looked over at Jason, who was as ashen as the sky.

The fields full of seething, jagged rocks outside the window revealed themselves as the cause of our jarring ride. The grass was thick, and curled like bright green waves. It must have been hell trying to carve a road through that land, and whoever did it had good reason for giving up. The memory of Jason and me singing "Green and Grey" with Stubbs at the Ivy House in Sunderland came back to me as the bus rolled deep into the countryside.

I became lost in the events of the past weeks with idealism arcing in my mind and spinning like the wheels below me. There's an ease with which my mind wanders, and I'm helpless to its movement. Dreaminess is a force I never could escape from. It's okay because I never want to escape. It's everything else that puts me on the run. If strangers had seen us heaped like waste in the train station, our trip may have appeared foolhardy and coarse. Passersby saw only our beat-up eyes and dishevelled appearances. But they didn't see us drifting on the train ride from Belgium that brought us to the U.K. and showed us how beautiful life could be. They didn't see me at peace in the warmth of a Scottish hillside filled with understanding. They didn't see the two humans in the apex of life somewhere in a dark harbour in Skye, bewildered by the power of our surroundings. And I felt good about that, because it was our secret. Maybe the most beautiful, most honest experiences aren't obvious. Some are disguised so not everyone will find them, like cracking open that geode. There's something in having to work a little for the discovery and having to peel back the layers.

Because without effort it wouldn't be the same. Our trip was like a Leatherface song, where buried beneath a gruff exterior something grander was unfolding, and like the lyrics, we wouldn't understand the magnitude of our journey for years to come.

I kept thinking how we ended up in their jam space listening to them write music, the esoteric roads that led us there. It seemed like it was supposed to happen. Like a passage through the gates. My mind wandered to the night we met Stubbs on his home turf. That old expression "never meet your heroes" was singing. The first real encounter with Stubbs destroyed the image I had built of him. The reckoning felt clashing, yet humbling and cathartic. But I also knew better. You can't write those kind of words without spending time alone.

I thought about my embarrassing sixteen-year-old self that lied to my brother when I was high. How I'd wanted his acceptance so badly. But the truth is that I was searching for something much different. I hungered deep down to find my own voice through words. And if those expressions could be as resounding with others as Stubbs's were with me, well, what a gift it is to imagine. I longed to contribute to this cycle. As rough as that memory of my younger self is when it hits, I forgave that kid for his foolishness because I knew what the lie meant. The ancient wound didn't feel as tender as it once did. I came to understand that the expectations of my hero were really projections of the things I longed for, reflections of who I strived to be — what I was searching for in life.

"A time when everything was evergreen. Evergreen and seemingly ideal."

I wanted to live inside those lines. I still do. Understanding this made me thankful that I met Stubbs, and grateful that their music came along when I needed it most. I took out my notebook and pen and started answering the call from that buried tomb. What felt like a realization had me sinking deeper into it all. It was indulgent, but a life not romanticized is a life not worth living. The vision was clear and the dream-like notions spilled with the falling rain.

EPILOGUE

It's been thirty-one years since I first heard *Mush*. I listened to the original pressing of the record the other night before leaving for British Columbia. My heart still races like it did that afternoon long ago, and it's the only album that does this to me. The urgency, passion, and sincerity still speak so loudly. Something new reveals itself with every listen. Each time I feel inspired. It's the sound of my youth personified, but is somehow also who I've grown into.

I know now it was the idea of poetry that I was hearing within it all along. And how much power can be found in so few words. How it can resonate through the years like the ringing of a bell. The way it attaches itself to your psyche and becomes a part of you. Stubbs has this ability, especially when he delivers it with such desperation.

When I found Mary Oliver, I found Stubbs again. When I found Stubbs again, I fell deeper in love with Oliver. When I discovered her poem "The Sun," in which she pleads with the reader, "or have you too / turned from this world — or have you too / gone crazy / for power, / for things?" I hear Stubbs biting back in "The Scheme of Things," "I have many things, I have dreams." So much impact with so little said.

I take a moment away from typing. Wild roses move in the wind, and beyond them is a valley of cedars and firs. Beyond that is the ocean. I watch a white ferry glide like a citadel through the blue below. A crow glides overhead with wings like a slow-moving propeller. The distant tree line's reflection in the water makes the shape of a sound wave, and I wonder if the song is in a minor key.

ACKNOWLEDGEMENTS

Thank you:

To the Toronto Arts Council, whose generous support gave me the time to complete this project. For this I'm truly grateful.

This book would not have seen the light of day without the guidance, expertise, and love from Michael Holmes and Dave Bidini. I think you know how much it means. Thank you for your friendship, and for taking another chance on a rogue like me.

Thank you, Janet Morassutti for helping me navigate new waters. You're so cool.

Jen Albert, Jessica Albert, Victoria Cozza, Jen Knoch, Caroline Suzuki, Claire Pokorchak, Carrie Gleason, and all the staff at ECW Press who helped make *Days and Days* come alive. I'm so thankful for your time, attention, and efforts.

This book, of course, wouldn't exist without the members of Leatherface (past and present). Thank you for being you, Frankie

Stubbs, and for letting me have at it. There's no way I got it all right, from lyrics and facts, but know that I came with heart. Thank you, Graeme Philliskirk for your generosity and time. I couldn't have done it without you. Thank you, Andrew Laing, David Lee Burdon, and Leighton Evans for trusting me with your endearing stories.

Jason Dwyer, who urged me to be adventurous, for the miles and memories, and for introducing me to one of the greatest records ever made.

Megan Tilston for your endless patience, motivation, and for setting me at ease on the days when I'd say, "What am I doing? Nobody's going to read this." You're my light, my best friend, and I love you forever.

Frances MacDonald for the infinite inspiration and the custom Leatherface LP. Keep being incredible.

Austin Lucas, Chuck Coles, Chuck Ragan, Chris Wollard, Cactus, Damian Abraham, Davey Quinn, Duncan Redmonds, JDM, Sean Forbes, Sergie Loobkoff, Siobhan McCollum, Jack Rabid, and Simon Wells for your insight, contributions, and excitement.

Ty Trumbull for braving the first draft, and for your encouraging critique.

Cone McCaslin for being excellent.

And to all my friends and family for their support.

Leatherface's music can and should be purchased from
Little Rocket Records at www.littlerocketrecords.co.uk.

Entertainment. Writing. Culture. ────────

ECW is a proudly independent, Canadian-owned book publisher. We know great writing can improve people's lives, and we're passionate about sharing original, exciting, and insightful writing across genres.

──────────────── **Thanks for reading along!**

We want our books not just to sustain our imaginations, but to help construct a healthier, more just world, and so we've become a certified B Corporation, meaning we meet a high standard of social and environmental responsibility — and we're going to keep aiming higher. We believe books can drive change, but the way we make them can too.

Certified

Corporation

Being a B Corp means that the act of publishing this book should be a force for good – for the planet, for our communities, and for the people that worked to make this book. For example, everyone who worked on this book was paid at least a living wage. You can learn more at the Ontario Living Wage Network.

This book is also available as a Global Certified Accessible™ (GCA) ebook. ECW Press's ebooks are screen reader friendly and are built to meet the needs of those who are unable to read standard print due to blindness, low vision, dyslexia, or a physical disability.

This book is printed on Sustana EnviroBook™, a recycled paper, and other controlled sources that are certified by the Forest Stewardship Council®.

ECW's office is situated on land that was the traditional territory of many nations including the Wendat, the Anishnaabeg, Haudenosaunee, Chippewa, Métis, and current treaty holders the Mississaugas of the Credit. In the 1880s, the land was developed as part of a growing community around St. Matthew's Anglican and other churches. Starting in the 1950s, our neighbourhood was transformed by immigrants fleeing the Vietnam War and Chinese Canadians dispossessed by the building of Nathan Phillips Square and the subsequent rise in real estate value in other Chinatowns. We are grateful to those who cared for the land before us and are proud to be working amidst this mix of cultures.